A Harper Rogers Cozy Mystery Collection

Murder at Palm Park

Murder at Jax Beach

Murder at the Pirate Museum

Southern Chick Lit
Sharon E. Buck

Copyright © 2024 by Sharon E. Buck

All rights reserved.

No portion of this book may be reproduced in any form without written permission from the publisher or author, except as permitted by U.S. copyright law.

For more information, or to book an event, contact :
sharon@sharonebuck.com

To join my VIP Newsletter and to receive a **FREE** book, go to http://www.SharonEBuck.com

Cover designs by Steven Novak, NovakIllustration.com

Contents

Murder at Palm Park

Murder at Jax Beach

Murder at the Pirate Museum

Murder at Palm Park

Sharon E. Buck

Southern Chick Lit

Copyright © 2024 by Sharon E. Buck

All rights reserved.

No portion of this book may be reproduced in any form without written permission from the publisher or author, except as permitted by U.S. copyright law.

For more information, or to book an event, contact :
sharon@sharonebuck.com

To join my VIP Newsletter and to receive a **FREE** book, go to http://www.SharonEBuck.com

Cover design by Steven Novak, NovakIllustration.com

Contents

1. Chapter 1   #
2. Chapter 2   #
3. Chapter 3   #
4. Chapter 4   #
5. Chapter 5   #
6. Chapter 6   #
7. Chapter 7   #
8. Chapter 8   #
9. Chapter 9   #
10. Chapter 10   #
11. Chapter 11   #
12. Chapter 12   #
13. Chapter 13   #
14. Chapter 14   #
15. Chapter 15   #
16. Chapter 16   #

More Books   #

More Books - 2 #

17. About the Author #

18. Acknowledgements #

Chapter 1

Sarah was slumped over the table, her coffee with an obscene amount of liquid sugar in it was dripping off the edge, so was red fluid. The new barista, well, let's just say he wasn't going to be making any coffee drinks ever again.

I threw up as I was punching nine-one-one. My hand was shaking so badly that I now only had about half a cup of coffee left. I was now wearing the rest of it on my hand, arm, and the front of my shirt.

While waiting for the police to show up, it was only minutes but felt like hours, my thoughts dive-bombed my psyche.

I am a highly paid escort. I am young, cute, and deadly. I am an assassin.

No, no. That's not right. I am an opera singer. Yes, that's it. I open my mouth and beautiful, lyrical notes grace the air in the theatre.

I am a professional liar, and I am paid very well for it. What am I? I could be an actor, an attorney, in sales or advertising, a detective, or a writer.

"Seriously! Get out of your head. I can see story ideas bouncing around in your brain." Sarah had grumped at me. We've been friends since before breakfast. Actually, we've known each other since the fourth grade. We are not best friends...just good friends who know way too much about each other in certain areas of our lives. Still, when Sarah's not craving something to eat every two or three hours, she can be a lot of fun.

"What's wrong with you?" I grinned. It was just so much fun to see how much I could annoy Sarah, especially when I knew she was skating on the edge of crazy without her morning caffeine and sugar fix.

She grabbed her cup of coffee from the new barista at Coffee & Cupcakes, took a sip, put it back on the counter, and pushed it back to him. "It doesn't have enough sugar in it. I specifically asked for six shots. You didn't do that."

The guy inhaled deeply through his nose, letting the air out slowly through his nostrils, "Do you want me to put more in this cup or do you want a new one?"

Sarah snapped, "What do you think?"

"Hey, Sarah, chill." I held up three fingers to the guy. "Just put that many in the cup."

She started to say something, and I decided to shut her down. "Stop it! Tip the man."

Glaring at me, she snatched the mug that now had more sugar in it than our ancestors had had in a year, "No!"

Deciding our friendship probably needed a break, a long break, I tipped the young man. Taking my coffee and ignoring Sarah seated at one of the little tables, I started for the door.

"Hey!"

I ignored her and kept walking.

Looking back on it, I was amazed at how unobservant I was...or, just call it being too self-absorbed with Sarah's bad manners that I wasn't paying attention to the tall individual coming through the door. I was already out on the sidewalk trying to decide if I was going home to start writing a new story or if I was going to go pet the new puppies at Ronnie's pet store when I heard two double shots.

It took a moment for it to register that those were gunshots that I heard. Behind me. In the coffee shop.

Turning around, I rushed through the door. I don't know that I was thinking anything when I entered the store. My brain stops having coherent thoughts when I'm scared.

That's when I saw Sarah and called the cops.

Detective Sam Needles, really that is his name, walked over to where I was now sitting inside the store. "Please tell me you're not rehearsing a scene for a new book or something."

I shook my head. There was a small, unfortunate incident that had happened several months earlier when several mothers at the local park had observed me, Ronnie, Sarah, and Ruthie acting out a scene for a new book, thought we were trying to kill each other, and called the cops. We were but it was because I was trying to figure out the action details and how to describe it in a chapter. I'm a visual person and I needed to see a person's movement before I could write it.

Sam had been dispatched because the local patrol officers were off getting coffee and donuts or something.

Let's just say he wasn't amused when I told him those nosy mothers should have been paying more attention to their precious little progenies rather than adults on the other side of a public park who were minding their own business.

I told him what had happened.

"Was it a man or a woman coming through the door as you were going out?"

I shrugged. "I think it was probably a man because he was so much taller than I am."

Sam tried to keep from snorting. "You do realize you're only about five-three on a good day."

Huffing and trying to stand taller, there's only so much vertical height I can do even with taking deep breaths and blowing it out. "I'll have you know I'm five-four. Don't make me any shorter than I already am."

"So, the person was tall. What were they wearing? Did they have anything in their hand? Hair color or where they wearing a hat? Can you describe anything about this individual?"

Shaking my head, I said, "Um, I was kinda not paying attention. I was irritated with Sarah's poor manners with the new guy, the new barista."

Sam nodded his head. "Did Sarah have any enemies? Anyone she was having a problem with? Owed money to?"

I suddenly realized how little of Sarah's personal life I actually knew. When we got together, all we did was talk about everyday things, nothing important, and nothing really personal.

"Sarah was dating or, rather, had gone out on a coffee date with a guy she met online. But I don't know anything about him."

I hadn't been wild about her picking men out of a lineup on a dating website and told her so. I didn't know the guy's name or anything about him. She told me I was an old fuddy-dud. Seriously? Who even uses words like that anymore? We had exchanged unpleasant words and today was the first day we had seen each other in a week.

With her being so snarky at the barista, I hadn't even cared enough to stay and ask her what was wrong. Maybe my subconscious had picked up bad vibes or maybe it was just me deciding that I'd had enough of her negativity. Whatever it was, I didn't want it in my life.

Maybe I should feel badly about my thoughts and feelings but, to be honest, I really didn't. I was sad she was dead, had been murdered, but I wasn't freaking out about it. My throwing up was more about seeing blood than anything else. I have a notoriously weak stomach when it comes to seeing body fluids, even seeing a kid spit on the ground can cause me to want to vomit. Go figure.

No expression on Sam's face. "Thought you had been friends for years. How could you not know who she was dating?"

Did I dare say we didn't have that type of relationship because that wouldn't make sense...or maybe it did. Just because we were women and friends for years didn't mean we shared all the details of our lives. Or, at least, I don't.

To share all details, intimate details, of my life involved a level of trust that I just simply do not have for most humans. Dogs, yes; humans, no.

Also, I must admit, I truly wasn't that interested in who Sarah was dating right now. Since my own dating life was minimal...who am I kidding? It's non-existent, which means, I wasn't remotely interested in who she was dating. It was different when we were both dating someone because then we had things to talk about but with me not having anyone in the romance department at the moment, I didn't care.

I wasn't sure how to respond to Sam's question, so I shrugged.

Raising his eyebrows slightly, he asked, "You do know where she lives, right?"

Snorting, I gave him the address. "Before you ask, no, I have no clue on any of her passwords or anything. I don't even remember which dating website she was on."

"Do you have a key to her apartment?"

"Um, I think there's one over the door frame." I only knew that because we had been out partying one night, I had been the designated drunk driver, and we had somehow managed to stagger walk up the four steps into her apartment building while giggling where I had to semi-lift her up to get the key.

Where was the apartment key and why didn't she have it with her? Because we had both left our purses with the bartender where he had kindly stashed them under the counter for safekeeping. The key was in her purse.

"Does she have any relatives nearby? Who is her next of kin? Do you know how to contact them?"

A red-haired woman entered the coffee shop, dabbing at her eyes with a tissue, stopped, and took a slow look around the room.

"Sam. What happened?"

"Lisa, do you have security cameras anywhere?" Sam ignored her question. I wondered if Lisa was a special kind of stupid since it was pretty obvious that two people had been killed in her business establishment.

I had known Lisa since middle school. She wasn't that bright then either; however, let me be fair and say that she did have the proverbial green thumb on growing successful businesses in our little town. The coffee shop was success number five.

Not willing to admit that, although my IQ was higher than Lisa's, her ability to connect the dots in life and become a successful business owner did cause a little bit of ugly jealousy within me.

I am a word ho, I sell my words for a living. Sometimes I'm making really good money and other times, I was eating beanie-weenies for a week while waiting on a royalty commission check. There were days where the thought tap danced its way into my mind that I'd probably make more money by selling my body on the street. I was never going to do that, but the thought did occasionally enter my brain.

Lisa pointed at a door with a plastic Employees Only sign on it. "There."

Sam walked over to the door, turned the knob, looked back at Lisa, and said, "Would you unlock the door?"

I could tell he was mentally struggling not to roll his eyes at her. The joys of living in a small town and knowing each other way too well was that we all knew each other's tells.

"Oh, yeah, yeah, sure." Lisa grappled with the door, finally holding up the key she had been trying to jam in the lock, and said, "Um, I don't think this is the right key. I'll have to go home and get the right one."

"Lisa, you mean you don't use the same key for all of your stores?" I was incredulous. It seemed perfectly logical to me that you use the same key for all your stores or, at the very least, have a key ring with all the stores' keys, color-coded of course, in your purse or car at all times.

A Bambi in the headlights look crossed her face. Shaking her head, "It never occurred to me to do that. Thanks, it's a great idea. Sam, I'll be back in a minute."

She scurried out the door. Sam and I looked at each other dumbfounded. I swear I don't know how this woman is such a money-making guru. Maybe I overthink things too much.

"What you want to bet that either the security camera doesn't work or that you can't see anything on it?"

Sam ignored me, walked behind the counter, and poured himself a coffee.

Maybe I was in shock or maybe my mind had already warped into brain fog, I don't know, but I was already mentally writing a new scene for my book because that seemed like the most logical thing for me to do.

"Harper!"

I started, looking around to see who had shouted my name.

It was Sam. He was holding out a cup of coffee. "I wanted to know how you wanted your coffee."

"Black with two shots of vanilla."

Lisa was back, frowning at us like naughty children who had been caught shoplifting expensive candy. Her stern death scare look had zero effect on either one of us. Sam had probably seen more hateful looks in his law enforcement career pulling speedsters over in our small town.

Me? It was nothing like the death stare I received from my now-deceased mother when I informed her many years ago that I was going to make my living by writing novels.

"Just because I named you Harper does not mean you need to be a writer," she sniffed. "I just liked the name – nothing more, nothing less."

Hateful looks did not intimidate me. I just used them in my next book.

Lisa's lips were tight as she walked over to the Employees Only door. On the fourth key, she finally managed to get the door open.

Entering, I glanced around and resolved to never order food from here ever again. There were open containers of cupcakes from a wholesale big box store sitting on metal shelving, crumbs were all over the floor, and open jars of frosting on what should have been a clean countertop. That was covered with used paper towels, a dirty rag of some sort, and coffee cups that appeared to have been sitting there for hours on end if not days.

Sam looked at Lisa who appeared to be oblivious to the hundred and one health code violations. "Um, you do know..."

"The camera is back here." She went through an unlocked door where there was a desk, a chair, a computer, and two camera screens. There was only enough room for one person, two if one was sitting in the metal folding chair.

Sam sat down in the chair, Lisa stood directly behind him, and I was scooched over to the side. Lisa gave Sam the password and told him how to get into the system.

We watched silently as the man entered the store, yes, it was a man, lifted his right arm and shot Sarah twice before turning to the new barista and double-tapped him. The man walked past the countertop and out through the back.

Sarah had barely glanced at the man as he came through the door. I guessed she was more intent on determining whether the new barista had put the ridiculously obscene amount of sugar in her coffee.

How did I surmise this? You could see Sarah's head bent downward as the man approached.

The barista gave the man a welcoming smile as he came through the door. When he shot Sarah, the barista had taken a step backward and raised his hands in surrender. I would hazard a guess that the poor guy thought he was being robbed. Unfortunately, not.

"Do you know him?" asked Sam pointing at the man on the screen.

Lisa didn't say anything. One tear escaped from her left eye and was slowly edging its way down her cheek.

Sam half-turned in his chair. "Lisa, do you know this man?"

"Um, I don't think so."

She was lying. I knew it. I could feel it in my bones. The question was why.

"Okay, I'm going to email this to..."

"Um, I can't let you do that." Lisa was suddenly all businesslike. "I need to talk to my attorney first."

Sam stood up, looking somewhat puzzled. "Why, Lisa? I'm trying to solve a crime, a murder that was committed here in your store. There's nothing incriminating on this tape for your store."

We all backed up from that postage stamp size room.

She shook her head. "Get a search warrant and I'll be happy to give it to you."

Lisa was punching numbers in her phone, looked up, and said, "You can leave now."

Sam stood there for a moment. "Lisa, do you really want to do this the hard way? It's starting to appear that you know the murderer and are protecting him."

She pointed at the door. "Come back when you have a search warrant."

Sam shook his head. "Crime scene. We're not leaving until we've completed what we need to do. On the security tapes, I'll get a search warrant for that."

"Are you being shaken down, Lisa?" Something didn't make sense and my brain was clicking on anything that might get her to talk.

"What part of leave do you guys not understand? If you don't exit my premises within the next thirty seconds, I'm going to have my attorney file harassment charges against the both of you."

I held up my hands in surrender and started walking toward the door. Sam had moved over to his two officers as they were collecting evidence, and they were talking in low tones.

Ideas were swirling in my head on how I could use this in a book. Somewhat oblivious, once again, I literally bumped into Ronnie as I exited Coffee & Cupcakes for the second time today.

"Oh, honey! Are you okay?" He was holding a teacup Maltese puppy. I melted looking into those sweet, innocent eyes, and her beautiful white long hair didn't hurt either. "Here, honey, hold Paige for me."

She was a bouncy little thing. She wanted to lick my face but settled for my neck when I moved my head back. My insides turned into an ooey gooey puddle of love. Little sweet dogs do that to me.

"What's going on, Harper? I heard the sirens," he paused. "Where's Sarah?"

I hugged Paige. I struggled to tell Ronnie what had happened. Instead, I asked, "Did you see anyone before you heard the sirens and saw the blue light special?"

He kind of snickered at the blue light special reference. "Those stores don't exist anymore. Nope, I was busy in the store and didn't see anything. Where's Sarah? I know you two were supposed to have coffee this morning."

Ronnie was busy looking through the plate glass windows when he yelped, "Oh, my goodness! Oh, oh, oh! Is that...is that Sarah laying on the table? Noooo!"

He put his hands to his face and started to cry. "Not Sarah, not Sarah, not Sarah."

Ronnie is definitely always in touch with his feminine side and isn't afraid to show his emotions. In all honesty, he was probably better with them than I am. He's always telling me to feel my feelings. I would except I don't know what I'm supposed to be feeling or how to do that. I don't have a good frame of reference for them. Oh, I can write about them in my books; but, in my real life, eh, not so much. This probably explains my lackluster dating life.

"Honey, I need a hug." Poor Ronnie had a cascade of tears running underneath his glasses and dripping into his beard.

"Um, will your, um, beard lights short circuit or something with your waterworks?" I was more curious than anything else.

Yes, Ronnie had his own sense of style and having brightly colored lights in his beard just added to his special uniqueness.

Hugging me tightly, I didn't hear his muffled reply because I was more concerned that he was going to squish Paige and then we'd have another death today. I could handle Sarah's untimely death but a dog dying…I'd cry buckets and buckets…for days.

I am very sensitive when it comes to animals. Humans, not so much.

Apparently, Ronnie felt Paige squirming between the two of us. "Oh, sweetheart, I am so sorry!" He was cooing to Paige and took her back from me.

"How much is she, Ronnie?" Maybe that's what I needed in my life, a cute, little four-legged dog to love.

"Harper, you can't have her."

I was indignant. "What do you mean I can't have her? I love animals."

"Honey, I know you do," he nuzzled the top of Paige's head, "but you'll forget to feed her or take her out. You're not a responsible pet owner."

Ronnie held up his hand as I started to howl in protest, "Admit it, Harper. You love animals but you'd make a lousy dog mama because you get so involved in writing that you forget about everything going on around you…including your friends."

Did this flamboyant pet store owner just shade me twice? It takes a lot to rile me up but once I am…well, let's just say it's not pretty.

"Did you just call me a witch with a 'b'?" I demanded, attempting to give him the death stare. "Also, what do you mean I don't pay attention to my friends?"

Much as I hate to admit that while he was right on the second part, I still didn't want to have a confirmation.

"Oh, please, girl. You are stressed. Go home and write it out."

That was probably a good idea; however, I didn't want to go home.

"Ronnie."

Grinning, "Yes, I'll see if I can get us two coffees to-go. I'm guessing you've been kicked out since it's a crime scene." He warned and thrust Paige at me at the same time, "You'd better be standing right here when I get back."

He bounced through the doors. I could see him talking to Lisa who kept shaking her head no. She half-turned from him, probably thinking Ronnie'd get the idea and leave. That was a bad, very bad, assumption on her part. I knew what he was going to do and started to laugh.

Ronnie scooted his bottom up on the countertop, swung his legs over, poured two cups of to-go coffee, and started to walk around the counter before Lisa even realized what he'd done.

She was furious. I could see her shouting and waving her arms at him. He blew her a kiss, I opened the door for him, and he handed me a cup.

Lisa took her outrage and aimed it directly at Sam and his crew. He ignored her.

"Here you go, sweetie. For obvious reasons, I didn't put any creamer or sugar in it." Ronnie took a sip of the steaming coffee. "Let's go back to the store and you can tell me everything you know."

Once in the store with all of the cute dogs running around in their playpen, Ronnie set up a metal folding chair next to his padded stool behind the counter. "Tell me everything."

I finished and looked at him. Emotion was starting to take hold of my little gray cells in my brain. I shook my head; I didn't like this feeling. It meant I wasn't in control, and I always like being in control. It's comfortable for me.

"Harper, it's okay, honey, you can cry if you need to." Ronnie was always good for a hug, and I leaned into him. After a few moments of feeling safe in his arms, he pulled back and kissed me on both cheeks.

"Did Tommy get coffee with you and Sarah?"

I jerked my head back. "Wha...what did you say?"

"Tommy King stopped in here before heading down to the coffee shop. I told him you were having coffee with Sarah this morning."

Standing there, I blinked my eyes several times trying to compute what Ronnie was telling me. Tommy King was back in town? I wondered why.

Ronnie was prattling on about Tommy. Most of it was not even registering until he said, "Did you know he's lost over one hundred pounds on the Go-Slo diet? I almost didn't recognize him."

My head whipped around. "Do what?"

"Harper," Ronnie sighed, "please pay attention. I said I almost didn't recognize Tommy because he'd lost so much weight."

I was afraid to ask but inquiring minds needed to know. "What was Tommy wearing?"

"All black from head to toe."

Chapter 2

"I need to talk to Sam." Dashing out the store, I ran the three stores down to Coffee & Cupcakes. Sam was still in the store. Lisa had put up a hand-written sign on the door that said, "Due to unforeseen circumstances, we will be closed today. Opening tomorrow at 7 a.m."

I tapped on the door to get Sam's attention. Lisa gave me the three-finger salute. I was thinking less and less of her adult behavior, it went hand-in-hand with her low IQ.

Apparently, we were going to be playing charades. I pointed at Sam and waved my hand for him to come to me. Lisa grinned, shook her head, and gave me another three-finger salute.

I don't do well with stupid. It tends to bring out the worst in me. I tapped on her door one more time, Lisa looked at me with a snarky smile. I pulled my lipstick out of my purse, and before she could reach the glass entryway, I wrote "You Suck!"

On a very childish level, I took great delight in doing that. On an adult level, that was a complete waste of my dollar store lipstick. I'd never use it again. I was also annoyed that I had let myself be manipulated to do something that emotional.

"What do you want?!" screamed Lisa as she opened the door.

I pointed at Sam, "I need to talk to him."

"You're going to clean that off my door!" snapped Lisa. I ignored her.

Sam came striding over. "Come on, Harper, out here." He looked pointedly at Lisa, "Where we can have some privacy."

She turned the key in the lock on the door, effectively locking us both out.

Sam sighed, "What?"

I told him about Tommy King being at the pet store, dressed all in black, and how Ronnie told him that both Sarah and I would be having coffee this morning.

"What do you know about Tommy?"

Pulling up memories from high school that I'd tried hard to forget, not that high school was all that bad or that long ago, but I wasn't interested in rehashing an old life. But it had nothing to do with my existence now of throwing letters up on a blank laptop screen with fictional characters that only existed in my brain...or, maybe, it had everything to do with it. Sometimes I overthink things; okay, most things. The question becomes does it serve my everyday life in a positive way? My brain had skittered off into Never Neverland.

"Harper, do you need to go to the ER? Shock can do strange things to people." Sam's voice was gentle.

"Huh? Oh, yeah. What was your question again? I was thinking." I had done a deep dive back into those pesky high school memories.

"What do you know about Tommy King?"

I took a deep breath and let it out slowly. "Tommy was a popular kid in high school and dated a lot."

"Did he date Sarah?"

"Well, yeah. I also went out with him a couple of times." Gee, did I sound too defensive? My dates with Tommy were just to a movie and a hamburger. No sparks of teenage hormones threatening to lead either one of us down the primrose path of sin, no goodnight kiss either, no nothing.

Sam wasn't interested in my dating Tommy. "Were Tommy and Sarah a thing, an item?"

This was a little complicated. Time has an interesting way of distorting events, things people said, and how we actually remember the situations.

"They had an on-again and off-again relationship." I was careful about my choice of words. Their dating life wasn't exactly volatile, but it wasn't exactly healthy either. Teenagers are growing bundles of emotions tap dancing their way into adulthood that threaten to erupt on a minute-by-minute basis. Throw in a healthy dose of hormones from both genders and you have a mish-mosh of teenage angst that should probably stay in the blender of life until they're in their early twenties.

Sam was taking notes. "So did they date," he looked at me, "off and on through their high school years?"

I was trying to remember when Sarah first started dating Tommy. "I think they started dating at the first football game when we were sophomores."

"How serious were they?"

Shrugging, I started to say go ask Sarah, but she was not in a position to give him a verbal response. "You never knew with those two. One week they were fine, the next week they hated each other. Typical teenage dating, I guess."

"Did they date after high school? Had Sarah seen Tommy recently?"

Again, I shrugged. "As far as I know, Sarah hasn't seen or talked to Tommy in years. We've been out of school for ten years."

Sam glanced up from his notes. "Were you guys having a ten-year reunion this year?"

I had to stop and think about it. I hadn't been contacted but, then again, I'd only been back in town about six months or so. Maybe my invitation had gotten lost in the mail.

"Not that I am aware of, Sam." Trying to be coquettish, flirty, and not the uninspired writer I was at the moment, "Are you hitting me up for a date?"

Blinking his eyes rapidly for a few seconds, "No, Harper, I'm trying to find a connection to the murder."

I mumbled something, who knows what. I felt rejection once again from the male populace. I need to figure out why I make such futile inane attempts to flirt with unattainable men. I'd ask Ronnie later... maybe.

"Last question and then you can go," Sam smiled. Yes, he had a very nice smile with a cute little dimple in his right cheek. Maybe he wasn't rejecting me after all.

"Tommy's been gone for years?"

I nodded yes.

"Why do you think he was back in town?"

That was a loaded question...and one I didn't want to answer. So, I answered it the easiest way possible, "No clue."

"When was the last time you saw or spoke with Tommy?"

"Sam, thought you said that was my last question and I could leave. Now you've asked another one." I was trying not to sound panicked. "If the person who came through that door and murdered Sarah was Tommy, don't you think he would have said something to me? You know, like hello."

Answer a question with a question, it's what all the top guru negotiators said to do. I hoped it worked.

Cracking a smile, Sam answered, "You're right. I did say that. Okay, go but, don't leave town."

He smiled, I smiled. I didn't have anywhere to go.

Chapter 3

Pondering the morning's events as I drove the few minutes back to my apartment, I wondered if Tommy's suddenly being back in town really did have anything to do with Sarah.

I hadn't heard, seen, or even thought about Tommy in years. The last I heard he was working for some obscure company creating high-tech computer simulators. Sarah and I had laughed over coffee about nerdy Tommy constructing role-playing games for adults. I didn't even know what industry it was for. But this was several years ago, and I didn't have a clue as to what he was doing now.

My phone rang. I didn't recognize the number but so few people called me anymore, including telephone solicitors, I figured it had to be someone whom I had given my number to.

"Hey, it's Sam. I know you're a writer but what did Sarah do? What type of work?"

It suddenly dawned on me that I really didn't know. I knew that she had worked for several companies online but, specifically, I didn't know. Maybe Ronnie was right. I did tend to be oblivious to a number of things. Maybe I am too self-centered.

"Um," I semi-stuttered, "I'm not really sure. I know she had just recently changed jobs. She works from home, she works remotely."

I could almost see Sam rolling his eyes through the phone.

"Ronnie might know." I was trying to be helpful.

We hung up and I immediately punched Ronnie's numbers.

"Hey, sweet'ums." Ronnie was always upbeat and perky.

I quickly told him about my call with Sam. "I hate to say you're right, Ronnie..."

He giggled.

"But what new job was Sarah doing?"

"Honey, Sam's calling. I'll call you back."

Walking into my apartment, I noticed it seemed empty, lonely. I didn't have a lot of knickknacks gracing my décor. They would just be something to dust. I didn't want to think about how my interior life matched the external aspects of my apartment.

Flipping on my laptop, I decided to google Sarah. Maybe that would tell me what new job she was doing. Surprisingly, there was nothing on Sarah Gnome... anywhere. Not on Facebook, not on Instagram, not on YouTube, not on Twitter/X, and not on TikTok. The only two social media platforms I knew she frequented were Facebook and Instagram, but her pages appeared to have been deleted. They had been up just a couple of days ago because I had looked at them. This wasn't good.

Sitting there, thinking, I wondered if Tommy and Sarah were working on something together. That would be strange. Maybe that was what she wanted to tell me over coffee.

With her social media pages being deleted, it meant someone had access to her passwords or maybe even her apartment.

Probably not one of my better thoughts but I decided to go to her apartment. I felt sure Sam would go there. Maybe I'd beat him and could figure out what was going on.

Not seeing any cop cars outside her building, I went inside, found the key over the door, and let myself in. Sarah wasn't the tidiest person in the world, but she wasn't a slob either. Her apartment, on the other hand, was very messy. It didn't look ransacked per se, but it very definitely looked like someone had been through her stuff.

The sofa cushions weren't put back into place, her kitchen – the one place that was always clean – one of the cabinet doors was slightly ajar. Sarah on her worst day wouldn't have left it that way. Papers on the coffee table were askew. Her yellow legal-size pad that she always kept random notes on was not on her desk. Her laptop was gone.

I heard someone rattle the doorknob. Fear rushed through my body like a runaway freight train. For someone who normally never sweats under eighty-two degrees, I was drenched in my body fluid. I was paralyzed with fear. Standing next to Sarah's glass-top desk, I was in full view of the door as it opened.

"Sam!" I gasped, beyond happy it was someone I knew. I went over to the sofa and sat down. I was actually shaking and hoped he wouldn't see how badly scared I was.

His eyes swept the room as he entered. "Not surprised to see you here. What did you notice?"

I told him about the general messiness. "I haven't looked in her bedroom yet or the bathroom."

"You okay to walk or are you still in shock?"

I shrugged and headed to Sarah's bedroom. I wasn't going to dwell on feelings that I didn't know what to do with anyway. I could compartmentalize and think about them later...maybe.

"She always made her bed." I pointed at the pulled back, rumpled up sheets, and duvet. "Sarah never ever didn't make up her bed. Even after sleepovers as a kid, she always made up her bed before we went down to breakfast."

Sam pointed at the dresser drawers. "Doesn't like look those were opened. Here," he tossed me some latex gloves, "open them. Oh, by the way, did you touch anything in the living room?"

I shook my head. "Only the door when I came in. I'd only been here for a couple of minutes before you."

I opened the drawers, nothing looked like it had been touched. Her closet didn't look like anything had been moved around either. This was odd. The living room I could understand but why only the bed and nothing else in her bedroom?

Going into the bathroom, I blinked a couple of times. "Um, Sam, think we've got something here."

On the mirror, in red lipstick, was "You know. Why?

Chapter 4

I noticed the punctuation immediately. Since I'm a writer, that would be my natural first observation. I pointed it out to Sam.

"What do you think it means, Harper?"

That was a no-brainer question for me. Maybe I should become a detective. Better yet, maybe I should become a crime scene writer. I wondered if their books sold well.

"It's someone who's intelligent and made sure they used proper punctuation, which indicates to me they do that on a regular basis, it's a habit. They don't have to think about it.

"It also conveys a sense of betrayal, which means they knew each other. Probably fairly well based on the why question. What it also means is that whoever did this knew where Sarah lived.

"Since the door didn't appear to be jimmied when I got here, it means that someone knew the key was over the doorframe, used it, put it back, and then left. The question really is did someone do this before or after Sarah was murdered? Was she supposed to see it? Was it a warning? But what it specifically means or refers to, I don't have a clue."

Sam smiled, "Good suppositions. While it indicates the individual knew Sarah, it was not an emotional response."

I must have looked somewhat quizzically at him because he said, "If the person was angry, the lipstick would be smeared. Whoever did this took their time to write it, they weren't in a hurry. See how straight up and down the letters are? If they were upset, the letters would be slanted."

"It's almost like they were sad," I added. "Betrayal."

"Harper, you never answered my earlier question about why you thought Tommy might be back in town after years of being away."

"I said no clue, Sam." My heart started beating a little faster. This was a road I didn't want to go down. I honestly didn't think it had anything to do with Sarah's murder.

"You're lying." A flat statement from a small-town detective. Although I had lived in a large city for a number of years before returning here, I had not mastered the passive look of non-interest when someone, anyone, asked me a question.

"Why don't you ask Lisa about him? After all, they dated off and on for three years after we graduated."

"And?" Oh, great, now I was going to have to connect the dots for Sam. Well, at least a few of them.

Taking a deep breath and exhaling, I said, "Could we sit out on the sofa instead of standing here in the bathroom?"

A few minutes later, I was still trying to gather my thoughts on what to share.

"Harper," Sam prodded, "are you going to tell me or not?"

"Okay, Tommy was sorta dating Sarah while they were both in college. They were going to two different schools. Sarah found out that Lisa was also dating Tommy. He was alternating weekends with them. She just happened to come home on a weekend that he wasn't seeing her and saw him and Lisa cozying up at the movies."

I didn't want to tell him that Sarah had become completely unglued seeing Tommy's arm wrapped around Lisa and that they were smooching. That's too tame a word, they were going at it hot and heavy.

I didn't tell him that Sarah took the extra-large bucket of popcorn with extra butter that we had just gotten along with the baby bucket-size soft drink, got up from our seats, went down to the empty row behind the two lovebirds and dumped both the popcorn and drink on the two of them. She took the empty popcorn bucket and smashed it on top of Tommy's head. She also screamed some rather unkind remarks at him and Lisa.

Tommy struggled to pull the popcorn bucket off his head. Lisa tried to climb out of and over her rocking chair seat to get to Sarah who punched Lisa in the nose.

I almost dragged Sarah back up the aisle so she wouldn't be charged with assault. We went out one of the back exit doors.

As far as I knew, Sarah had not spoken to Tommy or Lisa ever again, which is what made it interesting that she wanted me to have coffee with her at one of Lisa's businesses. Maybe she didn't know Lisa owned Coffee & Cupcakes. That was unlikely since Sarah had come back a little more than three years ago.

"What else?"

"That's it."

"Did Tommy ever try to get back in touch with Sarah?" Sam was relentless but I guess that was required to be a detective.

"He tried calling her, but she wouldn't take his calls. In fact, she blocked him. He tried to see her on campus, but he wasn't allowed in her sorority house."

"What about you?"

I shrugged. "Yeah, he called me and wanted to get back with Sarah. I told him that she said she never wanted to see or hear from him ever again. That was it."

I didn't lie. She still held a bit of a grudge against him. Her version was if only he'd been honest and said he was also dating someone else, she'd been okay with that. Now, THAT was a lie. She was also dating other guys at school and hadn't told Tommy about them either. So, you had two liars dating each other. Even with my limited dating experience, I knew that relationship was never going to work long-term.

I inwardly sighed. If only I had applied that to my own life, I probably wouldn't be divorced and living back in a small town named Palm Park with only four palm trees, hundreds of oak trees, and too many pine trees to count. Northeast Florida wasn't conducive to healthy palm tree life.

City life felt too overwhelming. At least the memories here were not as devastating as those in the city. That's what I told myself. I had to believe that.

"What did Sarah major in?" Sam ran his hand through his wavy black hair. "I'm trying to find the connection here. There's got to be one."

"Well, what about that new barista guy? Maybe someone was after him and Sarah just happened to be in the way." I probably sounded a little defensive of Sarah. I guess I just didn't want to believe someone had targeted her specifically.

"He's a nephew of Lisa's and had just graduated from college. He was working there until he found a job in Jacksonville. Chances of someone explicitly gunning for him are not high."

Sam held up his hand. "He wasn't into drugs or anything like that. He graduated from college in three years, not four. He was a nose-to-the-grindstone type of kid."

I am a persistent person if nothing else. I don't have any better sense than to keep plugging away at something until I have an answer.

"What about someone warning Lisa? If that's the case, then she'd be playing in a pretty high-stakes game." Yes, the thought had crossed my mind that maybe the murders of two people, who had nothing to do with each other except to be in the wrong place at the wrong time, were a warning to Lisa.

Sam was impassive. No sign that he had even heard me. Cops aren't supposed to acknowledge anything, I guess.

He exhaled. "Harper, why don't you answer my questions without skirting around? Seems like you have avoidance tendencies."

I hadn't thought of myself that way before. Maybe I could work it into my latest book. I'd have to google the symptoms. I vaguely wondered if they could be cured.

"It's called 'squirrel', I'm easily distracted by new thoughts." I smiled.

"Nope, it's called you're trying to avoid giving me answers that might help solve this case because you don't want to cast anyone in a bad light."

Well, there was that.

"Sarah majored in art, but it wasn't schoolteacher art. It had something to do with mechanical art." I had to search my brain. Sarah liked things that most people wouldn't call art. I didn't think mechanical drawings were art, but I am a word artist, and I would hazard a guess that most people wouldn't think of that as being a writer.

"She mentioned something about three or four weeks ago that she was working on something called geovisual art. I don't even know what that means." I dropped my shoulders and raised my hands palms up.

"Here's someone you've known your whole life and yet you seem to know so little about her, Harper. Doesn't that strike you as more than a little odd?"

Um, no, it really didn't. Was I just that obtuse about my friends? Maybe. Did this mean my brain just shut down about any human interaction that didn't involve me or what I was working on? I didn't think so but perhaps I wasn't the best judge of that. I'd have to ask Ronnie about that also... maybe.

"I hate to say it, but maybe you're right." I exhaled slowly. "I didn't understand what Sarah did and she really never talked about her work. I know that she worked for some pretty decent companies because I do remember her saying on a couple of occasions that whatever company she was working for wouldn't let her put in but so much money in her 401K. So, to me, that means she was making good money."

"If she was doing so well, why was she living in an apartment instead of owning a house?"

I laughed, "That's easy, for the both of us. It means someone else has to take care of the maintenance and you don't have to pay for it. Owning a house, you have to have someone do the lawn, pay for repairs, and you have a mortgage. Living in an apartment is a low-stress decision."

"You're not building equity in anything."

"True but it's not worth the hassle. Besides, her investments seemed to be doing well." I added, "So are mine."

"So, you knew she was working for a new company about three or four weeks ago then?"

I nodded. "But I don't know the name of it or what she was doing. I did notice last week when we were talking on the phone that she seemed a little stressed. She's the one who suggested we hook up for coffee today. Said she wanted to run a couple of things past me. I just assumed it was about that new guy she met on the dating website." I had a thought. "Maybe Ronnie knows something."

Looking around the apartment one more time, Sam said, "Okay, nothing else looks out of place to you?"

I shook my head.

"Keep the key with you. If we need to get back in, I'll let you know. Go home, Harper. Sooner or later, all of this is going to hit you like a ton of bricks and you should be somewhere where you feel comfortable and safe. If you think of anything else, here's my cell number." He wrote it down on the back of his business card and handed it to me.

Grinning, "Don't go see Ronnie. Let us do our work. In fact, I'm going to follow you back to your apartment."

Rats! I'd just call Ronnie when I got home then.

Sam did follow me back home. In fact, he followed me all the way to my door.

"Did you want to come in?" I was semi-struggling to be nice. I really just wanted him to leave.

"Yes, I want to check and make sure your apartment is okay."

That someone might want to invade my apartment had never occurred to me. I cautiously opened the door, peeking my head carefully inside. "Nope, don't see anything."

Sam walked past me, surveying the living room/dining area, poked his head in the bedroom, and then checked out the bathroom.

I was actually a little amused. It reminded me of all the Law & Order tv shows I had watched. "Everything clear, Detective?"

He grinned. "Yes. Just making sure. And because I know you're going to call Ronnie the minute this door is shut, tell him I'm on my way."

Smiling, I nodded. Punching the numbers in as I heard the door click, it struck me as a little unusual that Ronnie didn't answer my call but maybe he was waiting on a customer. I left a message and didn't think anymore about it.

I wish I had.

Chapter 5

An unknown number popped up on my phone. Literally, that's what it said. I surmised it was probably Sam. A weird thought sprouted in my brain; I wondered if he was calling me for a date. Why would I even think that? Obviously, I rationalized, my emotions had short-circuited, and errant thoughts were running rampant through my mind. I shook my head trying to clear those peculiarities from taking hold.

"Hello."

I was right. It was Sam calling. I smiled. Except he couldn't see it. He also didn't sound happy.

"Did you actually talk to Ronnie when you called?"

Fear and a tremendous sense of foreboding washed over me. I didn't like all these emotions that kept insisting on visiting my brain today.

"Ah, no. I left a message for him. I thought he might have been with a customer." I paused, "Why?"

"Someone beat the crap out of him. He's on the way to the hospital."

I gasped. What was going on? Ronnie was the sweetest guy in the world. He would not have argued with a robber, he would give them anything they wanted as long as they didn't harm the animals in the pet store.

"Are the dogs okay?"

"What? Yeah, they're fine. The two little white ones were cuddled up next to Ronnie. It looks like he may have been trying to protect them. There's blood all over them. It's Ronnie's blood, not theirs. Does he have anyone else who looks after the store when he's not here?"

"Donnie does sometimes." I gave him the number. I was shivering. "Sam, I'm going over to Ronnie's house and..."

"Harper, you need to stay out of this. Ronnie lives over on Pinewood in the little bungalow, right?"

I nodded. Duh! Sam couldn't see that. "Uh, yeah."

"On second thought, Harper, meet me there but don't go in until I'm there."

Disconnecting the phone, I started to cry. This was not my standard wimpy cry-once-every-three-years-for-five-minutes-whether-I-needed-to-or-not routine. This was from a previously untapped deep well of emotion. I didn't know I could feel this way. I didn't even feel like this after my divorce. This hurt. It was a physical, emotional, and spiritual hurt.

I cried for Sarah and my lost friendship. I cried for the barista who was just starting his life when it was terminated so abruptly. I cried for Ronnie and prayed that he would live. I borderline wailed for the little puppies who were probably traumatized beyond belief. And, lastly, I cried for myself. That part I wasn't sure about me crying for myself except that it felt like I needed to.

Wiping the tears from my face and honking like Canadian geese flying south for the winter into a tissue, I half-expected Sam to call and ask where I was. Surprisingly, only ten minutes had passed since I had my total emotional breakdown.

Taking a handful of tissues, stuffing them in my purse for future use, I shut and locked my apartment door. For whatever reason, I reached my hand up to the doorframe and did a quick swipe. I don't know why I did that because I had never put a key up there. I wasn't prone to locking myself out of my apartment and there really was no need for anyone else to have a key.

My fingers bumped something as I swiped, and a key fell on the floor. That was weird...and scary. I picked up the key. My brain was not comprehending what I was looking at. I just stood there, blinking, nothing was registering on why a key would be over my door. I put the key in the lock, and it easily unbolted my door.

I needed to see Sam and tell him what was going on. He was sitting in his car when I got to Ronnie's.

"What's going on, Harper?" He was semi-frowning. "You look like you've seen a ghost."

Stuttering, which I'm prone to do when I'm scared and that doesn't happen very often, I explained how I had found the key over my door.

"This is so not good," I finally managed to get out. "Before you ask, I have never given anyone a key to my apartment. Not Sarah, not Ronnie, not Ruthie, not anyone."

"Where's Ruthie?"

"Oh, she's a flight attendant and only comes home about once a year. I don't know where she is at the moment."

"Her parents?" Sam asked. He had his phone out and was texting.

"Dead, have been for many years."

Sam stood there, tapping his first finger against his chin. "Harper, when you guys were acting out the scene for your book a couple of months ago, did you notice anyone..."

I started to interrupt and tell him those nosy mothers should have been keeping an eye on their kids versus watching us.

He held up his hand. "Other than the mothers at the park, did you notice anyone else? A man? Someone who didn't look like they belonged there?"

Blinking my eyes several time and exhaling through my nose, I shook my head. "I don't think so. I don't remember for sure. We were just very slowly going through the motions so I could write it down as it was happening. I really don't remember seeing anyone else there."

My brain was whirling around with the slightest of all possibilities that maybe all of this had something to do with one of my books...except I don't write murder mysteries. I write somewhat steamy romances where sometimes two guys fight over the girl.

While I had a decent following on social media, I was nowhere close to being a megastar. No stalkers that I was aware of. No one wanted to kill me that

I knew of, and, if that were the case, whoever killed Sarah could have easily shot me dead in front of the store.

"Harper, stand behind me," Sam ordered as he tried the knob. The door opened easily, and he cautiously leaned in through the door.

"Hello. Police."

No answer, no rustling, no sound. It was quiet.

"Does Ronnie always leave his door unlocked?" Sam turned back to me before proceeding further into the house.

"Yes. His opinion is if anyone is going to steal anything, he'd rather them just take it instead of breaking the door or window. Plus," I sort of laughed, "he always says he doesn't have anything worth stealing."

"What about a TV or laptop?"

I looked around the living room. "He has one in the bedroom, and I don't know about a laptop. I think he has one at the store though."

Walking through the fastidiously clean living room and kitchen, I didn't see anything out of place. Noticing our yearbook on his coffee table, I did point that out to Sam.

"Was that always here?"

I shrugged. "I don't know. I rarely ever came over here. We always met at different places, like I did with Sarah."

We walked around the little house not seeing a single thing that looked like it had been disturbed from its normal place.

Sam laughed, "Did Ronnie decorate the house himself or did he have an interior designer?"

I laughed also. "Ronnie did it all himself. I don't think pet store owners make enough to hire interior designers. I know that he sometimes went to Jacksonville and designed some homes."

Holding up my hand, "No, I don't know any of their names."

"Is this a side hustle for Ronnie or did he have a degree, training, whatever it is called for interior design?"

I vaguely remembered Ronnie saying something about going to Atlanta a long time ago and taking some courses. Since I've only been back in town six months or so, I was still catching up on others' lives. I touched base with friends over the years since high school but nothing in-depth with their personal lives. It was the old standard of "Hey, how you doing? Whatcha been up to, etc." type of calls.

Honestly, I kind of thought it was rude to delve too much into others' lives. I guess that was part of my emotional disconnect with people. What I thought of as being kind and considerate they viewed as not being interested and, therefore, didn't share much about their lives. I wasn't sure how to make that connection to others. Maybe I needed to go to therapy.

Answering him, "Yes, I think he did at one time. Lisa might know."

Sam snorted, "She's lawyered up on everything. If I ask her what time of day it is she'll say, 'Talk to my lawyer.' That's a waste of time. Would Donnie know?"

"They run in the same circles. Probably."

Doing a slow turn in the middle of the living room, Sam pointed at the light fan combo. "Why does Ronnie have a camera there?"

I looked. "Maybe in case anyone does try to steal something, he has a picture of them. I don't know."

His phone buzzed and he answered it. "Yeah, okay. Keep me apprised. I'm going back to the pet store."

Turning to me, "Ronnie's on life support."

"I can't do this," I murmured, "I can't do this." I sat down, on the floor, in the middle of the living room.

"Harper, Harper." The voice sounded very far away. It felt like time had been suspended in the universe. I saw colors floating slowly around me. I could still feel myself breathing. Maybe I had died, and this is what heaven looked like. I heard someone talking but it didn't make any sense, it was only sounds, a vibration of some sort being offered up into the air. I was faintly aware that my body was being moved. I didn't know where. I didn't care. I shut my eyes and again wondered if I had died. Time ceased to exist.

Chapter 6

Opening my eyes I felt moderately refreshed. It took a moment for me to realize where I was. The emergency room. The one place I didn't want to be. I was pretty sure no one wanted to be in the hospital, especially the emergency room.

I wondered how I had gotten here. I noticed an IV stuck in my arm, that explained why I felt somewhat better than I had earlier in the day. I pushed the call button that was in my hand.

A smiling nurse came in. "Hi, there. Good to see you awake. Can you tell me your name and where you are?"

I wondered what she would do if I gave her a name out of one of my books rather than using my real name. I decided to test it out.

"Mary Savoy. I'm in Bright Springs, Florida."

She kept her smile, glancing at the computer screen. "Do you remember hitting your head?"

"No."

She left the room and Sam came in with her a minute later. He gave me a look that was probably practiced on prison inmates. A poker face that I was having a hard time reading, it was stern, passive, and not remotely amused that I had given the nurse the wrong name.

"So, you don't remember your name and you live in a fictional town?"

Maybe he'd go away if I shut my eyes. I didn't hear them leave so I kind of opened one eye in a slit to see if they were still there. They were.

"You know I can have them put you in a room overnight, don't you?" Sam sounded bored. "Do you want to play nice and go home or do you want spend the night here?"

I'd rather be anywhere but in the hospital. I took a deep breath and let it out slowly. "I'm Harper Elizabeth Rogers and I'm in the ER with Detective Sam Needles."

Sam burst out laughing. "Your initials are H.E.R., HER?"

I rolled my eyes. "What can I say? My mother had a perverted sense of humor."

The nurse laughed also. "Okay, Harper. Tell me how you're feeling now."

I semi-groaned and tried to reposition myself on the bed. "I think I'm better. What happened? Why am I in here?"

"What's the last thing you remember, Harper?" Sam asked, his face muscles had relaxed a little.

Trying hard to remember, my brows furrowed together, and my lips were in a tight line. "We were in Ronnie's house, you said something about a camera. Uh, you got a phone call and said Ronnie's on life support. That's all I remember."

"Okay, that's good." Sam did an up nod to the nurse. "How soon can she get out of here?"

The nurse left to go confer with the powers that be...at least, that's what I was assuming. I still had on my clothes from earlier, so I didn't have to worry about wearing a hospital gown on the way home with Sam.

"Are you going to tell me what happened or not?" I tried to sound demanding. This whole thing was embarrassing. I just wanted to go home and hide.

"You fainted, probably due to the shock of Sarah and the coffee guy being murdered..."

"Barista." I hate it when people don't use the right word to describe something. I'm sure I make mistakes also with the English language, but I strive not to.

Sam ignored me and continued. "Finding out that Ronnie had been beaten up and was on life support, that's when you collapsed on the floor. You went into shock, and I called for the ambulance."

"Oh, great." I semi-snorted, "This is beyond embarrassing, Sam. Just take me home and let me hide."

"You're going to be cleared shortly but I don't think you should go back to your apartment. Do you have anyone you could spend the night with?"

"Why?"

"Safety reasons."

I scrunched up my face. "Um..."

"One, I want someone to keep an eye on you for tonight in case you have any other reactions to what's happened today. Two, in case someone decides to pay a visit to your apartment. And three," he smiled, showing off the dimple in his cheek, "I don't want another murder on my hands."

Well, I couldn't argue with that logic. I didn't want anything else happening to me either. I couldn't think of anyone who would let me spend the night. They either had children, which I'm not overly fond of, or they were somewhat newly married...for the second or third time, or they weren't the type of friends who I could ask something like that.

I knew a lot of people but just not ones I felt comfortable enough asking or that I liked well enough to even spend one night at their home.

"Just take me to the Holiday Inn Express and I'll spend the night there." I grinned, "And since you've been so nice..."

Sam rolled his eyes.

"Because I know you're going to take me home so I can get some clean clothes before taking me to the hotel, I'll spring for a nice dinner somewhere if you can take an hour off to eat."

Sam had his hands in his pants pockets and rocked back on his heels, grinning. "Harper Rogers, are you asking me out on a date?"

Okay, that really wasn't the word I had in mind, but I could sort of understand where he was coming from. I guess it may have sounded like that to a guy. I was somewhat confused by my sudden burst of social niceness but then decided it wouldn't hurt to have another friend. At least, that's what I was trying to tell myself. He was cute.

I sniffed. "Call it whatever you want. I was merely trying to be nice."

He laughed. "Let's get you out of here. I'm starving."

Chapter 7

About thirty minutes later we were sitting in the local steak house and, much as I hate to admit it, it did feel like a date. We made small talk which, surprisingly, wasn't awkward. It felt like we had known each other for years. We kind of did. Sam was a couple of years behind me in school and, obviously, we had not stayed in touch throughout the years. Everything was fine until he asked the one question that made me want to lie.

"So, what brings you back to our lovely little town?" He grinned as he speared another piece of his ribeye. "I thought you were going to become the next New York Times best-selling author."

I slightly huffed. "You know, you can still make good money without being on the New York Times list. I have a friend who writes romance novels and is consistently pulling ten to twelve thousand dollars a month and I guarantee you've never heard of her."

Sam leaned back, and put his hands up in mock surrender. He was still smiling but it was a warm smile, not the kind that made you want to punch his lights out. "No offense, Harper. I thought that was the dream of every writer."

Shaking my head, "Not necessarily. It would be nice, but my goal has always been to have people enjoy my work. Plus, as Dolly Parton says, 'I ask God to give me some to share and some to spare.' I do okay, I'm not rich but I also don't have to eat beanie weenies on a regular basis."

Looking at me with very kind eyes, "If this isn't in your budget, I can pay for it, Harper. It's not a big deal."

Now, I was almost embarrassed. It made me sound poor. I thought I was putting to rest so many people's perception of writers that we were all poor, starving artists unless we had some big success like the New York Times list. I wanted to slap people who thought that writers on that list made beaucoodles of money. Some did, but I also knew several writers who barely made their advance money from the big-name publishing houses.

Attempting to educate this one person of the public, I said, "Self-published authors can make more money than being published by a traditional mainstream publishing house.

"Also," I sniffed, okay, I'm a snob, "I can maintain control over all my work and then if I want to sell my books to a big house, I can. But," I held my finger up, "unless someone's offering something in the high six figures, I'm going to keep doing what I'm doing."

"Actually, that's very interesting." He put another piece of steak in his mouth. "I wondered how all of that works. Maybe I'll write a book one day."

I couldn't leave well enough alone. No, I had to spill my guts about being an author. "Writing's the easy part. The hard part is constantly marketing your books and getting readers to buy them."

He nodded. "So, are you going to write a book about these murders? You know, something like 'Bloodstain on Elm Street' or 'Rustic Secrets of Pinecrest.'"

I couldn't help it, I started to laugh. "Those titles sound like a Freddie Kruger movie. Actually, I write fiction, not non-fiction but," I shrugged, "you never know. Of course, now that I have an in with local law enforcement. That might be a thought to pursue. It depends on how this all turns out."

Suddenly, there was a little tension in the air between the two of us. "Sorry, I, I, I didn't mean to overstep my bounds," I stuttered. "I, I just meant..."

He smiled again, the dimples were back, he wasn't mad or, at least, I didn't think so. "No, don't worry about it, Harper. I was just thinking there's so much we don't know at this point. You saw Tommy King, our primary suspect, yet nothing's happened to you."

"Well, I didn't actually see him, remember? The guy who walked past me wasn't Tommy. Yeah, well, I'm not planning on anything happening to me either," I snapped.

"I hardly think Sarah or the coffee guy or Ronnie thought anything was going to happen to them either," Sam said drily. "Most people don't wake up thinking this is the day I'm going to die or get shot or get beaten up. There's a connection here, I just haven't found it yet."

Unexpectedly, I was bored, tired, and no longer wanted to be around people. My ability to be engaging in public and around people took a nosedive heading south. I just wanted to go to the hotel, take a shower, get in bed, and pull the covers up over my head. That was a do-able exercise.

"Sam, would you mind taking me to the hotel? I think I've had all the fun I can stand for one day."

He slid out of the booth. "No problem, let's go."

"Wait, I need to pay for the meal." I hadn't seen the waiter except to fill our iced tea glasses from several minutes ago.

"You can pay next time, Harper." Sam smiled, his eyes twinkling. "This one's on me and, before you ask, I had a free meal coming to me anyway."

He held out his hand helping me out of the booth. Maybe this was a quasi-date.

Chapter 8

Pulling around to the hotel's back entrance door, Sam hopped out of the car. "Stay here, I'll be back in a minute."

I tilted my head back against the headrest and promptly fell asleep.

A few minutes later, Sam opened the door. "Come on, sleepy head. I've gotten you a room on the second floor. It's under the name of Mary Savoy."

I grinned. "Thanks for using one of my characters but why a different name? I actually kind of like my own name."

"Because I can't have anything happen to you." He grinned, "We get rooms periodically to protect people and you're now a protected person."

Struggling to get out of the car, I smiled. "So, I'm in the witness protection program now?"

"Kind of. You're the only connection in this investigation right now. Ronnie was a year behind you in school. You, Sarah, Tommy, and Lisa were all in the same class." He scratched his head. "Honestly, there may not be an association between y'all or there may be the tiniest bit of one but until we figure out what's going on, I need to keep you safe."

Actually, it was kind of exciting to be in the witness protection program even if it was on a local level. Apparently, my sense of adventure, always on the lowest rung of the totem pole to begin with, was spiking. I knew I was going to find a way to work it into one of my books.

We got to the room door, Sam opened it for me, took a cursory look around, double-checking the bathroom to make sure no one was hiding behind the shower curtain, and said, "You've got the room for five days. If you need to or want to go somewhere, check with me first."

Walking out the door, he turned, winked, and said, "This'll give you an opportunity to work on a new book...or finish whatever you're working on. Night."

The door shut and I walked over, pushing the long u-bolt over the door safety guard. Popped in the shower and then fell exhausted in bed.

I heard a light tapping at the door, groaning, I rolled and squinted at the phone to see what time it was. It was three twenty-seven. Even in my groggy state, I knew something was wrong. If it were Sam, he would have called first. I immediately texted him.

The tapping was insistent, but it had a rhythmic beat. My heart was pounding. I was also annoyed because I had taken a shower hours ago and now I was drenched in sweat. I didn't want to take another shower.

Easing my way out of bed, I padded over to the door. I had already silenced my phone so when the light flashed indicating a new message, I wasn't alerting whoever was on the other side of the door.

"Keep them there as long as possible. On my way."

"Uh, yeah, who is it?" I tried to sound sleepy, which I no longer was. I was also standing next to the door hinges. I had read somewhere, maybe in one of my books, that if someone were going to shoot you, don't stand by the doorknob.

The voice was muffled. I tried to look out the peephole, but it was covered. That was definitely not a good sign.

"I didn't order pizza." I was trying to sound confused. The tapping continued. If the fool who was tapping on my door thought I was going to open it, they were beyond stupid.

"Hotel security. Open the door, ma'am."

"Wait. Okay? I've, I've got to put some clothes on." I really didn't want to give this guy any untoward ideas; however, I was trying to stall as long as possible so Sam could get here.

Oh, lord! This sounded like a romance novel where the damsel in distress needs the knight in shining armor riding on a white horse comes to her rescue. I think I live in my head too much. I could semi-justify my errant thoughts because of everything that had happened in the last twenty-four hours, although it felt like a week, but my brain had turned to mush, and bizarre thoughts that had never once entered my brain in my entire life were now bouncing around like an Olympic Chinese ping pong match.

The tapping suddenly stopped. I heard loud voices in the hallway and then a slam against my door. That was it! My nerves couldn't take it anymore. I ran into the bathroom thinking if someone did manage to get through the locked door, they'd have to go through the locked bathroom door. Surely, I wasn't worth that much effort...or I hoped not.

Now a different knocking on the door. My heart was still pounding. I'm not a drinker but I was thinking I definitely needed something to calm my nerves...at three something in the morning. All of this craziness was beyond out-of-the-box life for me. I was in a snow globe that was being shaken. In one sense, it was thrilling and exciting; and in the other sense, I absolutely hated it.

"Harper, Harper! It's safe. It's me, Sam. You can open the door now."

"Stand in front of the peephole," I demanded. I didn't want a masked intruder entering my room.

Standing on my tiptoes, I looked through the little hole in the door. Sam was standing back and had a guy in handcuffs turned sideways so I could see him.

I unlocked the door.

"Do you know who this is?" asked Sam. The handcuffed guy was about six feet tall and thin, but he didn't look like anyone I knew. I shook my head.

"Do I know you?" I was perplexed. He didn't answer.

"Was this the guy who walked past you into Coffee & Cupcakes?" Sam was all business.

"I, I..."

"I want an attorney." Finally, the man spoke.

All Sam had done at that point was handcuff him. All I had done was stutter and now the guy wants an attorney? This made absolutely no sense. Why would he lawyer up this quickly?

He caught Sam off-guard because he raised his eyebrows at me. "We can do that down at the station."

A uniformed officer came strolling down the hall. "Detective?"

"Take him down to the station. Disturbing the peace."

The officer did a curious side eye glance at Sam, nodded, and motioned for the man to start walking down the hallway.

Turning to me, Sam asked, "Are you sure that's not the man from the coffee shop?"

I hated to admit that I wasn't paying any attention when the guy pushed past me. "I honestly don't know, Sam." I gulped, "I really was thinking of other things." That sounded lame even to me, but it was all I could come up with.

"Was that Tommy King? Also, can we go into your room and not do this out here in the hallway?"

"Ah, yeah, of course, um, sorry."

"Well?" Sam had sat down in the desk chair. He kept his eyes on my face. I was wearing pajamas instead of my normal tee shirt; otherwise, I'd be beyond embarrassed about my lack of clothing.

I raised both eyebrows. "Well, what?"

Sam was exasperated. "You know, it's really annoying how you answer a question with a question or deflect a question altogether and change topics. Was. That. Tommy. King?"

I shook my head. "Tommy's much heavier."

"Ronnie said he had lost a lot of weight. Would that be Tommy King with the weight loss?"

I thought for a moment. "No. That guy didn't have Tommy's face. Plus, Tommy's eyes are blue. That guy had brown eyes."

Nodding his head, he tapped his chin thoughtfully. "I don't recall seeing that guy in the lobby when I checked you in. There was no one in the hallway when we came up in the elevator and no one was in this hallway when I opened the door. You're not registered under your own name."

He snapped his fingers. "Harper, did he use your name at any time before I got here?"

"No. The only thing he said a couple of times was hotel security and he wasn't very loud. He was kind of hard to hear. He had also put his hand over the peephole because I tried looking out to see who it was."

Sam knit his eyebrows together. "This just keeps getting curiouser and curiouser."

"Alice in Wonderland." I popped up with, smiling. "I know that book."

"What?"

He wasn't amused. I guessed it would hard to explain to him that playing Jeopardy on a regular basis was almost an aphrodisiac to a writer...and nerdy people. I guess I need to admit to myself that I am nerdy. I preferred to think of myself as an intellectual who can't be bothered with those pesky plebeians whose IQ is in the same realm as Lisa's. Now I am an erudite snot. What was going on with all these weird thoughts? I've obviously short-circuited my brain somewhere along the line in the past twenty-four hours. I had to admit that maybe, just maybe, that's not a bad thing.

I've been in the doldrums for several months and maybe all this activity, as horrible as it was, was what I needed to re-establish myself back in the land of the living. Poor choice of words with two people dead and one on life support. I started to chuckle.

"You do realize that none of this is funny, Harper." Sam's tone was sharp, and it was a statement, not a question.

"I'll explain it some other time to you." I took a deep breath. "What's next?"

The corners of his mouth turned downward slightly before becoming a small smile. "It's too early for breakfast here. I'm wide awake and I have to be at work in a couple of hours. No point in me going back home and trying to sleep. You're up. We might as well go to Huddle House for breakfast."

He wiggled his eyebrows. "At least you can always come back here and take a nap."

It didn't sound like a bad idea. "Um, let me change into some jeans and a shirt." I grabbed my clothes and changed in the bathroom. Were we starting to connect on a personal level? That was scary. My last relationship, my marriage, ended in disaster. I wasn't willing to risk my emotions again. Emotions are fickle...and they lie...a lot. Push back, close off, shut down, compartmentalize, those things I could do well. After all, that's what I've been doing for months. It was comfortable. I knew deep down I was lying to myself, but I also wasn't willing to change. Not right now anyway.

I came out of the bathroom with a minimal amount of makeup on and I had run a brush through my hair so I didn't look like the wild woman of Borneo. A runway model I'm not but I'm in small town USA and who cares if I'm not a fashionista? I certainly don't and I don't really think Sam cares either. Unless you're dog ugly, I don't think most men pay much attention to a woman's makeup. I could be wrong, but I don't think so.

Chowing down on a grease-laden, cholesterol-filled breakfast, Sam mumbled something.

"Sorry, I didn't catch that," I said taking a sip of coffee.

"I said you never answered my question from dinner about why you came back here." His eyes twinkled, "Remember, I said you're good about deflecting questions and changing topics? You never answered my question."

Not wanting to pursue this unwanted topic of conversation, I went back to poking my food around on the plate. No longer hungry, I didn't want to admit failure in any part of my life. People used those debacles to remind me of how inferior I am in the universe. I realize I'm not perfect, I'm human, but I do try to keep my mistakes down to the bare bone minimum.

"Divorce." Maybe that one word would keep Sam from asking any more questions. Unfortunately, I added more to it. "I can write anywhere."

Looking up from slathering an ungodly amount of butter on his toast, he asked, "Why come back here then? I would think a large city like Jacksonville would offer far more benefits in terms of culture and artistic friends than here."

I really shouldn't have added 'I can write anywhere,' now it opened up the door for more conversation than what I wanted to explain.

My lips were set in a tight line and I just kind of nodded my head. "So, what kept you here in Palm Park? Didn't you ever have a desire to leave?"

"Nope."

Our eyes searched each other's but no magic knowing of our own inside secrets. Just two people looking at each other. No more, no less.

Pulling out his phone, he glanced down at it. "Ronnie's off life support and is breathing on his own. He's still in ICU though. Looks like he's going to make it."

He chuckled and looked at me. "Donnie's arranged for the gay brigade to have someone posted outside his room until he's better."

I grinned. "Ronnie's friends will definitely take care of him and, by the way, not all of his friends are gay."

Sam held up his hands in mock surrender. "I was not casting dispersion on anyone. It actually makes my life a lot easier to have his friends around taking care of him. We simply don't have enough people on the force to post someone outside his room and keep him safe. The ICU team is great, but they can't keep their eye on every patient a hundred percent."

We chatted a few more minutes and I could see the sun starting to push its way through the inky darkness of night and turning it into day. I loved watching the pink and soft blue rays poking their way into wakefulness. Morning was my favorite time of day.

On the way back to the hotel, Sam glanced at his phone again. "Do you know a Danny Willis?"

My stomach dropped to my feet. I gasped. The world started spinning. I felt faint.

"That...that...that was Danny Willis?"

Chapter 9

I sat in stunned silence. Even though I'm not a best-selling author, I do sell a fair number of books and make a decent living at it. I suppose at some point every writer has a stalker. I've never had a fan show up at my door before and that was more than somewhat disconcerting, especially since he showed up at the hotel. I did wonder if he was the one who had broken into my apartment or had put the key over the door. How had he gotten a key? That was the scary part.

"I take it you know him." Sam's tone was flat. "Why didn't you tell me you knew him, Harper?"

"I don't, I didn't," I stuttered. "How, how did he find me?"

"Tell me, from the beginning."

"Um, well, he started following me on social media. Then he started sending fan emails. I typically respond to people." I started to twist my hands. "He then started saying he loved me and wanted to take me out on dates. I ignored those and didn't respond."

Taking a deep breath, I continued, "I also really don't put anything really personal out on social media, so I didn't think much about it."

"What happened?"

"He started sending me photos of places where I had been, photos of me with friends, photos of me and my ex-husband...before he became my ex-husband. He'd say things like 'I could be here with you' or 'We'd have so much fun together.' Then he sent me pictures of my husband with another woman..." I paused, it was still very painful and even harder to verbalize, "in a compromising position."

"Sheet Olympics," murmured Sam.

I nodded. "I haven't heard that term before but yes. Danny said he loved me and would never do to me what my husband was doing, that he would never cheat on me."

"Did you report him?"

I just looked at Sam. The thought of 'you're a special kind of stupid' bounced around in my brain. Instead, I said, "What do you think? Yes, but you and I both know virtually nothing is going to be done. It only shows a paper trail on the off chance that I'm murdered or something. Then everyone will lament about how the system has failed once again, how the system is broken, what a nice person I was, blah, blah, blah."

Sam merely nodded his head in agreement. "Harper, how do you think he found you?"

Almost breaking down in tears, I hate all these emotions that keep springing up, I semi-wailed, "No clue. That's your job. You find out how he's done this. I'll file harassment charges against him. Send him back to wherever he lives. Make him leave me alone."

Sam looked a little awkward, which was kind of surprising considering all the strange people he encounters. Maybe he doesn't run into emotional females very often. *I* don't run into this side of me...ever.

"Is this the reason why you moved back to Palm Park? Danny Willis caused you to get a divorce from your husband and you figured here was better than Jacksonville?"

Well, Sam did have a way of shortening everything down to a few words.

I was defeated. I didn't want to admit to Sam that my marriage had been over for a while. I knew it but simply didn't want to acknowledge it because then it meant I'd have to take action and actually do something about my miserable existence. I wasn't actually living a good life. It was empty, lonely. My marriage was a sham after the first year. I knew it, he knew it, but we were both economic slaves. We needed to stay together because the cost of living in a decent area was high. I vaguely wondered what I ever saw in him. I was pretty sure he probably thought the same thing about me.

I was happier being back here in small town USA knowing I could always escape to the larger city if I wanted to. People here genuinely cared about each other. It wasn't all smoke and mirrors. The fake facial façade that so many wore in the city wasn't running rampant here. Oh, people would still smile and stab you in the back – it's a small town after all – but you always knew right where you stood with them. You never had to guess. Pros and cons to everything.

"Close enough, Sam." I sniffed, "Is there anything you can do about Danny Willis?"

Chuckling, he said, "Well, I can try to put the fear of God in him but, I'm guessing, since he's lawyered up, he has a fairly good idea of what we can and can't do."

Trying to remember what I had written in a book, I asked, "Can you put a tracking device on his car so we know where he is and if he's stalking me?"

"Not legally."

His phone vibrated. "Yeah, okay, yeah." Turning to look at me, "Yeah, she won't press charges if he promises to stay away from her. There's another stipulation. He's got to tell you how he knew exactly where she was. Uh huh, yeah, okay. Call me when you find out."

"Well?"

Sam dipped his head and ran his hair through his hair. "You writers."

"What?" Then it dawned on me, I laughed. "He put some type of tracker on my purse. Ha! I'd make a good detective."

"Give my guy a minute or two and...wait. That's him now. Yeah, okay. How did he get a key to her apartment? Gotcha. Okay, let him go but put the fear of God into him."

I looked at him.

"Danny said he had bumped into you several days ago in a store and stuck the tracker on the bottom of your purse. As to the key, he stuck some type of putty stick in the lock, got an impression, and had the key made. Apparently, he was going to surprise you with a candlelight dinner at some point in the near future." Sam laughed, "Romantic little devil, isn't he?"

I sputtered, horrified. "But you're letting him go!"

Sam nodded. "I seriously doubt he'll ever bother you again because we now have documentation, and he won't want that showing up in court.

"Do you remember him bumping into you?"

Stopping to think, I couldn't remember but, then again, I bump into stuff and people by accident fairly frequently and my doing that doesn't normally register with me. It was totally possible he had bumped into me, and I simply wasn't paying attention.

Sam stuck his hand out for the card key at the hotel door. I handed it to him.

"At least, you can go back to sleep, take a nap, rest, or do whatever it is you writers do while I go back to work."

"Can I go home now?"

"Danny's not the one who murdered Sarah, the coffee guy..."

"Barista."

"Whatever. And he's not the one who beat up Ronnie. You need to stay here. Do not, repeat, do not let anyone in."

I held up my hand. He ignored it. "I don't care if it's someone you've known forever and three days, text me before opening that door."

"Okay." I went into the sterile hotel room designed by some highly paid interior decorator to look personal, it failed, to contemplate life. Opening up my laptop and trying to write on my book, I just looked at the blank screen totally unmotivated to do anything. Shutting it, I murmured, "Oh, well, I tried." Then mentally slapping myself, I said out loud what the great philosopher Yoda pontificated. "Do or do not. There is no try."

I don't like him much. I took a nap.

Chapter 10

The phone started playing its annoying little song waking me up from a sound nap.

"Wha...what? Hello?" I managed to eke out. I hadn't looked at caller ID.

"Harper, we need to talk." Female voice, flat, demanding.

I was struggling to come fully awake. The voice was familiar, but I couldn't place it.

"Who is this?" I snapped. I felt absolutely no need to be polite. My phone, I could answer it however I wanted to.

"It's Lisa. Where are you? I went by your apartment, but you weren't there. We need to talk."

Bells, whistles, and fire alarms were going off in my head. Why was Lisa calling me? I didn't have anything to do with the murders.

What was even more disconcerting was that Lisa not only knew where I lived but had gone there. Obviously, to confront me about something. Why?

"Lisa, whatever you have to say, you can tell me now." I was still peeved and a wee bit on the snappish side.

Lisa sounded annoyed and was still demanding. "No, Harper, we need to meet in person."

"No."

She sounded shocked that someone would dare say 'no' to her. "What? What do you mean no? You have to meet with me."

I could almost see the small-town business mogul stamping her feet or throwing something at a wall. She wasn't used to not getting her way, she was a bully. Well, I wasn't buying what she was selling, and the buyer is always the one in control.

Grinning, although Lisa couldn't see it through the phone, I answered, "No is a complete sentence. What part of that did you not understand?"

A moment of silence, then she snarled, "Little Miss Goody Two-Shoes, always thinking you're better than the rest of us. You might be intellectually smarter than I am, but you don't have the sense God gave a goose in real life. You'll be sorry."

I started to laugh, feeling like I had the upper hand, then realized she had disconnected the call. That was annoying and a little frustrating. It also meant she thought she was in control. That was the part I didn't like.

I texted Sam. He called a couple of minutes later. I gave him the low down and ended with, "She was threatening me. Can I do anything about that?"

Almost chuckling, he answered, "She didn't actually threaten you, Harper. She insulted you but she didn't say she was going to kill you or anything. The fact that she hung up the phone on you means she's emotional, a control freak, and not used to people telling her no. But I am curious as to what she wanted to discuss with you. Maybe..."

"No."

"Harper, it may help us to solve the murders."

"No is a complete sentence," I snipped. "Also, when did it become we in solving the murders? You're law enforcement and I am not. This is your job, not mine."

"Meet with her."

"No."

"Yes."

"No, it looks like I'm capitulating. It makes her in control." I was being stubborn, maybe somewhat childish but if Lisa had arranged the murders of Sarah and her nephew, the no-name barista, what would she do to me?

Sam laughed. I envisioned his dimple becoming even more pronounced. "You do know that saying 'giving up' has less letters in it than capitulating, don't you?"

He was becoming annoying. "I never counted, besides, capitulating is a perfectly acceptable word," I huffed.

"Changing topics. Good news on Ronnie, he's still in ICU but he has opened his eyes."

I was silent, saying a private prayer for Ronnie and wishing a thousand stinging ants invade the crotch and cause unspeakable pain to whoever had beaten him up. Ronnie was such a gentle soul, he wouldn't have argued with anyone about anything and would have given them whatever they wanted. I was still in shock and, if I had to admit it, grief over what had been done to him.

"Harper," Sam's tone was a little softer, "you can't go see him yet. There's a very short list of who can see him. Everyone else will not be allowed in ICU."

I inhaled deeply and let it out slowly. "Can he talk yet? Tell him, tell him," I choked up, "tell him whatever he needs, I'll get it for him."

"Got it."

I sat for a moment after our call. Was I curious as to what Lisa wanted? Sorta, maybe, yes. Was I curious enough to return her call knowing that she was going to be making snarky remarks about me, my writing, my intellect? Not really, however, I was going to have to ponder on it.

A tidal wave of emotions hit me. Ambush grief it's called. Although I had thought about putting Sarah on the back burner of my life for a short time, it never once occurred to me that I might never see her again. The murder of my childhood friend, I didn't even have the words to express how devastating I felt at the moment. I puttered about the hotel room and finally made a pot of coffee. The pot was about the size of a little girl's tea party set. It had the capacity of a Styrofoam cup and a half. It would have to do and, to be honest, I didn't even really want it. It was simply something to do.

I was numb, almost like sitting in a snow globe waiting to be shaken. Shaking my head slightly, I dug deep inside myself and resolved, one way or the other, to find out who murdered Sarah and put Ronnie in the hospital. There was no doubt in my mind that they were related in some way.

Looking at my phone, I mustered up my courage, found Lisa's number in recent calls, and punched it.

Lisa, ever the epitome of graciousness, snarked, "About time you called me back."

Trying very hard to keep my temper reigned in and not say words that only Marines and sailors use, "What is it that you want, Lisa? I don't know anything, and I don't want to waste time for either one of us."

"I'm not talking about it over the phone. Tell me where you are, and I'll come to you."

Um, no. Something was definitely off, and I didn't want her to know where I was staying.

"Lisa, I am willing to meet you anywhere in public. Just give me a time and a place."

"What's the matter? You afraid of me?" She was deliberately taunting me. She didn't realize I had been through many years of this type of emotional abuse...because that's exactly what it was. Bullying is one term, narcissism is another.

"Where do you want to meet, Lisa?" I was calm. I lowered my voice and tone slightly, letting her know she couldn't rattle my cage. I was an expert at deflecting people's questions.

"Fine," she snapped. "Meet me at Athenian Owl in thirty minutes."

I grinned. I knew George, the owner, or as he liked to call himself Adonis the Greek God. He was cute but, more importantly, I was sure he wouldn't let Lisa do anything harmful to me.

Texting Sam where I was going to be, I pulled up the Uber app and put all my info in there to be picked up.

A few minutes later, I was walking through the door of the Athenian Owl. It was a small family-owned Greek restaurant where the food was very good and the prices reasonable.

"How are you today, my dear?" George gushed as he escorted me to a booth. His delightful Greek accent, his warmth at greeting me as a friend and not as a customer, and his happiness in life always made me feel welcome.

"George," I paused, looking around, "Lisa is joining me."

A slight frown crossed his face, "I'll take care of you, not to worry."

Grinning, "Do you want me to spill some water on her?"

I laughed. He understood. "No, but it's a thought."

Lisa barreled through the restaurant door and into the restaurant. She was a woman on a mission – a frown on her face and had all the subtlety of a debutante who had been kicked off her sorority board of directors.

She slid into the booth, ignoring George. "Water with a slice of lemon and not the end of it either," she ordered, flicking her wrist as dismissal at George.

He rolled his eyes and left. I just looked at her, my poker face mask was on. This was another expression I had perfected over the years with my ex-husband. It had annoyed him to no end and, thus, provided a modicum of pleasure for me.

"We need to talk." She didn't even bother to acknowledge George's presence when he returned with her water. I, on the other hand, told him 'Thank you' for my iced tea. Good manners will win out every time.

"You know I own five businesses, right?" No preamble, no nothing. This was a woman who expected everyone to cater to her whims. I wasn't going to be one of them.

"So?" I took a sip of my tea and proceeded to look at the menu. It was merely a diversionary tactic; I knew the menu by heart, and I typically ordered the same thing every time I came here...the lamb shank exohico.

Out of the corner of my eye, I saw Mama, George's mother approaching our table. I smiled. Mama was always so sweet to everyone.

She leaned over and gave me a hug. Lisa was visibly annoyed and made absolutely no pretense at hiding it. "Eleni, what kind of barely edible food is the least likely to make me sick today?"

Whoa! Lisa had the social grace of someone looking to have the kitchen staff deliberately spit into her food.

I didn't know Mama's name was Eleni, she'd always just told me to call her Mama. All of the other patrons called her that. Obviously, Lisa wasn't going to do it.

Mama's smile never slipped nor wavered. In her heavy Greek accent, she said, "Lisa, so nice you come to have wonderful meal here."

"Humph."

I was bordering on severely disliking Lisa even more. Honestly, how hard is it to be nice to others? Well, there's always that odd moment in life where niceness flies to the moon but, generally speaking, how difficult is it to be reasonably polite to someone?

For Lisa, on a scale of one to ten with ten being easy, she was at a negative two on the niceness scale.

"Mama, you know what I like." I smiled. Mama hugged me again.

"I get waiter for you." She ambled off to another table.

"The food is despicable here."

I was ready to slap Lisa into oblivion but wanted to know what she wanted to talk to me about. Throwing caution out like discarded bath water, I semi-snapped, "You suggested this place which, by the way, is one of my favorite restaurants. Now, what was it you wanted to talk about?"

The waiter showed up before Lisa could say anything. She ordered soup.

After the waiter left, Lisa leaned back in the booth, tapping her red nails on the table. "You know I date Vinnie Piasano. Well..."

Shaking my head, "Who's that?"

Blinking her eyes rapidly, she slowly breathed out, "Of the Piasano family." Seeing my confused look, she did a slow eye roll. "Out of New York."

I shrugged.

"Oh, come on, Harper! You can't possibly be that dense...or that stupid. The Piasanos are one of the top five mafia families in this country."

"Lisa, I don't hang around criminals so, therefore, I have no clue on who's on the top ten list of whatever." I was semi-smug. Really, she was dating a mafioso guy? And, for the record, yes, I had heard of the Paisano family. Plus, I couldn't resist the little dig about her hanging around with criminals. She said I was stupid, I'm not, although I do have ambiguous moments from a lack of clarity from time to time.

If looks could kill, I'd be twenty feet underground. She continued on while glaring at me as if I were wearing a red pointy hat and holding a pitchfork with flames dancing around my feet.

"I am also dating Tommy King."

Shut the front door! Tommy could have cared less about Lisa in high school. Now, in college, that was a totally different thing. The boy had a hard time keeping his pants zipped during those teenage years and, according to Sarah when she dated him in college, he was even more randy after high school. I wondered if that continued into his adult life. Chances were the answer was yes.

"When did he come back into town?" I was surprised I hadn't heard anything about him or even seen him in town.

"He's not. He comes into Jacksonville a couple of times a month and we meet then."

"Okay, so?" I shrugged again.

A deep sigh, "For a writer, you're incredibly dense. Vinnie saw us at dinner in Jacksonville."

The puzzle pieces started to fall into place.

Chapter 11

"Vinnie was jealous? Did he kill Tommy?" I was incredulous. Would this explain why no one has been able to find Tommy? Would a guy kill just for the sake of his girlfriend having dinner with another male friend?

Lisa grinned, "He's Italian, what can I say? Vinnie's very passionate."

I snorted, "I know plenty of Italians and, yes, they can be loud and emotional but..."

"No." She paused, fiddling with her linen napkin, and looking at the tabletop. "I don't think so. I mean, I think Tommy's in Jacksonville this weekend."

I interrupted her, I was angry. "No, that's not true. You know perfectly well Tommy went to see Ronnie."

"Um, yeah, okay. I had told Tommy I wanted a Maltese puppy and I think he went to see Ronnie to get me one." She glanced up at me, slightly moving her eyes to the right.

I am a graduate of several different neurolinguistic programming courses. It was time I had a little come-to-Jesus with Lisa. I was blunt and made absolutely no effort to conceal my disgust with her. "You're lying."

"No, no. No, I'm not." That last sentence was a pathetic attempt to sound strong and confident in her words. I could see through her like I could a water glass.

"You're lying, and, honestly, Lisa, this is a complete waste of my time to even be here." I started to slide out of the booth to go home. I knew George or Mama would put my meal in a to-go box. I looked around but didn't see them at the moment.

"Wait, Harper," she sighed. "I did want the puppy, Tommy did go to see Ronnie about it but then left for whatever reason."

My eyebrows arched up.

"Okay, Tommy called me after that and said he couldn't afford Ronnie's prices. Now, Harper," she leaned forward with both hands clutching the edge of the table, "I know Tommy makes almost two hundred thousand dollars a year. HE CAN afford Ronnie's prices...easily. Apparently, I don't mean enough to him to spend money on me for a cute, little, white Maltese puppy."

I was flabbergasted. Was she nuts? I just sat there and looked at her for what seemed like an eternity but was actually only for a few seconds.

She ignored my silence. "He and Ronnie talked about their diets and how Tommy had lost over one hundred pounds on Go-Slo. Then Tommy left. I haven't seen him since then and he's not returning my calls."

I coughed, my mind a jumble of thoughts. "Um, did you tell Vinnie all of this?"

Somewhere between the time we sat down and the food arriving, I must have grown a unicorn in the middle of my forehead because Lisa was looking at me like she had never seen me before.

"Well, duh, yes, of course, I did."

"Lisa, what kind of game are you playing?" My tone was cold. I could barely believe what I was hearing. Had she had Sarah murdered over jealousy between two men and her wanting a puppy? This was sick, demented, and unbelievable.

"If you date me, then you need to know I'm not cheap." She tossed her hair and smiled. "You better pay, so you can play."

The callousness of this woman defied any logical explanation I could ever come up with. I would never even begin to think of writing something like this in a book because no one would believe me.

"Sounds like a ho." The words escaped my mouth. I guess I should care but I didn't.

"What?" Lisa's tone was icy cold, her eyes pierced mine. "What did you just say, Harper? What are you implying?"

I was seething. "I'm not implying anything, Lisa! I am flat out saying the only difference between you and a girl out on the street is your price!

"Furthermore, did you have Vinnie kill Sarah and your nephew as well as having Ronnie beaten up because you were upset with Tommy? Was Vinnie so jealous that he took his anger out on poor innocent people?"

I was shouting at this point, the other restaurant patrons were turning their heads and looking at our booth. George was hurrying across the dining room to our table.

Okay, I might not have thought of all the possible consequences of what she might do to me. She threw her water at me and proceeded to scream some rather nasty words and questioned my ancestry.

George wrapped his right arm around her right shoulder and pulled her out of the booth. "Out!" He pointed at the door. Mama came out of the kitchen with a broom in her hand.

"Lisa, you ride broom or get out before I sweep you out." Mama's tone brooked no nonsense.

Lisa, still shouting obscene words, left the restaurant. Some of the patrons were clapping.

George pulled out his handkerchief and handed it to me to wipe the water from my face. I grinned, "Thanks, George! Mama, loved how you to told her to ride the broom." Mama winked and went back to the kitchen.

He slid in where Lisa had been sitting. "My dear, do all of your fans act like this upon meeting you in person?"

We both laughed. I leaned over the booth and tapped the gray-haired man behind me. "So did you get enough information to arrest her?"

Sam slid out of his booth and in next to me while pulling off his silver-gray fox wig. He fluffed his own black hair slightly. "I had it on crooked. Good thing she wasn't paying the slightest bit of attention to me.

"But, in answer to your question, I need to run everything by the state attorney first and then see what we can do."

We high-fived each other.

"Of course, the real trick is going to be getting Vinnie to admit anything; and that's between slim and none and slim went to the Bahamas. He's got some very high-priced attorneys, so that part's doubtful. But we basically have Lisa knowing or even instigating a murder-for-hire situation and that we can do something about."

"Hopefully, that witch will roll on Vinnie to save her own skin." I added smirking.

"We'll see. Now, George, what do you have for dessert?"

George bounced up like a Jack Russell terrier. "I think we still have some baklava cheesecake."

Chapter 12

As predicted, Lisa tried to roll on Vinnie. Also, as predicted, Vinnie disavowed any knowledge of the murder of Sarah and Lisa's nephew. In fact, he said he had met Lisa on a dating website, but they had only gone out a couple of times.

He had been adamant, through his attorneys of course, that they weren't dating, and he barely knew who she was.

Ronnie was still in ICU but was, hopefully, going to be moved into a regular room within the next couple of days. He was allowed to have visitors if and only if his gay brigade knew the person; otherwise, they wouldn't let anyone in to see Ronnie. I was allowed to see him.

He was still hooked up to all sorts of tubing that made little gurgling sounds from time to time, but his smile outweighed anything he was going through.

"Oh, honey, how are you?"

I leaned over and gave him a hug. He couldn't hug back but I heard a sniffle and that was good enough for me.

We chatted about nothing for a couple of minutes before I asked him, "Any clues?"

"No, as I told the cops, Detective Sam, I don't really remember anything. I was playing with the puppies in their little playpen when the door opened. It was a guy dressed all in black and when I stood up, he punched me in the face, and I fell down on the floor."

Ronnie's eyes welled up with tears. "Harper, he just kept punching me over and over. Then he started kicking me, I screamed but, you know, no one can hear anything in another store, it's too far away. I told him to take the cash in the register, but he kept saying, 'Where is he? Where is he?' I have no clue who he's talking about, Harper. I told him to take the money, but he just kept wailing away on me."

Ronnie's tears were rapidly exiting his eyes and running down his cheeks. He sniffled, "Honestly, Harper, he could have had anything in the store. I wasn't going to fight him."

Tears were now pouring down his face. "Honey, I like to think I'm brave but I'm a big old wimp. I covered up my head and curled up in the fetal position, trying to protect the puppies. I must have passed out. I don't remember anything other than that."

I swallowed, hard. I patted his hand. Then I started to cry. What is up with all of these emotions I keep having?!

Ronnie tried to wipe the tears from his eyes, but he had so many IV lines in him that he couldn't do it. Donnie must have suspected something was up or he was listening outside the door because he came into the room, glanced at me, and then proceeded to press a tissue against Ronnie's eyes.

"Harper, honey, I think Ronnie's tired." He was being so gentle. I nodded.

"Harper, it's okay to let your emotions out," Ronnie whispered as he tried to smile between the tears. "You've been wrapped up too tight for far too long."

Rats! Tears were now cascading down my cheeks. I didn't like these feelings, but Ronnie was probably right. I had been hiding from these emotions for far too long. Maybe it was time to feel the feelings. Inwardly, I smiled because I hated that term. It reminds me of stoned hippies from a bygone period of time.

"One last thing, Harper."

I turned to look at him while blowing my nose.

"It wasn't Tommy who did this to me. I do know that much."

Nodding and zombie-like, I left Ronnie's room. I was halfway down the hallway when Donnie ran up and tapped me on the shoulder.

"Harper..."

"I'm sorry. I didn't mean to upset him." I sniffled.

"No, no, that's not it." Donnie looked around to see if anyone was near by or even paying attention to us. There wasn't. "I have the security camera tape."

I whipped my head around to look him full in the face. "I didn't know Ronnie had a security system in the store."

"No one did," he whispered. "I had just set it up a couple of days before he got beat up."

"Donnie, did you recognize the guy who beat up Ronnie?" I held my breath.

He grabbed my hand. "Oh, honey, it was so hard to watch. I threw up." He paused, "I've never seen that guy before. But here's the thing, Harper, the only other male who'd been in the store that day was Tommy. Do you think that's what the attacker meant when he kept saying, 'Where is he? Where is he?' I mean, that's the only thing I can think of."

Could it possibly be two different people, and these were actually two separate incidents? Unlikely in my mind. Maybe this whole thing had nothing to do with Vinnie but everything to do with Tommy and Lisa. What was the connection?

"Donnie, did Ronnie tell you what he and Tommy talked about?"

Donnie lifted his shoulders and let them drop. "He said they talked about that Go-Slo diet, and that Tommy had been seeing Sarah but that they wanted to take their time and see if things might work out again for them."

"Was he seeing her in Jacksonville?"

"Yes, they'd gone out a couple of times. Apparently, they were on some dating website and re-discovered each other." He kind of giggled. "Not like he couldn't have picked up the phone and called but whatever."

I smiled. Sarah would have let him make the first move on doing that. Interesting that they connected on a dating website. I wondered if this was what Sarah wanted to talk to me about...dating Tommy again. I'd never know. Maybe I wasn't being a good enough friend to Sarah by becoming annoyed at her and not staying long enough to listen to whatever she had to say. I did feel sadness and remorse.

"Apparently, they ran into Lisa at one of the restaurants. Tommy told Ronnie he met Lisa on the same dating site that he did Sarah, and they went out a few times, but he decided she was too possessive and didn't want to date her anymore. He asked Ronnie how he could get rid of her because she was blowing up his phone with text messages."

Everything suddenly jumped into high gear for me.

Chapter 13

Sitting across the table from Sam, I was excitedly telling him what I thought had happened.

He scratched his head and lifted his coffee to his lips. Pausing for a moment, "That's a possibility, a little convoluted but a possibility."

"Don't you see how Lisa has manipulated all of this?"

"Harper, you're forgetting an important thing here. Why would Lisa have her nephew killed? That makes no sense."

I shook my head. "Maybe it was an accident..."

"No, that was a deliberate murder. The perpetrator shot Sarah, walked over, and shot her nephew. There wasn't a pause, a slowing down, nothing. It was intentional."

"What about Lisa's sister Ellenore? Is she blaming Lisa for her son being murdered?"

Sam held up his hand. "Harper, I can only tell you so much. This is an ongoing investigation. Did you know Ellenore in school?"

"No. She was several years younger than me. I don't really remember her from school."

"Only thing I'm going to say is that they aren't, um, close." Flashing his dimple at me, yes, he smiled. "So does our having coffee again mean that we're dating?"

My cup was halfway to my mouth and I'm sure I looked like Bambi in the headlights. I was flustered and sputtered, "Wha...what? Um, no, I...I don't know. Are we?"

The caffeine in the coffee must have unleashed ping pong balls in my head because I couldn't put two coherent sentences together and sound reasonably intelligent.

Sam laughed. "Stop sweating, Harper. I'm not asking you to marry me. Coffee dates are just two people getting together, nothing more, nothing less. Don't read anything into this. I'm just messing with you."

Okay, this cop finally had a sense of humor. I guess that's a relief. My hand was still shaking as I took a sip of the now lukewarm coffee. Apparently, the adrenaline rush caused my hands to absorb all of the heat from the cup.

"Okay, since that threw you for a loop," Sam was still laughing, "let's go back for one last thing. Vinnie Piasano is an innocent bystander in all of this."

I nodded. I had already figured that out. This was all on Lisa. That conniving, evil woman. Who did she date in high school? I couldn't remember. Why? Probably because I didn't care and, more than likely, I was wrapped up in my own intellectual snobbism. Maybe she didn't even date in high school. A lot of us didn't.

Looking up a number in my phone, I discovered I did have it. I was surprised. It was from so long ago I wasn't even sure if it was still in existence. I punched it.

"Yes?" The voice was wary, flat, and while not particularly friendly, at least it wasn't hostile.

Summoning up my courage. I asked, "Did you date Lisa in high school?"

"No."

"Do you know if she did and, if so, who did date her?"

"Don't know."

This was equivalent to pulling embedded teeth. "Do you know anyone who might know?"

"No."

"Do you want to meet? To talk about all of this?"

"No."

I felt defeated. No point in pursuing this any further. I started to hang up.

"Maybe." The tone had softened slightly.

Cautiously ecstatic, I asked, "What if we happened to bump into each other at BDubs around three in Jax?"

"I don't want company."

"Totally understand and I don't either. If that happens, go to our backup place."

The phone disconnected. I semi-chuckled. Unless Lisa had my phone bugged, unlikely since I kept it with me at all times, or maybe had bugged my car. I didn't think she'd do that, but I didn't know for sure, and I specifically didn't know if she even knew how to do that.

I called for a rental car, and they said they would pick me up. It was going to be cutting it tight to make the three p.m. time but I was determined to do it.

Walking into BDubs, I looked around for a booth, spotting my person, I walked over and slid into the red-vinyl booth.

I smiled, "It's been a long time, Tommy."

Chapter 14

He smiled back. **The tension** on his face was evident but he didn't look like he had aged since high school.

"Harper, good to see you."

"You really have lost some weight."

He grinned, looking down at his beer. "Well, I put on twenty pounds in college. You know, the old freshman year weight gain thing. I just kept on pounding the beer and eating fast food like crazy after college and the next thing I knew I was seriously fat. Plus, I felt like crap all the time. Not to mention, I couldn't get any dates."

Mr. Romeo not getting girls? That was a revelation, and, not to mention, was probably a devastating blow to Tommy's ego.

He had thoughtfully ordered me a beer and I took a sip. I hadn't had a beer in years and thought back to the last time Tommy, Sarah, and I had been at a bonfire and drank a couple. That was a fun memory.

"Anyway, I decided I needed to," he looked up, "wanted to change things in my life. I'm not getting any younger..."

"We're not that old," I interrupted him.

"True, but I was thinking I wanted to get married, have a couple of kids, and be part of the American dream."

Really? I never thought Tommy would ever have any desire for that. I always figured he would be a playboy until the day he died.

"Anyway, so I took part in the Go-Slo diet program, worked out in the gym..."

"Yes, I noticed your muscles," I said admiringly.

He blushed slightly. "And started dropping weight like crazy. No pills, no steroids, no nothing. Just cutting gluten and sugar out of my diet, eating a lot of fresh fruits and vegetables, and then giving myself one cheat day a week. This beer," pointing at it, "is on my cheat day for this week. I can have two, no more."

"So, how did you and Sarah hook up again?" I prompted him.

He named the website. Yes, I knew the one. Sarah had dated a couple of men from it and was always telling me this was the way to get back into the dating scene after my divorce. I had been reluctant at best to do it. Maybe I should have.

"You know," he looked at me shyly, "I never did stop loving Sarah."

I started to interrupt but he raised his hand. "We were both young, foolish, teenage hormones and emotions running rampant. Neither one of us was ready to settle down. But now," he opened his hands and waved them outward," we were both at a different point in our lives. We talked quite a bit on the phone before deciding to meet in person.

"Harper, I was straight up and told Sarah I was dating several women, one who was Lisa, and she said she was dating several men as well. We had run into Lisa at a restaurant, and she invited us to have coffee at her shop in town. I haven't been in town much since we left school, and it sounded like a good idea. Of course, I knew the gossip would start the minute anyone saw me and Sarah together.

"Honestly, Harper, we were just going to meet to have coffee and talk. We were still in the catching up phase and getting to know each other as adults."

"Was Lisa okay with you dating Sarah?" I almost whispered.

Tommy frowned and rolled his eyes. "I did tell every woman that I was seeing that I was dating other women. I was being honest and upfront with that.

"Initially, Lisa seemed to be okay with that. We only went out two or three times. And, before you ask, no, I did not sleep with her. We only went out to eat in Jacksonville."

"Donnie told me that you had talked with Ronnie that she was being too possessive. What happened?"

He shook his head and shrugged. "I really didn't understand why she got upset when I said I thought it was best for us to part as friends and date other people.

"Honestly, Harper, there just wasn't any chemistry and I didn't want to waste my time. Also," he sighed, "she isn't the easiest person in the world to talk to, and I hated the way she was so dismissive to waiters."

"She's rude." I jumped in there.

"Yes. Anyway, I did call her and let her know we should go our separate ways in terms of dating. I didn't text her." He laughed.

"You have grown up," I giggled.

Nodding, "Told you. Anyway, she seemed to be okay with that and then about a week or so ago she started blowing up my phone with messages saying she missed me, that she thought we had something special together, blah, blah, blah. Then she said she wanted a Maltese puppy."

I raised my eyebrows.

"Yeah, I was thinking what does a puppy have to do about anything? Anyway, she invited me and Sarah to have coffee in her shop. I thought that meant she was being nice. So I told her yes, Sarah and I were going to have coffee at her place. That was it."

"Tell me about the puppies. She said you were going to buy her one."

Shocked. "Really? No, I was way early for meeting Sarah and decided to stop in and see Ronnie for a few minutes. I love puppies and all animals in general, but I never had any intention of purchasing an animal for Lisa." He semi-laughed, "I thought she'd make a rotten pet mom. Ronnie thought the same thing. No, I wasn't going to buy an animal for her."

"Did you tell her that?" I was curious. More bells and whistles were going off in my head.

"Yeah, sure I did, but she said if I'd buy her a puppy, she'd leave me alone. Essentially, Harper, that's blackmail and once that starts, it never ends. I wasn't going to do that."

Oh, Lisa, Lisa, liar, liar, pants on fire.

A thought occurred to me. "Do you know if Lisa was ever married?"

"Um, I don't think so. Based on what she was telling me, she just, ah, dated a lot. If I had wanted to, it would have been easy to sleep with her. I just didn't want to go that route. Something kept stopping me." He grinned and winked, "See, I have grown up."

Raising my barely touched beer, "Indeed, sir, you have. I'm proud of you."

"I just can't figure out why anyone would want to kill Sarah." Tommy was genuinely sad. His eyes watered for a moment.

"Tommy," I didn't know how to ask this but proceeded anyway, "why was Sarah so grumpy and anxious? You already know I was going to have coffee with her. She seemed really out of sorts, almost mad."

Blowing air through his nostrils, "She had texted me early that morning and said Lisa had messaged her saying to leave her boyfriend alone because she wasn't going to have another woman stepping into her place. Sarah wanted to meet somewhere else for coffee, but I said Lisa told me she never came into Coffee & Cupcakes, and I didn't think it was that big a deal to keep our appointment."

"I feel so guilty about this, Harper," Tommy's voice broke. "What if we had gone somewhere else? Sarah would still be alive."

"Do you think Lisa had anything to do with this?" I was cautious because I was trending on thin ice with this question.

Tommy shook his head. "She's possessive, just like she was in college, but I can't imagine she'd do something like that. Plus, she would have had to hire someone to do it."

"Why do you keep looking at the door?" I had noticed over the course of our conversation that his eyes kept flickering to the door every time it opened.

"I just want to make sure Lisa doesn't barrel in here. I don't want a scene."

Something wasn't right. I started to feel a slight prickle at the back of my head. There were starting to be some inconsistencies.

"Okay." I needed to go back to the hotel and make some notes on paper. I needed to see everything written down. There was something obvious I was missing.

"Tommy, I know this is so hard." I was trying to be sympathetic. I did think he was sad about Sarah's death but was it for the same reason that I was? I wasn't sure.

He nodded with a sad expression.

"Changing topics," I said brightly, "what are you doing these days? What kind of job do you have? I'm writing, a book author, as you probably know from Sarah. I have ten books out now."

"Hey, that's terrific. On me, just kind of boring stuff. I'm a computer video programmer."

"That sounds interesting."

He laughed. "You don't have to humor me, Parker. You're into words and I'm into coding with a lot of strange symbols and numbers."

I snickered. "Okay, you got me, Tommy. I was trying to pretend to be interested in that. But you're right, I don't understand it and I don't care. Listen, I need to go. I'm on deadline with a new publisher and I need to get something out to her before she wants her advance money back."

Tommy's eyes narrowed. "Thought you were an independent publisher."

He'd done his research on me.

"That's true under my real name. I am also a ghostwriter for a small publishing house, and she wants the two chapters I've been working on." I lifted my hands up. "Hey, a girl's gotta do what a girl's gotta do to make money in the writing biz."

As I slid out of the booth, he asked, "What's the topic?"

"Mortgages, it's for a guy out of Chicago."

He nodded. "Take care, Harper."

As I walked out of the restaurant, I could feel Tommy's eyes boring a hole in me. I almost sensed he didn't think I believed him on everything.

I didn't.

Chapter 15

Tried calling Sam on the way back to Palm Park, but it kept rolling into voicemail. Finally, I decided to leave a message.

I also did a voice to text message, and it was a good thing I looked at it before I hit send. It had a lot of incorrect words. I tried correcting them as I was driving but it wasn't working out well and caused me to spew a lot of naughty language. I finally just deleted the text message. He either would or wouldn't call me from my voicemail message.

Everything was swirling around in my head. Occam's Razor theory kept bouncing around in my head. The simplest answer is usually the right one. Maybe I was overthinking everything. As a writer, I tend to do that because I live in my head. Thoughts are the horses on the merry go-round. They go up and down while going endlessly in a circle.

I was almost back to the car rental place when Sam returned my call.

"Yes?" I heard a smile in his voice. "Are you wanting to go for coffee again?"

I couldn't help it, I laughed. "What about dinner instead? I've got tons of info, stuff, to run by you."

"Do you want to do steak again or do you want seafood?"

"Wherever we go, I want anyone spying on me, us, to know we're out in public but," I paused, "we need to be in a booth so I can spread out some papers for you to look at."

"Steak. Can you be there in twenty or thirty minutes?" I could hear him smirking. "I'm guessing I need to bring paper and a couple of pens. Am I right?"

"B-I-N-G-O, B-I-N-G-O, B-I-N-G-O, and bingo was his name-o." I singsonged.

"Have you been drinking?"

Giggling, "Two sips of beer does not constitute drinking, so the answer is no. See you in a few minutes."

I had the car rental place drop me off at the steak house. At some point, I was going to need to pick up my car from Ronnie's. As I entered, the hostess had her pasted fake smile on with the menus in her hand, turned, and waved for me to follow her.

Sam was already seated and had placed sheets of paper with several different pens on the table.

The server brought us iced tea and left.

"Sam, I think this whole thing with Sarah, Ronnie, Lisa, Lisa's nephew, Tommy, and the unknown killer is like a soap opera." I wrote each person's name on a separate piece of paper. "By the way, while we're sitting here, can you run a check on Tommy King and see what he does for a living, what company he works for, anything you can find on him?"

He looked at me for a moment, slid out of the booth, held his finger up, and walked out the door with his phone pressed to his ear.

I jotted down everything I could think of on each person.

Sam came back in, ignoring people looking at him, and said, "Done. Should have something within a couple of minutes. Meanwhile, back at the farm, what do you have?"

"Before we start, do you have any new suspects or more info?" I looked at him hopefully.

A slight shake of his head. He tapped his finger on one of the papers.

"Okay, here goes." I pointed at Sarah's paper. "Sarah dated Tommy in high school and off and on in college. They hooked back up through a dating website. Tommy allegedly made the first move on contacting Sarah, that I do believe. Sarah had used this website before but," and I held up my finger, "she never told me anything about who she was dating."

"I still can't believe you were friends since the fourth grade and you knew so little about her personal life," Sam mused.

Snapping at him, "I've told you before, that implies a level of trust I'm not comfortable with. Sarah and I had gotten into an argument last week about her using dating websites to find men. She told me she knew this guy and he was okay. She had dated him before and..." I let my voice trail off. I was thinking.

Somewhat shaking the cobwebs from my head, I continued, "She called me an old fuddy-dud. Us having coffee was the first time in a week we had talked or seen each other. Truly, Sam, I just wasn't interested in who she was dating."

Feeling what I thought was an irrational display of emotions, I immediately tried to compartmentalize it. What was this sensitivity I had? Guilt, remorse, anger? Maybe all of that and more. I just couldn't process it at this moment.

"Do you think it was Tommy she was referring to?" Sam asked.

"Um, maybe, probably but that doesn't explain why she was so grumpy. If she were dating Tommy and was happy about it, she'd be bouncing around. She was just flat out being witchy." I paused. "Having coffee at Coffee & Cupcakes was a normal thing for us. It's not like it was out of the clear blue sky."

I snapped my fingers. "Wait! Tommy lied."

Sam took a sip of his tea. "How?"

"Tommy said Lisa told him that Sarah never came into the shop. That's a blatant lie! We usually had coffee there at least every other week and usually once a week."

I was getting worked up. "I don't think Tommy even asked Ronnie about purchasing a puppy. He's lied the entire time.

"Sam, Tommy's the one who planned this whole thing, not Lisa!"

His phone pinged. He looked at me. "Yeah. Really. Okay. Thanks."

"What?" I was past curious. I was drumming my fingers on the tabletop.

"Tommy is a computer video programmer, works for a legit company in the Atlanta area, and is on vacation." Sam tapped his iced tea glass. "Harper, you're bouncing all over God's green acres on this. Let the police handle it. We do this every day, you don't."

I was rebuffed. We ate dinner in silence. It reminded me of so many times with my ex-husband when we went out to eat. I didn't like this feeling.

"Sam?"

Looking up from his last bite of steak, "Yeah?"

"Let me just run all of this through to see if it helps on anything."

He just nodded.

"Tommy found Sarah on the same dating website as Lisa. He was dating both of them at the same time. Lisa was possessive, according to Tommy, and Ronnie confirmed that. Vinnie didn't have anything to do with anything except for going out with Lisa a couple of times. With me so far?"

He nodded.

"What if Lisa was insanely jealous and didn't want Tommy dating Sarah anymore? And what if Tommy was going to dump Sarah and continue to date Lisa but Lisa didn't know he was planning on dumping Sarah? What if Lisa was so jealous about their relationship, a relationship that went back years, that she didn't think she stood a chance against Sarah unless Sarah was out of the picture?" I paused for air.

"That's a lot of ifs," said Sam drily, pushing back his plate. "You up for splitting a dessert?"

I nodded. I could let real food go but I was always ready for dessert. I was convinced there were two separate compartments in my stomach – one for food and the other for dessert. I could always find room for dessert regardless of how much other food I had eaten.

He flagged our server and ordered crème brûlée. I might could, maybe, fall in love with this man. Oh, no, no, no! What was happening to my brain and my emotions? It was the dessert thing, I kept saying over and over in my head. Shaking my head, hopefully eradicating those errant thoughts on consuming an ungodly amount of decadent sugar, I focused back on the murders.

"Harper, how do you explain the murder of Lisa's nephew? Also, what about the guy who beat Ronnie up and kept saying, 'Where is he? Where is he?', who or what is that referring to?"

Breaking the sugar shell on the crème brûlée, I didn't give Sam a chance to do it first. In my defense, he was a wee bit on the slow side, and I decided someone needed to break it first and it might as well be me. I spooned a mouthful of the delightfully sinful vanilla custard and allowed it to slowly melt in my mouth before I responded.

"Since I think Lisa is cra-cra..."

"There's no proof of that, Harper. That's called slander."

"Yeah, whatever, it's just us talking," I waved my spoon at him making sure there was nothing on it. I didn't want any of the ooey-gooey goodness going anywhere except in my mouth. "What if she thought Tommy was not going to leave Sarah for her and she hired a hit man to kill them both? Maybe the guy thought her nephew was Tommy and when he realized he had accidently killed the wrong man, he went after Ronnie thinking Ronnie could tell him where Tommy was."

Sam had taken his knife and sliced the crème brûlée in half. "Your side, my side. You can't eat what's on my side."

"Spoil sport." I grinned, happily digging into my side even more.

"So, this whole thing really just comes down to jealousy. That's what you're saying." He wasn't eating his side as fast as I was enjoying mine. "If Lisa couldn't have Tommy, no one could. Is that it?"

I nodded. "I'm guessing Lisa must have told him or texted him something to that effect and that's the reason why he kept looking at the door at BDubs. He thought she was going to kill him."

Sam just sat, looking at me and tapping his spoon on the side of the dessert plate. His brows were slightly knit together, he was thinking.

The sugar was causing my brain to go into overdrive, and I couldn't keep my mouth shut. "You know, it's not that hard to find someone to murder someone. You can find all sorts of unsavory characters on the dark web."

Sam semi-rolled his eyes at me. "Really? Unsavory characters and the dark web in the same sentence? Isn't that redundant, Harper?"

Well, yeah, it was. I could blame it on the sugar or the fact that I liked to do research for my books, and I just happened, it was an accident I swear, I found a website on the dark web where, theoretically, you could hire someone to murder anyone you chose. Coward that I am, I decided I didn't need to do any more research. That was the one and only time I went to the dark web. It's too scary for me.

"Yes, it is, however, you got to admit, there's a strong possibility I'm right."

"Maybe," he was non-committal. "You going back to the hotel or do you want me to take you home?"

Since I didn't have any weapons of mass destruction at home for protection and I wasn't overly excited that Lisa may want to visit me at an odd hour of the night, I opted for the hotel.

As we were driving to the hotel, I asked, "Can you subpoena Lisa's phone and computer records?"

Sam did a side eye glance, sighed, and said, "Harper, there's more to police work than having an idea and then trying to make it work or fit with preconceived ideas."

He smiled, "You've come up with some good ideas though. Maybe you can incorporate them in your next book."

A flash of inspiration came to me. "I'm right and you know it, Mr. Detective." I laughed.

He didn't say anything for a moment, then, "You could also be wrong."

I didn't say anything because, yes, I could be wrong, but I didn't think so.

Pulling up to the hotel, Sam unlocked the car doors, smiled, and nodded. "Don't let anyone in unless it's me."

No one was in the elevator area or in the hallway, I checked everywhere in the room where someone could hide. I was alone.

Blame it on the sugar rush but I had an idea to start a new book. When I'm in the zone, I am absolutely oblivious to the time. Stretching, I thought I had only been writing for an hour. It was more like six hours. No wonder I was tired.

Making sure the door was safely secured, I turned in for the night. I had just gone to sleep when the fire alarms started going off. I was so groggy, that the piercing sound of the alarms barely penetrated the reptilian part of my brain, I rolled over and went back to sleep.

Chapter 16

Around ten a.m. my phone started its annoying little happy music alerting me that someone was up and needed my attention.

"Yeah." I was barely coherent.

"Harper, I wanted you to be the first to know that Lisa has been arrested and charged with the murder of her nephew and Sarah."

Sitting up quickly caused the blood flow to my brain to drop sharply. I could feel my eyeballs trying to focus.

"Sam? Really? How? What?"

A soft chuckle, "Were you sleeping?"

"Yes, I didn't go to bed until somewhere around four, I was writing on my book." I was trying to wipe the sleep out of my eyes. "Details, Sam, give me details."

"Lisa went by your apartment last night, you weren't home, and she decided you had to be in a hotel somewhere.

"Apparently, she thought if she started a fire in the hotel, you'd have to run down the stairs, and she could talk to you."

"About what?" Lisa was sounding more and more unstable to me.

"She's convinced that you were trying to take Tommy away from her. First, Sarah, and then you."

"You're kidding!" I was flabbergasted. "I wouldn't have Tommy for a million dollars."

Sam chuckled. "Anyway, when you didn't come down the stairs, she had a total mental breakdown in the stairwell. Security called us and we arrested her for destruction of hotel property. And that's when it became very interesting." He stopped talking.

"Seriously, Sam, you just stop and don't say anything else." I tried to sound annoyed, but I was actually kind of laughing because it sounded funny. Honestly, if I wrote this in a book, no one would ever believe me. The crazier something sounds, the more likely it is to be true.

"What did she want to talk to me about?"

"Said she wanted to let you know that Tommy was in love with her, and you should stop seeing him."

"Seriously, Sam, I've only seen him less than a handful of times since college. Yesterday was the first time in years I've seen him. Wait! How did she know I'd seen him?"

"He called and told her. Anyway, she suddenly spouted out that she was going to do to you what she'd done to Sarah. At that point, we Mirandized her and she yelled she didn't need an attorney. She kept shouting that Tommy loved her, he didn't love anyone else. He didn't love Sarah, he didn't love you. He loved only her. If she couldn't have Tommy, no one could..."

"There's your answer," I said. "Just what I said."

There was a slight groan, "Are you going to say I told you so?"

I smiled, although he couldn't see it through the phone. "Probably not if you'll take me out for crème brûlée."

"Why Harper Rogers, I think you're flirting with me!"

I felt like Bambi in the headlights again. This time I think one of the girly girl genes must have sprung loose from wherever it had been hiding...for years. "Um, ah, huh, ah..."

Sam laughed, "Don't worry about it and, yes, I'll take you out for steak and crème brûlée again."

Finally finding my voice, I asked, "Did Lisa admit to hiring a hit man?"

"Yes," he sighed, "she did. She thought if she killed both of them, then she'd never have to worry about Tommy pining for Sarah instead of loving her. Her nephew was killed by accident. The phone number she had for her gun-for-hire is, of course, gone. It was a burner phone. She apparently lost her marbles when she realized her nephew was murdered instead of Tommy."

"She was so calm, though, Sam."

"True, but she was in shock and that could explain her reaction. Also, remember, she wasn't close to her family.

"Anyway, she called him and told him he murdered the wrong man. Since he had seen Tommy in Ronnie's pet store, he figured Ronnie would know where Tommy was or where he was staying. Ronnie, of course, didn't know either."

"How come Sarah's apartment was trashed?"

"She figured if it looked like a robbery, nobody would connect it to the murders."

"Sad, so sad." I could feel tears forming. "I don't think Sarah had any intention of ever hooking back up with Tommy. Maybe that's why she was grumpy or maybe it was because of her new job. Guess I'll never know."

"It's okay, Harper," Sam's voice was soft. "You can't blame yourself. There's no way you could have known any of this."

He paused again. "Lisa's in jail. If she's convicted, which is months away any way you look at it, she's looking at hard time for years."

"All this for someone being jealous. Unbelievable."

"True." Sam paused, and took a deep breath. "Now, about that steak and crème brûlée. When do you want to go?"

Purchase my books at your favorite retailer

Book 1
A Dose of Nice and Murder

Book 2
A Honky Tonk Night and Murder

Book 3
The Faberge Easter Egg and Murder

Book 4
Little Candy Hearts and Murder

Book 5
Lights, Action, Camera and Murder

Book 6
A Turkey Parade and Murder

Book 7
Cookies and Murder

Book 8
Flamingos and Murder

Book 9
Bowling and Murder

Purchase my books at your favorite retailer

| 101 Summer Jobs for Teachers | Kids Fun Activity Book |  Counting Laughs |

About the Author

I grew up in Palatka, Florida, traveled the Southeast extensively for years, and currently reside in Jacksonville, Florida.

To join my VIP Newsletter and to receive a **FREE** book, go to www.SharonEBuck.com/newsletter.

I absolutely love readers because without you I'd be eating peanut butter and crackers. I greatly appreciate you and your support. The best reward I get is when someone tells me my book brightened their day. People are always asking if I'm available for speaking engagements. The short answer is "Yes, of course." I can even do a Zoom event for your readers' group.

Would you be kind enough to review and recommend this book? I appreciate it!

Thank you for being a loyal fan!

Sharon (www.SharonEBuck.com)

Acknowledgements

Thank you to my wonderful support team and friends for your encouragement, words of reassurance, inspiration, and belief in me on those days when the blank computer screen would stare back at me like a one-eyed monster daring me not to write anything. I survived and conquered.

In no special order, thanks to the following individuals:

Kim Steadman – There should be a law about how much we're allowed to laugh on the phone. Thankfully, there's not. Thank you for your friendship and the time we spend talking about writing, books, the book business, and just chatting. Visit KimSteadman.com

Michelle Margiotta – Your music has lifted me up when I was frustrated with my writing process, when I had doubts, and it has nurtured the very depths of my soul. Your music is so filled with colors and swirls dancing throughout your compositions that one cannot help but to be totally enthralled and inspired by your incredible gift. Visit MichelleMargiotta.com

Cindy Marvin – my friend and attorney who tries (hard) to keep me out of trouble before I even get into it.

McDonald's Baymeadows @ I-95, Jacksonville, FL - Keisha and her morning crew for serving me vanilla iced coffee every morning. They jumpstart my day with their smiling faces. It's how I start my day.

Southside Chick-fil-A in Jacksonville, FL – Patty, the awesome marketing manager, and her team have hooked me on frosted coffee. I am now an addict LOL Every fast-food restaurant in America should take lessons in customer service from them. It's always a delight to go into a happy place of business. I am always treated like a friend, not a customer.

George at Athenian Owl Restaurant – Yes, there really is a George and Mama! My favorite Greek restaurant in Jacksonville and they make me feel at home every time I eat there.

And, lastly, thank you to all my loyal readers and fans. I love and appreciate you!

To God be the glory.

Murder at Jax Beach

A Harper Rogers Cozy Mystery

Sharon E. Buck

Southern Chick Lit

Copyright © 2024 by Sharon E. Buck

All rights reserved.

No portion of this book may be reproduced in any form without written permission from the publisher or author, except as permitted by U.S. copyright law.

This book is a work of fiction. Names, characters, businesses, organizations, places, events, and incidents either are the product of the author's imagination or are used fictitiously. Any resemblance to actual persons, living or dead, events, or locales is entirely coincidental.

For more information, or to book an event, contact: sharon@sharonebuck.com

To join my VIP Newsletter and to receive a **FREE** book, go to http://www.SharonEBuck.com

Cover design by Steven Novak, NovakIllustration.com

First Edition: March 2024

Contents

1. Chapter 1 #
2. Chapter 2 #
3. Chapter 3 #
4. Chapter 4 #
5. Chapter 5 #
6. Chapter 6 #
7. Chapter 7 #
8. Chapter 8 #
9. Chapter 9 #
10. Chapter 10 #
11. Chapter 11 #
12. Chapter 12 #
13. Chapter 13 #
14. Chapter 14 #

Murder at Palm Park - Chapter 1 #

Books #

More Books #

15. About the Author #
16. Acknowledgements #

Chapter 1

There was a surfer sitting on the edge of the ocean watching the waves. His board was next to him.

Only problem was he was dead. Well, he looked dead. Maybe he was just sleeping, and my imagination was playing tricks on me. That happens sometimes.

I had gone to Jacksonville Beach aka Jax Beach because I needed some alone time to think. My life was messed up and I figured the salty ocean air would help to clear my mind. Hopefully, add some sanity to it.

Finding a sitting-up dead body wasn't exactly what I expected to find at six a.m. on a hot, humid summer morning. Yeah, saying hot and humid in Florida is a little redundant since that's the way it is three hundred sixty-four and a half days in the year.

What made me think the surfer dude was dead? There was red stuff leaking from the back of his head down the back of his wet suit.

I looked around trying to see if there was anyone close by. Except for the seagulls darting about in the air and swooping down to land on the wet Florida sand, it was just me and the dead guy.

My idea of a tranquil morning walk dissipated faster than the sun was rising over the Atlantic Ocean.

I kind of wondered if the blond-haired guy was really dead as I walked a little closer to him.

"Hey!" I shouted. Nothing. "Hey!"

Easing up on his left side, I said, "Hey, buddy, you okay?"

That's when I saw the devastation caused by the hole in the back of his head. His face was gone. I hurled everything I had eaten in the past twenty-four hours. I have a notoriously weak stomach to begin with but seeing no face first thing in the morning...before coffee...was beyond unnerving.

My hands were shaking as I punched nine-one-one.

"What's your emergency?"

"Um, I, um, there's a dead guy on the beach."

"Which beach?"

"Jax Beach, just down from the pier."

After asking several more questions and, I'm sure dispatch was trying to keep me on the line and not run away, two beach guards came roaring up on their little four-wheel sand motorcycles. They got off and approached me cautiously. Their hands out to the side. I could see what appeared to be tasers but I couldn't tell if they were actually armed or not.

I turned and threw up in the ocean this time. Probably wasn't a wise thing to do with the incoming tide but at least it was in the ocean and not on the sand.

"What's going on here?"

My brain had already gone into massive overload. I wanted to ask him if he was a special kind of stupid but decided that might not bode well for me.

"Um, um, I was walking and saw this guy and, um, um..." I turned and hurled again into the ocean.

If I'm going to throw up, I'd rather do it in the privacy of my apartment and not in a public place, much less in front of guys who were about my age. This was beyond embarrassing.

My brain shut down, everything zoomed into a narrow tunnel. I was desperately trying to make sure I wasn't throwing up on myself. When I finally looked up there were police officers from the Jax Beach Police Department everywhere. They were all standing a healthy distance from me. The good news is no one was laughing at me and my situation. I'm guessing they've all seen this before during spring break and the summertime with the hundreds of over-indulging young people.

Squinting my eyes shut and taking a deep breath trying to quell the nausea, it occurred to me that a throwing up female must pose a serious threat to them since they were all standing about eight feet or so from me. The only weapon I had was whatever was spewing out of my mouth into the ocean. Yeah, big threat.

"Ma'am, do you have anything on your person we need to know about?" This was from a slim, reasonably attractive female officer. Shaking my head, she came over next to me. "You, okay?"

"No. There's a dead guy with no face." I was finally able to stand up straight and look at her. "How can a dead guy be sitting up?"

She ignored my question. "Is there someone you want to call?"

Even with the overwhelm of seeing a dead guy first thing in the morning, my brain was swimming up and down but not in a straight line. It was bobbing like a cork on the ocean waves.

"What? Are you arresting me?" my voice had gone up several notches.

"No. You look like you're in shock and I wanted to know if you needed a friend to come be with you."

The only person I could think of was Sam Needles, a Palm Park detective I had sort of become friendly with over the past several months.

My brain was screaming at me that I had friends in Jacksonville. It made more sense for me to call one of them instead of Sam. I don't know why I thought of Sam first. Maybe because he was a police officer, and I thought any little bit of law enforcement help would me.

"Um, do you know Detective Sam Needles in Palm Park? He, um, might come."

The female officer rocked back a little on her heels. She semi-smiled. "Sam Needles? Black hair, cute dimples?"

I nodded while my mind was frantically trying to figure out if this officer and Sam had dated or were a couple or what? All of that based on a simple smile.

Meanwhile, I was mentally slapping myself silly. Why was the only person I could think of calling was another police officer in another county an hour away? It's not like I didn't have friends here in Jacksonville. They just weren't the kind you'd invite to a death-on-the-beach party. My brain was shutting down. I was re-evaluating my life once again.

"Um, what did you say? I think my brain rode out on one of the waves." I was trying to be funny which went over like a lead balloon. She wasn't smiling, just standing there looking at me. She probably looked at dead fish bait like this, impassive.

"I said do you have his phone number?"

I handed her my phone. "He's in there somewhere."

I never handed my phone over to anyone. Why do it now? Everything seemed to speed up and then slow down. It wasn't from the fresh salt air whipping around my face. I was having too much external stimuli with seeing the dead guy.

Watching her do a mental eye roll, I'm sure she probably thought I had lost my marbles or was mentally ill or just a female whacko on the beach.

I watched as the police officers were cordoning off the area with the dead guy. One guy was busy snapping pictures from different angles like a person on speed. The minions from a local funeral home showed up in a brand-new white minivan with the funeral home's name prominently displayed on the side. If caterers can promote themselves and their restaurants, there's no reason why a funeral home shouldn't be able to do the same thing, I thought. Although, admittedly, it was probably in poor taste.

She had found Sam's name, spoke to him for a moment, and handed me the phone.

"Another dead body and you called me?" His voice sounded slightly amused. "How did you ever survive the first thirty years of your life?"

Okay, that was just wrong...and maybe that's what I needed to shake the cobwebs from my brain. Anger can do that to a person.

"You know perfectly well, I'm only twenty-eight and you're..."

He laughed. "I know how old I am. I also know how old you are. The question is what happened?"

I quickly explained what I had seen. The lady police officer was paying close attention to my explanation. I ended with, "For whatever reason, the only person I could think to call was you."

There was an amused semi-snort on the other end of the line. I could tell Sam was struggling not to laugh. "Do tell. Okay, tell Cherise I'll be there in about thirty minutes. I actually happen to be at Town Center."

I was annoyed. Why? Well, I couldn't really explain it and now was not the time to overanalyze every aspect of my life, which, unfortunately, I was prone to do on a daily basis. Analysis paralysis is what the so-called psychobabble gurus call it. I prefer to call it a creative use of overindulging my brain cells in a time vacuum.

"Is your name Cherise?" Well, that was just stupid on my part. She was the only female on the beach besides me.

She nodded, brushing her hair off her forehead. I could see little beads of sweat forming along her hairline. Humidity rarely, if ever, leaves Florida weather regardless of where you are in the state.

"Sam said to tell you he'd be here in thirty minutes or less."

"Did you know the deceased?" an officer wearing cargo police shorts and a short-sleeved shirt walked up and asked me.

"No."

Cherise proceeded to give him the rundown on what I had said over the phone to Sam.

I know it's Florida, I know it's always hot and humid, I was sweating profusely, it wasn't even seven a.m., but these cops were working at the speed of a turtle laying eggs. They were sloooow.

They didn't seem to be particularly interested in doing much of anything. Most of them seem to be just standing around and shooting the breeze with each other. Our precious city government dollars at work.

I spotted Sam ambling over the sugar sand dune and coming down to the hard-packed beach sand. He was carrying three cups of coffee. He handed one to Cherise, gave her a lazy smile, and a much bigger smile to me as he gave me the coffee. "I figured you both could use one."

Cherise thanked him and went over to the group of men just standing around and appearing to be doing nothing. Perhaps they were thinking, there wasn't any physical motion needed for that. Maybe they were solving the case. They were just watching the coroner lift the body up into the gurney.

I started to ask Sam a question, but he held up a finger. "Drink the coffee, Harper. Let me see what the guys have to say."

My hand was shaking so badly that if the cup had not had a lid on it nothing would be left in the Styrofoam container.

Watching Sam out of the corner of my eye, I was still trying to process everything going on. My nerves could have ridden a pogo stick as much bouncing up and down they were doing.

Walking back over to me, he asked, "Harper, you know who that is, don't you?"

I frowned and shook my head sipping my coffee.

"They think that it's Mickey Rogers' son Mason."

Chapter 2

Shocked I didn't know what to say. There was empty space floating around in my brain. I know the old saying that nature abhors a vacuum didn't seem to be true in my case. There was air in my noggin. No dots were being connected; no straight lines were aligning with anything. It felt like my very being was a black hole in the universe where things disappeared forever.

I hadn't heard the name Mickey Rogers in years, and it took a moment for it to connect.

"You, they, think it's who?" I finally managed to stutter out. Then I turned and threw up in the ocean again.

How did this happen? This was my biological father's son? I didn't know he had any children.

My dad had divorced my mother when I was two and rode off into the sunset to God knows where. I had never seen or talked to the man since he walked out the door.

My thoughts resembled a jumbled labyrinth of knotted strings. I vaguely wondered if my mother knew what became of him. It was always possible.

My mother had told me several times when I was little that she and Mickey, I'm not calling him Dad since

I never knew him, had had a major disagreement on my name when I was born. She said they'd had a lot of arguments before Mickey took off for good.

My name is Harper Elizabeth Rogers. Yes, my initials spell HER. She thought it was funny, and it was a lot better than Mickey's name choice of Harper Olivia Rogers aka HOR. Mom was adamant that her daughter's initials would not be compared to a lowly, jail-prone street walker. She won in the end.

Mom, however, wasn't amused when I told her I was going to be a novelist. "Just because I named you Harper doesn't mean you have to be a writer like Harper Lee," she sniffed. "I simply liked the name Harper."

Sadly, she died a couple of years ago before I had graduated from eating peanut butter and jelly sandwiches on a daily basis to eating out at decent restaurants several times a week. I like to think she would have been proud of me and my career choice.

It suddenly occurred to me why would Sam know that I was related to Mickey Rogers.

"Sam," I almost dreaded asking him, afraid of his answer, "how did you know Mickey Rogers is my biological father?"

I wanted to be excessively clear that I didn't know the man except by name only. He was simply a sperm donor as far as I was concerned. I hadn't thought about him in years and, honestly, I wouldn't recognize him if he were standing in front of me.

"He told me."

Oh, the day just keeps getting better and better. Then it occurred to me, why did the cops know Mickey Rogers and his son? And, more importantly, how was this connected to me? I don't like it when murders happen around me, it makes me nervous for a variety of reasons.

"Why?"

"Why what, Harper?" Sam had a slight smile on his face while tilting his head.

I groaned. Sam and I had flirted slightly several months ago. Yes, we have gone out several times since then but nothing serious. I was still trying to overcome the devastating effects from my divorce. I simply wasn't interested in a relationship. Well, platonic but nothing more.

"He's a decent musician and a lousy comedian. His comedic timing is atrocious."

I just stood there, blinking my eyes, trying to absorb this information about someone who was technically related to me but also someone I knew absolutely nothing about.

"He plays guitar in a cover band that periodically blasts through Jacksonville. I met him when," he nodded his head at Cherise, "she and I dated for a brief moment in time."

Score one for me. As a woman, we have the sixth sense in spades when it comes to knowing if another female has dated someone. Must be some type of pheromones that only we can detect.

"You had just come out with your book *Bowling and Murder* and were on Good Morning, America."

I smiled. That one morning show had taken me from eating very frugally to where I could eat out all the time and not have to stress about the cost.

Sam smiled and continued, "Cherise and I met him backstage at a meet-and-greet. He had asked where we were from. She said Jacksonville and I said Palm Park. He asked if I knew you. Well, I knew who you were and that you had grown up in Palm Park, but I didn't really know you. So, I said no. He said you were a very famous author, and that he was your dad. The line needed to keep moving, he turned, and started talking to someone else. That was it."

I almost couldn't breathe. Mickey Rogers actually knew who I was? I wondered why he had never bothered to contact me, especially after my mother had died.

"Sam, why would I know Mason Rogers? I didn't even know I had a half-brother until just now. In fact, I didn't even know Mickey was still alive. I'm still in shock from finding that out."

"Because there was a note in Mason's hand that said, 'If I'm dead, find Harper Rogers.'"

I fainted.

Chapter 3

Just call me wimpy. I am a writer. I don't go to the gym, I don't have Pilates muscles, I hide behind a computer and spew words out that, hopefully, people like to read. My fingers are exercised a lot every time the sun passes go. In general, if I jump up too quickly from a strenuous workout on the keyboard, I can become swimmy-headed. Finding out that a murdered man was basically accusing me of causing his death caused all my body's blood flow to head south to my toes. It was a sheer wonder that I didn't have seriously fat feet when I regained consciousness.

I heard voices but they were distant and, quite honestly, I didn't feel like opening my eyes. I was comfortable with my eyes shut. I was probably going to be arrested for murder. I wondered if I was allowed to write in jail. I was sure I wasn't going to look good in orange or whatever the color du jour was for prison uniforms. I didn't want to have to learn karate to protect myself inside government-issue human cages from people I would never ever have coffee with in real life. My brain felt like a dysfunctional marriage of Legos and Tinker Toys, nothing was matching up nor did it want to. Weird thoughts were running through my head at the speed of Einstein's theory of relativity. Maybe I had inhaled a cosmic ray of energy. I took a deep breath.

"Harper, I saw your eyelids twitch. Open them," ordered Sam. He was interrupting some seriously good non-productive thoughts.

Sighing deeply to let him know how annoyed I was, I opened them and then slowly sat up.

"Am I being arrested?" I timidly asked. I was searching frantically in my brain if I knew any attorneys I could call to get me out of jail. None came to mind. Well, that's not exactly true. I did know one, but I wasn't exactly sure if he'd represent me since he overheard me saying at a social function that he only handled schoolboard clients and they couldn't fire him regardless of the advice he gave them. Probably not the right thing to say at a public schoolboard meeting. I had tried to tell him I meant it as a joke. I don't think he has a sense of humor but, to be fair, I'm not wild about hearing someone criticize my writing either. Maybe he'd just attribute that unfortunate remark to my having a glass of wine that evening. I probably should never admit to him that I was only holding it and not drinking it.

"No, you're not being arrested," replied Cherise. Sweat was running in a straight line down the sides of her face, "but you do need to give me your statement again."

I arched my eyebrows. "How many times do I need to do that?"

"Until we're satisfied you're not lying."

Cherise wasn't smiling when she said that. I was not going to vote for her as a pseudo-Miss Congeniality. Errant thoughts were darting through my brain trying to piece together what was going on.

"Is Mickey here in the area?"

Sam and Cherise looked at each other and shrugged. One of the other officers gestured for them to come join their group.

I watched as they all turned and stared at the condo building behind the sand dunes. One of the officers pointed at it. I couldn't tell what floor he was pointing at, but it suddenly occurred to me I was in the clear. If they were pointing at the building, that meant someone had shot Mason. It also meant that someone probably had a high-powered rifle to shoot from that distance. I don't know much about guns, but I surmised a guess that whoever used the rifle, they were probably military or ex-military. I did know shotguns and handguns couldn't hit anything accurately from that far away. Was this a paid hit? What was going on? This was much more than just a random, theoretically accidental, homicide. And why, oh, why was my half-brother holding a note with my name on it? As far as I knew, I had never even seen him before. I certainly didn't know him.

"You can leave, Harper. We have all of your information and I'm sure someone will be in touch with you." Cherise held out her hand to pull me into an upright standing position.

Sam had his hands on his hips. "You going to finish your walk?"

"Wait!" I held up my hand. "This isn't making any sense. Why were you guys pointing at the condo?"

Then my sheer nosiness came alive and I blurted out, "Why were you at Town Center so early in the day? None of the stores open until ten a.m."

"Checking things out." Sam was very nonchalant. Realistically, it was a nunya – none of my business. I was trying to justify my nosiness as info for one of my new books I was yet to write.

One of the officers walked past us when Sam said just loud enough for him to hear, "Yes, I'll walk with you. I'll be your personal bodyguard."

Part of me wanted to believe it was his way of flirting, the other part of me was highly annoyed that he was posturing for another officer.

"It's a free country. You can walk wherever you want to," I snapped. Also, I was loud enough for the officer to hear. Childish? Yes, of course. Did it make me feel better? Absolutely it did.

Sam merely frowned, nodded his head up and to the right, "You walking or what?"

Gritting my teeth and finally giving up as we turned to walk side by side down the beach. "Why'd you say that to the cops?"

He grinned, showing off his dimple in his right cheek. "Do I have to have a reason? Come on, Harper, you really do need to walk with me."

It suddenly dawned on me, I'm blaming my mental slowness on all the unwelcome events of the morning, that Sam had information he was going to share with me.

"Yeah, sure," I said begrudgingly and started to walk.

As soon as we got out of ear range of the beach cops, Sam turned his head toward me. "We're pretty sure someone on the sixth floor of the condo shot Mason."

I was so pleased with myself for guessing that that I blurted out, "It had to be a high-powered rifle and someone with a military background, right?"

Sam did a side-eye glance at me. "You might not want to share that information. That puts you back in the category of knowing too much but, yes, you are correct. Mason was hit in the middle of his head. That means someone had to calculate wind velocity, wind direction, altitude, elevation, range to the target, ambient temperature..."

"In other words, the sniper was a pro and had to know what he was doing." I was so proud of myself.

Sam just nodded his head. "Yep. The question is why?"

"Um, that also means one of the cops knows about wind elevation, etc., right?"

Sam laughed, "Do you have any idea how many cops are ex-military? Any of them could have come up with the same solution."

I was walking in the ocean and Sam was a couple of feet away. He had on sneakers, and I was walking with just my bare-naked toes and feet in the coolish water. The water in Florida doesn't really get cold until January and then it only stays cold for about six to eight weeks. The temperature during the summertime averages about eighty-three degrees. The Gulf of Mexico, on the other hand aka the west coast of Florida, averages about eighty-eight degrees. I personally don't care for the west coast of Florida. The Gulf is like warm bathwater as far as I was concerned...and there were no waves. I've made more waves in a bathtub than you ever see on the Gulf unless there is a huge hurricane rolling in. It's boring.

The Atlantic Ocean by Jacksonville has a lot of waves, there are plenty of surfers. I seriously doubt most of them could surf California waves but it's still fun to watch them.

They were now starting to show up and paddling out to catch the swells. As hot and humid as it already was, the day was promising to be a scorcher, it was still only about nine in the morning.

"Why are you out walking so early, Harper?" Sam had small rivers of sweat running down both sides of his face. Let me point out that it's no longer called perspiration when that occurs. It's just pure out-and-out sweat. He was wiping the sweat off his face about every ten seconds. Yes, I counted because I was trying very hard not to do the same thing myself. I like air conditioning...a lot. I don't exercise in a gym because I don't like to sweat. I try to convince myself typing on a keyboard at a furious pace counts as exercise...with no sweat.

When I first started walking this morning I wasn't sweating. My original plan had been to walk on the beach, feel the sand between my toes, get my feet wet, and then head back home. I just wanted to walk and think for about thirty minutes. Finding Mason dead disrupted my entire morning and messed up my entire thinking process. How could one possibly think after stumbling upon a dead body? My thoughts were just going to have to continue to swirl in outer space with no destination.

"Are you even listening to me?" asked Sam wiping the sweat off his face, he sounded annoyed. He glanced over at me.

"Um," I was frantically trying to remember what he had said. "Um, why?"

Sam glanced over at me. This time he was visibly annoyed. "What do you have in common with Mason, your biological dad, and a sniper?"

I shrugged, thinking, "Nothing that I'm aware of."

"Harper, when was the last time you saw your dad?"

I didn't remember. I couldn't even pull up a memory of what he looked like. The man could have been standing in front of me and I wouldn't have been able to pick him out of a lineup.

It's weird how childhood feelings suddenly surface. They're not logical and, most probably, aren't even true except for what we believe about them. Maybe I screamed too loud as a two-year-old toddler. Maybe I didn't hug him enough. Who knows? All I knew was he was there one day and then he was gone. As far as I knew, I hadn't laid eyes on him in twenty-six years or so.

I shrugged. "I don't know. Maybe when I was two. Mom said he left and never returned."

"Any pictures of him or of the two of you together?"

Shaking my head no, "Why? You've seen him more than I have. Why would you need a picture?"

"Just curious." Sam kept his eyes focused straight ahead.

"Do you know something you're not sharing with me?" Rather than being aggravated, I was actually more curious. His line of questioning indicated to me that he knew something he wasn't willing to tell me.

We were almost back to where police personnel were still taking pictures and measurements.

Patience isn't one of my strong suits. "Well?" I tried to sound demanding, but it came out more like Alvin from Alvin and the Chipmunks. I cleared my throat and tried again. "Well?"

"It's a deep subject." He chuckled. "Harper, catch you later."

I just stood there trying to figure out what was going on. Nothing came to mind.

Cherise ambled over to me. "Harper, I'm sure we'll have some more questions for you at some point, but you can leave now."

"I have a question."

She turned. "Yes?"

"What do you think is going on?"

Poker-faced, she answered, "Police business, Harper, police business."

Weirdness is the only thing I could think of on the way back to my car. Walking up to the side of my car, I could see there was a note on my windshield. I grinned, maybe Sam wanted to meet for coffee or lunch but didn't want to ask me in front of Cherise or the other police officers.

Picking up the note from under the wipers, I flipped it open.

"You're next."

Chapter 4

That's not good. I turned and ran back down to the beach. I didn't see Sam anywhere, but I did see Cherise. I waved at her trying to get her attention. She spotted me but didn't wave back. I still wasn't going to vote for her as Miss Congeniality.

Huffing and puffing as I ran up to her, I hate running, I handed her the note. She glanced at it. "You know you should consider working out."

I snorted and tried to take a deep breath at the same time. "This was under my windshield wiper blade," I finally managed to say. Trying to find a spark of wit to craft a clever retort to her snide remark about my exercise habits, nothing fired in my brain cylinders at that moment. My most clever remarks often happen several hours later when I've had a chance to think about such things.

She barely looked at it and handed it back to me. "So?"

My nerves were frayed, they were not going to be put back together with disinterest, glue, or even chocolate. "What do you mean so?" I shouted. Pointing at some of the police techs, "Get one of them to dust it for fingerprints. Maybe it's from the killer, I don't know but DO SOMETHING!" My voice continued to rise until I was almost screaming at her.

The other officers were paying a lot more attention to me than what I probably deserved but, then again, in their line of work, they need to be aware at all times.

One of them started to walk over, Cherise waved him back. "I've got it."

Sneering, I snapped, "Got what? You haven't got anything, and you don't seem to be much interested in solving a murder and now a threat on my life."

"Miss Rogers, that note could mean anything and it may not have even been meant for you."

"You don't know that." I was livid. "It was on my car. Under my wipers. It says you're next. Just what exactly do you think that means, Miss Police Officer?"

Probably not the wisest thing to do is to antagonize a police officer while they're investigating an open murder case where you might be the prime suspect.

In my excitement or lunacy, I must have inadvertently invaded her personal territory because she held up her hand in the universal stop motion.

"Miss Rogers, you need to back up a few feet. We are investigating an active murder scene. We appreciate your cooperation and understand why you are upset. However, that note could have been left on your car accidentally. It may have been a practical joke..."

I held up my hand. She ignored it.

"That same note may be on several other cars. But you need to leave so we can do our job. Again, we appreciate your cooperation."

Great. She's not remotely interested. I wonder if Sam thinks anything about it, but I don't know where he's disappeared to or even what he's doing. He did say this was his day off. I probably shouldn't bother him for the rest of the day then. I think I am already blurring the boundary lines on personal versus professional time.

In my world, I ignore those boundary lines. I mean I do pay attention to the professional ones...most of the time. But a lot of my work as a writer involves research and creativity, therefore, those lines often overlap. Plus, I really don't care about crossing so-called boundary lines. If someone's a friend, I don't think anything about asking them about their job if it helps me with a plot or a character. Even if I don't know you as a friend, I still don't think anything about asking questions.

I was feeling thwarted by Cherise's lack of interest. I stomped off and left to go home. So much for my morning beach walk, clearing the cobwebs from my brain, and solving the world's problems.

Deciding I needed to do some research on dear old dad while driving back to Palm Park, I thought about googling him. Since Mom was no longer in the land of the living, I couldn't very well ask her. Mom had been an only child, so I didn't have any aunts, uncles, or cousins to ask. I couldn't recall us ever going to a relative's house for vacation or any holiday gatherings.

You might think we'd be like sisters or close friends. You'd be wrong. Surprisingly, Mom and I weren't really that close. She did her thing and I did mine. We saw each other at breakfast and dinner and that was it; otherwise, I was in school all day.

As a kid, it probably never occurred to me to ask questions about family. I could be obtuse at times. As an adult, I guess I simply didn't care. I often wore blinders and could be somewhat oblivious to many things that others took for granted.

I wasn't remotely interested in the 'Find Your DNA Match' websites. If I hadn't heard from someone in twenty years, I couldn't imagine why we needed to start communicating now. I could care less if there were so-called skeletons in the closet from a hundred years ago. It certainly wasn't going to do me any good now.

Musing about dear old dad, maybe I should see what the internet had to say about him.

He was a musician, just like Sam said. He did have a website. No mention of a son or daughter. It also didn't mention where he was based. He could live in Nome, Alaska for all I knew. Watching a couple of YouTube videos of him playing, I could understand why he played in bar cover bands. He was good, he just wasn't great. There didn't seem to be anything really special about his playing or singing.

Looking in the bathroom mirror while glancing at his website photo on my phone, I really didn't see any family resemblance. I guess that was a good thing because I didn't really have any impetus to continue searching for images.

An unknown number popped up on my phone. Since that was normally Sam, I answered the phone chirpily. "Are you calling for a coffee date?"

There was a slight pause before a robot-sounding voice answered. "Back off before you get hurt." The call was disconnected.

Pulling the phone away from my ear, I just stared at it for a few minutes.

This wasn't good.

Chapter 5

Punching in my friend Ronnie's number, I was hoping he'd answer quickly.

"Hello, honey. How you doing today?"

Ronnie was the flamboyant local pet store owner and we had been friends since high school. He welcomed me with open arms when I moved back to Palm Park from Jacksonville after a disastrous failed marriage.

I quickly told him everything going on and ending with, "Ronnie, did you know my dad?"

I could almost see him shaking his head. "No. I don't even remember Mama and Papa ever talking about him growing up. Have you talked to Sam about this? After all, he's a detective."

Almost a semi-snort, I answered, "He said he was at Town Center this morning and it was his day off. I asked him why he was there so early in the morning, and he never answered the question."

Ronnie laughed. "That's a nunya, Harper. It ain't none o' yor business. He might have been having breakfast with someone."

True, there were a ton of fast food and early-morning restaurants in that area. Maybe I had interrupted a date...a date that went from last night into this morning. A flickering of an emotion I did not understand or could really identify popped up in my brain. Maybe it was jealousy, maybe not. I didn't understand any of these emotions I was experiencing.

Was this a feeling of rejection? Maybe but Sam and I weren't dating. We did meet up for coffee periodically and did go to dinner once in a blue moon but none of those social interactions would constitute a date in my world. We flirted...sort of, maybe. I really wasn't ready to date, I was recovering from my divorce. At least, that's what I was telling myself. I felt like I was in an emotional vacuum and that was okay. I was trudging through life, that I could do because I had been doing it for years. I didn't need emotions. That was a lie. Deep inside I knew I did but I wasn't ready to confront or acknowledge them.

The thought did occur to me that I probably needed to get out more, see other people, make new friends, and not live in my head so much. I tried to justify that thought process by saying I was a writer, and I could live in my head as much as I wanted. I could play make-believe as much as I desired. After all, it's what makes great stories.

I tried justifying my reluctance to engage with others outside of my head. Then I tried to blame my lack of a robust social life on the death of my friend several months ago when we were meeting for a coffee date. I had to be honest, while Sarah's death was very upsetting, it had nothing to do with this funk I was in. I was already living in my head too much.

All these thoughts flitted through my brain at the speed of an adrenaline junkie as Ronnie was talking.

"Harper, honey, come on down to the store and I'll let you hold some puppies. They'll make you feel better."

I nodded and then realized Ronnie couldn't see me do that. "Yes, okay. Do you want me to pick up a butter pecan coffee for you?"

Ronnie almost squealed with delight. "Harper Elizabeth Rogers, if you do that, I'll love you to the moon and back."

With someone that happy, they couldn't help but elevate everyone's mood.

Laughing, I answered, "See you shortly."

Stopping at the Palm Park Coffee Shop, I got us both large coffees to go. The girls were friendly and seemed to be glad to see me.

"Oh, Harper, this guy came in a few minutes ago and asked if you came in here on a regular basis. I told him yes. He asked for me to give this to you the next time I saw you." She handed me an envelope.

I turned it over in my hands a couple of times. This was odd. It was just a plain number ten envelope with no writing on the outside.

Since I had a few minutes for the coffees to be ready, I opened the envelope. Pulling out a white sheet of paper. I debated about unfolding it and reading the contents.

Taking a deep breath, I hoped it was not a nasty note that was going to create an undue amount of stress on my already frazzled nerves. It said, "Meet me tonight at eight at the old house."

Chapter 6

Life was getting **curiosier and** curiosier to quote Lewis Carroll. I'd have to tell Ronnie about this. Maybe he'd go with me. I was assuming the old house was where I grew up. Even though I had moved back to Palm Park several months ago, I just never got around to going back and looking at the house I grew up in.

My living in an apartment reflected new decisions, a new way of experiencing life in new forms. The house had been sold years ago, and whatever the owners had chosen to do with the house...well, it was theirs. I didn't care. As far as I was concerned, it was comparable to owning an old coat I had given away to Goodwill. Good memories but no longer relevant to my current life.

Strolling into the pet store was equivalent to walking into a happy ray of sunshine. Ronnie was always happy. His smile could light up the entire state of Florida.

"Honey, honey, honey! Oh, I do love you for bringing me a butter pecan coffee." He promptly snatched it out of my hand. "I did get the right one, right?"

Nodding, I laughed. "Yes, I got us both a butter pecan today."

Placing the coffee on the counter, Ronnie reached into the puppy playpen and pulled out a very enthusiastic little Maltese.

I reached for her. I love puppies and I especially love Maltese dogs. I snuggled with her and let her lick all over my face and neck.

Ronnie grinned. "You still cannot have one of my dogs. We both know you'd forget about taking care of one of my babies."

Much as I hated to admit it, he was right. I'd forget to take the puppy out, I'd forget to feed it, and I'd probably forget its name within a matter of hours, particularly if I was writing a new book. BUT, I could love on any of his dogs as much as I liked.

"So, honey, what is that you need my advice on?"

I explained everything that had happened and ended with, "So, will you go with me to the old house tonight?"

Ronnie slightly frowned. "Harper, unless my memory suddenly has Swiss cheese holes in it, I think your house was torn down about a year ago. Someone was building a larger home on that lot, and I don't know if it was ever finished."

Looking up over his cup, "I'm assuming this means you never went back and looked at it."

I wiggled my eyebrows at him. "No point. I sold it and moved on."

He had a pensive look on his face. "You know, this could be dangerous. Maybe you should call Detective Sam and..."

"It's his day off," I interrupted him.

Ronnie tapped his first finger against his chin, thinking. "Harper, this whole area was chill until you moved back. Girl, what kind of nastiness did you bring back with you from Jacksonville? Please tell me you weren't involved in some weird voodoo stuff."

He looked at me and questioningly and then we both laughed. I wondered the same thing about the bizarre things that kept happening around me since I had moved back to Palm Park. Was this like a weird flu bug or some cosmic demonic fairy dust that somehow managed to find its way onto a poor, unsuspecting writer?

What were the odds of being around two murders in less than six months? It was bad enough when Sarah and I had gone for coffee, only for her to be tragically murdered by a mentally unstable business owner consumed by jealousy. She was now permanently ensconced at a long-term stay-cation resort courtesy of the state of Florida.

Now, I had this new murder that was suddenly in my sphere of existence. Was this the universe giving me a sign I should be writing murder mysteries or was it merely telling me I should stay indoors, write, and never let sunlight hit my pasty white skin? Does thinking these kinds of thoughts make me a double-minded person bouncing around on the ocean of life?

Ronnie was speaking. I could see his lips move but I was thinking. I don't think I multi-task well. So, I said the most intelligent thing I could think of at the moment, "Do what? I know you said something but I, um, was thinking…"

He grinned, "I said that you were living too much in your head, Harper. I also said meeting someone at night was probably not a wise thing to do. You definitely need backup."

Defending my going out at night, I snorted, "It's summertime, Ronnie. It's not going to get dark until about eight-thirty or so. As long as we can see what's going on, everything should be fine."

I wanted him to come with me. Thinking having a man accompany me would ward off any potential issues with meeting the stranger, I attempted to bribe him, I offered, "I'll buy your dinner at Hubba Bubba's."

Rolling his eyes, this was confirmation he was going to go with me, he beamed, "You certainly know the way to my heart. I love Hubba Bubba's. They have the best hushpuppies and fried catfish anywhere."

He sighed, "Okay, I'll do it. But we have to come back here before we go over to your old house. My babies need to be able to go out and do their job before bed."

I agreed. "I'll be back around six and we can go then."

Deciding to go by the old place after leaving Ronnie, I wanted to check the area ahead of time. I had offered to take one of the little, fluffy white Maltese puppies for a ride, but he was adamant that I wasn't a good choice for that. I was a little irritated about that but, in all honesty, I knew he as right. If, God forbid, I had an accident and something happened to the puppy, I would disappear and never been heard from again.

I thought about the house I grew up in and I had exactly zero feelings about it. Nothing. Not the slightest twinge, no emotional angst, no nothing. It was just something I was going to go look at.

Driving up the brick-lined street, I could see where the house had been torn down. It did appear to be under construction for a new home. The yard contained concrete blocks, wheelbarrows, and similar construction materials, but it appeared that work had been ceased for several months. I could see where weeds had grown up around the building material. Maybe the crew had been called to another job suddenly, but it was odd that no one had come back for their equipment and building material.

Since no one was around. I parked on the street and wandered around the area. There weren't any neighbors close by. The lots in this area had been huge, probably half a football field length or more between houses. I don't remember being overly friendly with neighbors as a kid. Chances of me knowing anyone now were between slim and none and Slim had gone to the Bahamas.

Carefully walking around, I didn't see anything that was screaming, "Danger, Will Robinson, danger!" There had been some concrete walls erected but no roof and the walls only extended about chest height. Maybe the new owners had run out of money, or the bank had taken over the property. Who knows? And I certainly didn't care.

Everything seemed relatively safe to me when Ronnie and I would come back tonight.

The thought did occur to me that I might need to bring a weapon of mass destruction back with me, but I didn't own one and I was fairly sure Ronnie didn't either. I certainly didn't think anything harmful would happen to either me or Ronnie.

I should have paid attention to that thought.

Chapter 7

Ronnie and I had a great meal at Hubba Bubba's Fish Camp. It was really just a rustic restaurant sitting over the St. Johns River. You didn't have to worry about accidental tourists finding this place. If they weren't native to Palm Park, the only way they would have found it was only because a local had brought them here. Hubba Bubba's didn't advertise. They weren't on social media. There weren't any signs posted on how to find them. It's just rural Florida at its best.

Ronnie was a little magpie, happy in his environment. The man knew everyone in town. Tons of people came over and spoke with him.

"Why haven't you run for office, Ronnie?" I was chowing down on the all-you-can-eat fried catfish special and I was up to number six. The catfish were as long as my wrist to the tip end of my middle finger. Some folks refer to them as fingerling catfish.

He giggled as he picked up another small fried catfish. "Honey, I don't want to be mayor. I want people to like me. I don't like politics. I just want to own my little pet store and have people know they aren't buying some puppy mill babies. These are little ones chosen by me, bred by responsible owners.

"Also, if I were mayor, I'd have to be in an office and that thought just makes me want to throw up. Nope, my furbabies might bark at me but they don't say ugly things and I don't have to worry about them hurting me."

I reached across the table and placed my hand on top of Ronnie's. He had been the victim of an unprovoked attack several months ago, spent time in ICU, and was fortunate to be back at the pet store.

Telling him what I found at my old place, I ended with, "Who and what do you think is going on?"

He laughed, "Are you sure you're not being pranked on some writer's tv show?"

I rolled my eyes.

"I don't know. Maybe you've gotten involved in a spy operation."

Choking on my iced tea, I managed to get out, "That makes absolutely no sense. I don't know anything that a corporation or the government would want to know about."

He arched his eyebrows. I must say he does it a lot better than I do. "Haven't you heard the old saying, 'I love my country, it's the government I fear'?"

I still didn't know anything. My brain was running at the speed of slow on trying to find a connection to any of these strange happenings. My ex-husband wasn't tied to anything to do with the government. I had no clue about Mason or what he was involved in since I had only just become aware of his existence.

Dear old dad, as far as I could tell, was a musician who just roamed the country visiting bars. Most musicians I know, and I only know two, were simply not the brightest bulbs in the box and I sincerely doubted the CIA, FBI, or any other scrambled letters of a governmental agency would want anything to do with them. They also smoked a lot of an illegal substance that most people in this country would like to see legalized.

It was still very light out when we arrived at the house. In the Florida summertime, daylight started at six a.m. and the bright sun could easily still be shining on everyone until about nine p.m.

There was a blue pickup truck parked in front of the property. No license plate. That should have been a clue that this might not have been one of my brighter ideas to do. I did, however, have the sense to take a picture of the truck with my phone.

I pulled up close to the truck but far enough back that I could escape quickly if I needed to.

We got out and Ronnie looked through the passenger window and announced, "Nothing here, nothing on the seat. It's clean."

We turned to go up the driveway when a man started walking toward us. I hadn't noticed him until just then. It was like he just suddenly appeared. He was wearing jeans, boots, and a tee shirt that said, "Only the good die young."

I smiled and quipped, "Billy Joel." I knew that song.

The man didn't say anything. He didn't look at the front of his shirt. I would have done that since I never remember what I put on in the morning.

Ronnie was being exceptionally quiet, which meant that he was trying to figure out if he knew this man.

The man beckoned us with his forefinger, turned, and started walking back to the far concrete wall. The wall was just tall enough to hide someone if they were crouching. I certainly hoped this wasn't the case.

We had walked forward and stopped just short of the back wall when Ronnie halted. He said loudly, "We're not going any further until you tell us what's going on."

The man either didn't hear Ronnie or he had decided to ignore us. He disappeared around a small shed in the back. I hadn't really noticed it before. The shade from the huge oak tree had hidden it. At least that's what I was telling myself because I hated to admit I wasn't being all that observant; I was more focused on the man. Who am I kidding? I wanted to be alert in case someone jumped out from behind the half-wall of the house.

"Ronnie, that shed wasn't here when I was a kid."

He shrugged. He was probably right, what difference did it make, especially since I had no intention of going that far.

"Unt uh, I'm not going somewhere that far from the street." I finally grew a spine. Too many weird things had happened, and I wasn't willing to participate in anything that might cause me bodily harm. I also noticed Ronnie had graciously allowed me to lead.

He's a wimp but, then again, I already knew that. I am too which is the reason why I can spot it in others so quickly.

Half-turning, "If you want to go ahead, I'm fine with that but I'm not going any further."

He grinned and bobbed his head. "Yoo hoo! Yoo hoo! Sir, sir, you need to come back out here."

Crickets. If whoever it was thought we were brave enough to wander back there on our own, they were sadly mistaken. We both had a yellow streak down our backs the size of the Ganges River. I was okay with being called a chicken. I'd stand up and own it.

The hair on my neck was a little damp. Maybe it was just sweat instead of my silly nerves...that's what I was trying to convince myself. I was trying to coax my nerves into believing that they were an early warning system for possible mayhem in my life but, much as I hate to say it, other than being a little sweaty, I wasn't getting much direction in the way of being in danger. Apparently, I have a lousy personal GPS system.

"Harper, honey, nothing's happening. Let's just go back to the car."

That's when I heard the cha-chunk of a shotgun pump. That's never a sign of welcoming hospitality. I turned and took off running down the driveway. Ronnie sprinted past me like a scared bunny in front of a bunch of hungry greyhounds.

He slid into the passenger side just as I dive-bombed into the driver's seat. My hands were shaking so badly that I was having a hard time even punching the start button on my car. Finally, it started, and we peeled off.

We both heard the shotgun explosion as stumbled into the car. What was even scarier was the dirt that bounced up and splattered against the car door. I was beyond grateful that neither one of us was digging little steel pellets out of our bodies. Buckshot could make anyone turn into instant hamburger helper.

Ronnie was hyperventilating, gulping in deep breaths of air before he managed to speak. "Harper, I don't like playing with you. This is dangerous. I'm not doing it again."

My neurological synapses were not firing on all cylinders. I was shaking. I was also not sure when the last time I had taken a deep breath. We were back on the main road, and I pulled into the McDonald's parking lot.

"Ronnie..."

"Nope, not doing it again," he gasped out. He was pale and shaking. I hoped I wasn't going to have to take him to the emergency room.

"Not what I was going to say," I semi-hissed out. I was lying. "I was going to say why do you think that guy used a shotgun on us?"

He shook his head. "Don't know, don't care. Not my circus, not my monkey. Take me home."

"Ronnie..."

He turned to me, tears in his eyes, "Harper, please take me home. My nerves can't take this. I'm already on medication from when that last guy tried to kill me."

His voice was steadily increasing until he wailed, "My babies need me. I can't let anything happen to my babies."

While I'm not normally an overly compassionate individual, I did experience sympathy for him. He had been traumatized several months ago when a man had beaten him up so badly that he ended up in ICU in the hospital. He was just getting back to being his old self.

"Ronnie, do you mind if we swing by my place real quick?" I paused for a moment, "I want to make sure no one broke in."

He could only nod while he was dabbing at his eyes with his blue and white silk handkerchief.

I started a nervous laugh and pointed at his handkerchief. "Ronnie, those colors look like they belong in the Kentucky Derby."

He was huffy. "These colors are very fashionable. I saw them when I was in Atlanta last week. But I'm glad you like them."

That's Ronnie, take a negative and turn it into a positive.

We both went into my apartment, checked all the windows, and, yes, of course, I checked the shower and closet. I had seen the shower scene in the movie Psycho, and it had scared the holy bejabbers out of me. I'm not sure what I would have done if someone was hiding behind the shower curtain.

I was standing in my bedroom thinking. I could hear Ronnie opening my refrigerator door.

"Harper, honey, I'm taking your bottle of Pinot Grigio home with me."

My eyebrows decided to meet in the middle. "What did you say, Ronnie?" Maybe I hadn't heard him right.

"I said I'm taking your bottle of Pinot home with me."

"Don't!" I shouted as I ran through the living room and into the kitchen.

He looked befuddled and held out the bottle to me. "I, I, I just thought it'd be okay," he stuttered.

"No, it's not that, Ronnie. You're certainly welcome to whatever's in the house but that's not mine. I don't drink white wine." I was trying to explain but everything came out in a rush.

Grabbing the bottle from him, I pointed at the top of the bottle. "Someone has opened it and left it here. That can't be good in any sense of the word."

Ronnie whipped out his phone. "Enough of playing games, Harper! It's time for the cops. There is just too much craziness going on. I'm calling Detective Sam." He was nervously tapping his fingers on the countertop.

I guess Sam wasn't answering his phone because Ronnie left a message. He texted a message to someone. "Please take me home, Harper, I've had all the excitement I can stand for one day."

Nodding, I couldn't blame him. My nerves were shot as well. My thoughts were bouncing around like ping pong balls during the Chinese Olympics. Nothing was making sense.

I didn't think anyone was actually trying to kill me. Scare me, yes; but killing me, no. But what were they trying to scare me off from? I didn't know anything...or, at least, I didn't think I did.

Arriving at Ronnie's cottage, I saw his friend Donnie's car. I did a side-eye glance at him.

"I need someone to come spend the night with me. Donnie was free for the evening. He's not going to let anyone get past the front door."

Grinning, "I need some of your friends, Ronnie. I want someone to protect me."

He harrumphed, "You need to make nice nice with Detective Sam and you won't have that problem."

All I could do was nod my head. I didn't want to have to explain why I didn't want a romantic relationship right now, although the thought had occurred to me on several occasions.

Donnie came out to the car. He had on blue camos. I didn't even know cammies came in any other color than green and brown. But, then again, I'm not a fashionista.

Leaving the two of them, I headed back to my apartment. Pulling into my parking spot at the complex later, I noticed Sam's unmarked police car several spaces down.

He was waiting for me by my apartment door. "I understand you need some help."

Chapter 8

It was all I could do to keep from having a silly schoolgirl grin on my face. What was it about this guy who kept getting in my head? Maybe I did want a romantic relationship with him that I was suppressing. He was cute, had a dimple in his cheek, dark wavy hair although it was short, and usually a very nice personality. I think I might test it on occasion.

Managing to suppress my ever-widening grin, I tampered down my emotional, wayward thoughts and merely answered, "Yep. Ronnie called you?"

"Yep."

Oh, great, now we're playing one-word games. I couldn't blame him since I was the one who had started it.

Plunging ahead, I wanted him to know everything that had occurred. "Sam, did he tell you everything that has happened? By the way, would you like some hot tea?"

"Harper, I'm not sure what's going on here." He scratched the back of his head and nodded his head for the tea. I turned on the electric tea kettle to heat up the water. Yes, I could put the cups in the microwave and heat the water that way except I'm somewhat of a purist when it comes to my tea. I wanted water heated in an electric tea kettle. It just seems so homey, so British, so authorish...it just makes me feel good.

Coffee, I just drink whatever is put in front of me. Putting a teaspoon of the Blood Orange loose tea I had recently purchased from Queen Bee June at Steapers in the tea ball, I turned and started to reach for a cup for each of us and realized Sam had already pulled two down from the cabinet.

He smiled and turned his palm over when I blinked in surprise at him. I was actually a little dumbfounded at his "Trying to be helpful."

I didn't know what to say. In the few years that I had been married, never once had my ex ever handed me any type of utensil - plate, glass, or cup. I guess he thought those things just magically appeared on the countertop or table for his dining enjoyment. He also never put anything in the sink or dishwasher regardless of how many times I asked him. I think we had separate lives long before we divorced. I don't what possessed either one of us to get married. We were misfits from the get-go.

I think my brain slid into some type of vortex, more like the spin cycle of a washing machine, but I didn't have the social coping skills on how to handle this nicety from Sam. This was something I never had happen before. I tried to think how Oprah would have responded to this back in her tv heyday. I couldn't recall if she had ever done a show on the social skills needed to survive for this type of situation.

Martha Stewart, now she's a demi-goddess of all things pertaining to the home, I had watched Martha a lot longer and much more often than I ever had Oprah.

What would Queen Martha do? Taking a deep breath, I breathed out a soft, "Thank you."

The tea kettle let its steam-generated long sigh out indicating that the water was ready to be poured into the cups.

How long had I been standing there contemplating the appropriate response to Sam? It seemed like hours but was probably only a couple of seconds when I said, "Thank you."

I felt like I was living in an alternative universe when he was around. There was real and then there was whatever was whirling around in my brain. Was I going crazy? Early dementia? Maybe I have undiagnosed Asperger's. I'd like to say it might have been all the weed I had smoked back in college except that would be a lie. The two times I had tried it, and I really did make a great effort to inhale the yellow smoke deep into my lungs because I so desperately wanted to be cool and fit in with my college roommates, it had made me incredibly drowsy to the point that I basically went to sleep right where I was. I had tumbled over on the couch, my eyes were shut, and I was snoozing away in la-la land almost immediately. I had been told I wasn't a fun, party person. So much for me being voted Miss Life-of-the-Party.

Sam raised his eyebrows. Okay, he must have asked a question. It probably had to do with him wanting to know if I had any sugar since we were drinking tea.

"The sugar and honey are in that cabinet." I pointed to the one next to the cups.

"Good guess but that wasn't what I asked," he grinned. That cute dimple in his cheek got me every time. Were these merely some type of emotions that I had kept repressed all these years? Perhaps it was some type of weird professional writer overload that I had never heard about.

"What I asked was if the man at your old house was your dad?"

I shook my head, hopefully, scattering my errant thoughts to the wind...although there was no wind blowing through my apartment, not even the air conditioning was on. "Even though I haven't seen him in years, there was absolutely nothing about him that would indicate he was."

I was befuddled, swiping my hand through my hair. "Sam, the guy never said anything. That's what was weird."

He blew on his hot tea before responding. A twinkle in his eye, "So, the fact that he pumped a shotgun at you wasn't strange? Is there something in your background you want to share with me?" He was almost laughing.

I flushed with pink creeping across my cheeks and grinned. "Yeah, well, I see your point. I was just going over everything in detail. Honestly, I kind of wanted it to be my dad, happy that it wasn't, and I'm more confused than ever about this whole thing. There is, literally, nothing that's making any sense."

He leaned toward me, his eyebrows furrowing. "I agree, Harper, but this is not random. The guy had the opportunity to kill both you and Ronnie. He had no way of knowing you were bringing anyone with you. If he kills one of you, he might as well kill both of you since, if he were ever caught, he'd be doing life anyway. This is more like a warning but the question what are you being warned about?"

I chewed the inside of my cheek. My hands were wrapped around the cup, the warmth felt good. It also helped to keep them still, not shaking. I didn't want to admit how much all of this was upsetting me.

"Here's something else for you to think about. The guy knew how to handle a shotgun. It wasn't like he accidentally let loose buckshot into your car door. He deliberately sprayed it into the dirt near your car. He meant to scare you." He was analyzing the details of what I had told him. I could tell he was concerned, his eyebrows were drawn together, his lips in a firm straight line, and his facial muscles were tight.

Chewing on my lower lip, I slowly dipped my head down in agreement. "You're right. I hadn't actually thought of it in that way."

"I be a detective."

We both laughed. The laughter felt good. Maybe I should try doing it more often. I'd have to ask Ronnie about all these errant thoughts that had either escaped from the nut house or were from outer space aliens trying to pollute the empty air inside my skull. Ronnie was better than a paid psychiatrist, he was also cheaper. Buying a meal here and there was well worth it to me.

Also, he was a cheap date. It's not like we were going to some high-end Brazilian steak house for one meal and where I'd have to be eating beanie-weenies for the rest of the month.

My tea was still very warm. "Well, 'Mr. I be a detective' what do you think is going on here?"

Sam looked at me over the top of his cup. "I don't think it's you this person is after. I think you're being used as bait."

Staring at him blankly for a moment, I finally uttered the only coherent thing I could think of. "Me? For what? I don't know anything."

"I don't think it's about what you do or do not know. I think someone thinks you're either in touch with your dad or you know how to get in touch with him. They, in essence, want you to lead them to him."

Snorting, I rolled my eyes. "Seriously, if that were the case, they know diddly squat about my relationship with my dad.

"In fact," I was gathering steam on this new thought, "there's virtually nothing on the internet that even remotely connects me with dear old dad."

Sam shrugged. "Who knows? Maybe Mickey said something to the wrong person or, more likely, he's up to his eyeballs in something and mentioned your name to keep him out of trouble."

I started to laugh. "Really?"

Sam took a big gulp of his tea. "You do know..."

"Come on, Sam, I've told you umpteen times, I know so little about the man that it's ridiculous."

He ignored me and continued, "he has an extensive arrest record across the country."

Chapter 9

That wasn't the best news I'd ever heard. However, I couldn't compute how that even applied to me. So what if he had umpteen arrest records? The man was a musician and travelled a lot...or, at least, I had surmised that he did. I had a now-deceased half-brother that I knew nothing about. I was taking a wild guess that dear old dad had probably populated a number of, um, fields from one coast to the other. Not my problem.

"So what? How does that affect me? I've only lived three places in my entire life...Palm Park, Gainesville at the University of Florida, go Gators, and in Jacksonville."

I was mildly curious. "Do I dare ask what he was arrested for? Wait!" I held up my hand. "Let me guess, drunk and disorderly conduct, public drunkenness, urinating in public."

The dimple showed up again. I felt squishy inside, not naughty squishy, but happy squishy. What was wrong with me?

"Mostly. But here's the crazy thing, his file shows up as classified on the FBI's website."

Shut the front door! What in the heck?! Wait. What does that even mean? My brain was shooting off bottle rockets of wayward thoughts, none of them exploding too brightly. They must be duds.

"Let me guess, way back in the day he belonged to some anti-Vietnam hippie group or something."

Sam shrugged. "Without me jumping through a lot of hoops, I don't know."

This was a lot like playing a puzzle without a picture of how the completed puzzle should look.

"What about Mason? What's his background?"

"Nothing much. Surfer dude, worked odd jobs here and there. Didn't have so much as a speeding ticket."

I guess I must watch too many spy movies because my thought was that Mason was collateral damage.

"He was used as a warning to Mickey."

Cocking my head at Sam, "What does that mean?"

My phone went off and showed an unknown number ID. Looking at Sam, "Hello."

"You left too soon last night."

It takes a lot to make me mad but whoever this was had just pushed the wrong button on this side of civility. "What do you mean? You tried to kill me last night!" I screeched.

A slight chuckle. "It was a warning. You've been warned." The call was disconnected.

I had already punched speaker on my phone so that Sam heard everything.

Looking at him with wide eyes. "Are there two different things going on here?"

The living room glass shattered. Sam grabbed the top of my shoulders and pushed me to the floor. I dropped my cup where it broke into nine million pieces. That was my favorite cup. Why do I wonder about weird stuff like that when someone just fired a shot through my window? Focus, Harper, focus.

For whatever reason, Sam tossed his cup across the now broken glass window area. I was going to have to buy another mug because that one died by death by high-powered rifle.

"Give me another cup."

Carefully opening the dishwasher, I handed him a dirty cup. If it was going to be shot, killed, and destroyed, it didn't make any difference if it was clean or dirty.

He tossed it in front of the window again. It fell to the floor. It broke instead of being shot.

Standing up, Sam said, "Whoever this is, they're a pro. To hit a coffee mug through a window requires some skill and precision."

"Military?" I questioned as I stood up.

"More than likely. You don't get that good without a lot of practice and ammo."

My phone rang again. I answered it warily. "Yes?"

"Toss up another cup. I need another practice shot." I immediately dropped to the floor on my knees and handed the phone to Sam. I'm a coward, what can I say?

His voice was icy cold as he punched the speaker button. "What do you want?"

The voice laughed. "World peace, Sam, world peace. I wondered how long it would take for you to get on Harper's phone."

Sam's brow furrowed. "Who is this?"

"Not your best friend. Good luck, buddy."

He stared at the phone for a few minutes after the caller disconnected before saying, "I've heard that voice before, but it's been a long time."

I gasped, "So, you know this guy?"

"Know probably isn't the best word to use, but, yeah, I think so. I've heard this voice before, I just don't know from where."

"Maybe you're the connection?" I tentatively offered.

He snorted as he walked over to the now breezy non-existent glass window. "If that were the case, I would have been dead by now."

Turning his back to the window, I actually cringed because if the shooter were still there, Sam was an easy not-to-be-missed target. He eyed the living room wall. I noticed a hole about the size of my thumb. "Um..."

He was looking down at the floor, picking up a casing, he examined it for a moment, turning it over and over in his hand. "Military grade."

I just nodded. I thought we had already established that fact. I guess it was a guy thing to announce that. It was just a smushed-up mushroom-looking piece of metal as far as I was concerned.

"Harper, he's just trying to scare you."

Snorting, "He's doing a fine job of it. If he thinks I'm going to lead him to dear old dad, I still don't know any more than I did before...which is nothing."

My phone pinged indicating a new message. I showed it to Sam who immediately put his finger to his lips as he searched under the coffee table, looked up at the ceiling light fixture, and pointed. There was a small square box at the top of the ceiling fan.

The phone pinged again. I swiped the message. "Where's the money?"

Pointing at the text, I said loudly, "Whoever you are, I haven't seen Mickey in years, and I have absolutely no clue what you mean about where's the money. If you think I can lead you to him, you're just a special kind of stupid." I drew out the word stupid so it sounded like stoopid.

The next text was just a finger pointing at me emoji. If Sam hadn't been there, I would have been a willy-nilly basketcase. My nerves weren't in the best of shape now but were vastly superior to what they would have been if I were home alone.

Sam stood up on my coffee table and pulled the small square box from the ceiling fixture. Grinning, he tossed it on the floor and brought his heel down crushing it. To make doubly sure it would not transmit sound ever again, he chucked it in the sink and turned on the water. Electronics and water are not a match made in heaven.

I was sweating buckets. This was way past lady-like perspiration. I asked, "Did you just sign my death warrant by doing that?"

He lifted his shoulders and then let them drop. "Doubtful. He could have killed you many times before now. He, or whomever he's working for, think you know something about Mickey."

Protesting as I started to pick up the large pieces of glass on the floor, "I don't know anything."

I hate housecleaning in general. The thought of cleaning up this mess was nauseating. There was nothing mentally or physically in me that wanted to scoop, sweep, or mop up the thousand and one little shards of glass now decorating my floor.

There was a knock at my door. I started to hyperventilate, my heart pounded and then tried to convince myself that if the sniper was going to kill me, he wouldn't do it by knocking on the door.

Sam looked through the peephole and then flung the door open as he stepped away from it. There was a box sitting on the welcome mat. I just looked at it, unsure what to do. I hadn't ordered anything online.

He picked it up and placed it on the kitchen countertop slowly turning it. "Got a label on it with your name and address."

Sam whipped out a knife from somewhere in his cargo pants and cut open the box. I peered over his shoulder. I gasped. Assuming that what I was looking at in the large, clear, plastic bag was not cane sugar or a vast quantity of baking soda, this was a gift that carried a felony charge of years to be spent in a government less-than-desirable resort if I was convicted. I don't look good in orange.

The fact that there was a law enforcement officer next to me looking at the same white, powdery substance didn't really make me feel any better since the box was addressed to me. I didn't know if Sam thought I was trafficking illicit drugs or not.

Let's face it, drug dealers make a lot more money than writers do. But, then again, why would I be living in an apartment if I were selling drugs? Hopefully, that thought had already occurred to Sam.

"Want to sell it and move out of the country?"

I hoped he was kidding when he said that although he had a poker face plastered on. My throat had seized up and I was trying to say something, but nothing was coming out. I shook my head. I could feel sweat running down my back. I vaguely wondered how much water weight I had lost in the past several hours. It had to be at least twenty pounds...hopefully.

There was absolutely no way I was going to jail...for any reason. I was trying to think of a way to escape. What countries don't have an extradition agreement with the U.S.? Given time, I could figure out what I needed to do but, standing next to a detective who had the power to take away my freedom, my brain went into meltdown mode. Three Mile Island or Chernobyl meltdown, where nothing no longer existed, were small compared to what was running rampant through my mind.

"Uh..."

Sam patted my hand, grinning. "You look like you've seen a ghost. I'm joking. There's no way I would even try to sell that much coke on the street."

Pausing with a slight smile and his eyes scanning my face, "You're fine, Harper. I'm not going to arrest you. I know you didn't have anything to do with this."

My phone rang causing both of us to jump. I punched speaker and cautiously answered. "Hello."

The voice was merry. "Well, hello, daughter of mine."

Chapter 10

I almost fainted. I felt like I was in the wind tunnel of a tornado. I was Dorothy in the Wizard of Oz, and I hadn't been smacked in the head. Taking a deep breath, I noticed Sam had placed his hand in the middle of my back. I was assuming it was because if I did faint, it would make it easier for him to guide me down to the floor.

"Mickey?" I managed to eke out, I couldn't bring myself to call him Dad. Why would I, given that I haven't seen or talked to the man in twenty-something years?

He sighed, almost giggling, "Well, I guess it is a little bit too much to expect you to call me Dad. Anyway, I sent you a box. I'm assuming that you received it."

Nodding my head and then realizing he couldn't see me. "Yes. Why are you sending hundreds of thousands of dollars of what appears to be cocaine to me? I don't do drugs and I certainly don't sell them."

"Which makes you the perfect recipient to receive my package. Please note, this is not a gift. That is my property."

Sam stopped himself from snapping his fingers and doing a high five with me. He had a big grin on his face. I wondered if he'd get a promotion after busting dear old dad on this.

He rolled his two fingers in a circular motion to keep me talking with Mickey.

"Yeah, so what am I supposed to do with this?" I snapped. "Does this have anything to do with Mason getting murdered?"

"That was very unfortunate, and it wasn't supposed to happen but certain, ah, people weren't willing to wait on some, um, items." Mickey sounded breezy. Mason's death didn't seem to faze him in the slightest. Either the man had a very cold heart, which did not bode well for me if anything nefarious came up...like a choice of whether I should live or die... or the man could hide his emotions very well. I was betting he had a cold heart.

Exploding, I slammed my hand down on the counter, "Listen, your son was murdered, and you don't have the slightest reaction to it? All you're interested in is the coke? What kind of mo..."

Sam was waving his hands at me and silently mouthing, "Don't."

Mickey's voice dropped and slowed down, "You know nothing about what's going on. Just for the record, Mason was not my biological son."

"Irrelevant!" I almost screamed at him. "He was still related to you! How can you be so heartless? Oh, yes, it's easy because you've done it before."

This time his voice was flat. "Bring the box over to the Cantina near the Naval Air Station. Ask for Fat

Freddy and give it to him only. No one else. Fat Freddy looks just like you would imagine him to look."

"NO!" I shouted. Sam was waving at me, his eyes wide. I ignored him. "NO! If I get caught with this, I'll go to jail and I'm not going to jail for any reason. And I'm especially not going to jail for you."

Mickey's voice was taunting, "I see you haven't lost any of your exuberance from childhood."

I disconnected the call and threw my phone across the room. I was breathing heavily. Tears had sprung to my eyes, more from anger than anything else.

"Harper, we have to get this guy." Sam's voice was urgent. "Call him back and agree to do it."

"NO!" I wailed. "What if someone screws up and I'm arrested on felony drug charges? I can't spend even one night in jail. No, no, no! This is my life we're talking about. Whoever these people are, they're willing to kill."

Breaking down into embarrassing deep, gut-wrenching sobs, I huffed out, "I don't want to die."

Surprising me, Sam wrapped his arms around me. It felt good. "Listen, I'm not going to let anything happen to you. This is a big-time drug deal. It means there's not just one or two people involved in this. Chances are there may be some Navy personnel involved as well."

I looked up at him, wiping the tears from my face. "Why?"

"You live in Palm Park. He's asking you to meet him near NAS at a club he's probably supposed to play at."

Interrupting him, "No. He said for me to give it to Fat Freddy. He didn't say the first thing about meeting him there."

"He's still probably playing there and whatever is going on will take the spotlight off him."

"Bait, I'm the bait dog," I grumbled as I looked at the kitchen countertop to see if I had a tissue box there.

The phone rang. It took several rings before I found where I had thrown it across the room.

"Yeah." I didn't see any point in being polite anymore.

Mickey picked up right where we had left off in the conversation. "Give the box to Fat Freddy and leave. That's it. Do it tonight somewhere between nine and ten. There's no reason for you to come and watch me play with my band."

I snorted. He ignored me and continued. "Fat Freddy will ask you who your favorite author is. Give him your name because," he paused almost laughing, "I'm assuming you are your own favorite author."

Rolling my eyes at Sam, I gave a three-finger salute to Mickey although he couldn't see it.

"Yeah, okay." I was reluctant.

"Harper, this is a warning. If you bring law enforcement, the FBI, or anyone else with you and Fat Freddy is arrested, you won't live to have your morning coffee." He hung up.

I was shaking so badly you could turn me into a walking massage machine.

"I'm going to die, I'm going to die, I'm going to die," I kept repeating over and over, totally unaware that Sam had placed both hands on each arm and was gently shaking me.

His voice was gentle. "Harper, you're going to be fine. We're not going to do anything that will jeopardize your life. Trust me on this."

My teeth were chattering. Fear does strange things to a human body. I was overwhelmed with sensory overload with my brain, my body, and my teeth. I wanted to hide. I didn't want to adult anymore.

I discovered I was sitting on the couch while Sam was making phone calls. I guess he must have placed me there. I was in the vortex of life seemingly, maddingly, spinning out of control.

"Okay, here's what's going to happen." As Sam explained the evening's plan, my brain slowly started to function. I only knew this because I felt a slight electrical surge indicating a new thought pattern. It was seeking to find what was wrong with the plan. Nothing, not one thing. Did I dare to hope that maybe, just maybe, I would be safe, and nothing would happen to me, and that maybe I could be eating pancakes or waffles in the morning?

"Oh, by the way," Sam interrupted my train of thought, "I'm having your window boarded up in a few minutes."

That was thoughtful of him. I was thinking I was going to be spending the night in a hotel where I could have a free breakfast buffet first thing in the morning. I could still do that. I know I would feel a lot safer.

That's my plan and I'm sticking to it.

"I know we have some clear packing tape at the office and..."

I sniffed, "The only loophole I see in the entire plan is getting that box into my car without me being killed."

"Not to worry. We're going to put the couch throw over it along with some of your clothes on top and put it in your car. It will look like you're moving out for the night."

"About that. I am. I'm going to spend the night at the hotel."

I expected an argument but didn't get it. Much as I hate to admit it, I was almost disappointed that I didn't receive any pushback about that.

"My cleaning lady is going to come over tomorrow morning and clean up this mess. Spending the night in the hotel is probably a good idea."

The only thing I've got to say is his mama trained him right. It was kind of strange that a detective had a cleaning lady but maybe...I could speculate on that topic for hours and still never come up with the right answer.

He was a gentleman; he did carry the box and my clothes out to my car. I followed him to the police station and parked in the garage.

Even though Palm Park is a small town, they did have a parking garage. Sam had already made arrangements for me to take an unmarked police car to meet Fat Freddy. Fortunately, this was an impounded vehicle that didn't have 'cop car' screaming all over it.

I drove the hour up to NAS, and found the club, it kind of resembled a strip club. It was in a dingy, tired strip shopping center, and walked in. It was dark. There was a band playing at the far end of the room. I made zero attempt to see if Mickey was playing. Scanning the bar area, I saw a very large man wearing a hideous Florida shirt with pink flamingos and green palm trees. He had an unlit cigar stuffed in the corner of his mouth. I walked over to him. He looked me up and down in a way that made me feel like I was naked.

I was nervous. "Um, are you Freddy?"

He didn't answer and continued to leer at me. It was loud in here. I never looked at the stage, I hoped if Mickey were on stage, he'd see that I was following his instructions. Maybe he didn't hear me, so I spoke louder. "Are you Freddy?"

Bobbing his head, he took his unlit cigar out of his mouth. "I'm Fat Freddy. You wanna drink?"

I blinked my eyes slowly trying to process everything while trying to act confident. I was scared. "Um, no, thank you."

"So, what's a classy broad like you doing in a place like this?"

Okay, this was the right guy, but he didn't ask any questions like Mickey said he would do. This still felt like a setup to me. I didn't want to be here any longer than necessary.

"I have something for you." Okay, this probably wasn't the smartest thing to say to a guy who was at least one hundred pounds overweight and apparently thought of himself as a ladies man.

If I thought he had leered at me before, it wasn't anything like he was doing now. There was sheer lust on his face, and he made no effort to conceal it. He was gross.

"Yeah, I'll bet you do, darlin'. Let's say we go in the back. I have a private room." Fat Freddy was almost drooling. Ugh, totally disgusting. I wanted to kill Mickey right now. He wasn't worth going to jail over but the thought was dancing at the forefront of my mind.

"I mean..." I was struggling to find the words to get the box out of the car and into this guy's hand. I wanted to be rid of this craziness. It's one thing to write about it in a book. It's another to have to live it. I like calmness. This wasn't it.

Finally, I spit it out. "I've got a box I'm supposed to give you. Do you want me to bring it through the front door or do you have a vehicle I can put it in?"

I could see it in his little beady eyes set in a florid face. He was greedy. Not my problem. I was told to give it to him and whatever happened after that wasn't my concern.

"Drive your car around to the back. There's a blue truck back there by the garbage dumpster. Put the box on the passenger's seat. Then you can leave or come back in here and we'll par-tay." He licked his lips.

I wanted to barf. I didn't say anything and turned around to walk out the door when he tapped me on the shoulder.

Turning back around, "What?" I glared at him.

"I don't know if I trust you, honey, but, if this is a setup, you'll wish you'd never been here." The lustful look on his face had turned into a hardened, threatening expression. He scared me. He wasn't just a fat boy with lustful thoughts, this was a guy I was sure had killed someone in his past.

"Trust me, I already wish that." I twisted around his hand and walked out the door.

Driving around the back of the building, I looked to see if I saw any police officers or anyone with guns. Not seeing anyone back there, I did spot the truck and pulled up close to it.

Looking around nervously, there really wasn't anyone back here and only a few vehicles. I opened the truck's passenger side door, left it ajar so I could put the box in there easily. I continued to look around as I picked up the box and then shoved it in the truck. I would not make a good spy, my nerves would do me in.

I also slid a tracker under the car seat before slamming the truck door shut. The sound was a lot noisier than I had anticipated. By this time, I was sure I had lost at least ten pounds in sweat alone just in the past several hours. I was more nervous than a cat on a hot tin roof. Getting back in the car, I borderline peeled out of the parking lot.

Taking deep breaths all the way back to the police station, I was making mental notes that I probably should take up yoga. Anything that would calm my nerves on a regular basis could only be a good thing.

Arriving, Sam greeted me in the garage. "How'd it go?"

I told him everything that had transpired. We had decided I wouldn't wear a wire in case I was searched.

"Nothing happened in the parking lot?"

I shook my head. "I've had all the fun I can stand, Sam. I'm going to the hotel."

An officer came through the station doors, spotted us, and waved at Sam to come inside.

Taking this as my cue to leave, I got in my car and left. Let law enforcement deal with whatever was going on. As far as I was concerned this was no longer my circus and no longer my monkey.

As I was driving to the hotel, I jumped when I realized there were flashing lights behind me. I was in sheer panic mode. What if the cops were going to arrest me now? Quickly looking at the speedometer, I noticed I was actually five miles under the speed limit. Surely, that couldn't be the reason for the flashing lights. I pulled over to the side of the road, four police cars went flying by me with blinking red and blue lights but no sirens.

My stress level was already way over the top. I'd like to say once the cars passed me, my nerves settled down, but I'd be lying. Yes, I vaguely wondered what was happening, but I didn't care enough to give it much more thought.

I wish I had.

Chapter 11

Checking into the hotel, all I could think about was taking a long, hot shower and then falling into bed.

That shower felt so good. Stepping out into the room, I discovered a man sitting in the chair, legs crossed, arms folded in his lap, and a shock of brown hair hanging down on his forehead, the rest of his hair was tied back in a ponytail.

I felt weak and grabbed the bathroom door frame.

"Who, who are you? How did you get in here?"

The man simply smiled before answering. "Thanks for delivering the box. Unfortunately, you now know what was in it."

"But, but..." I stuttered. The room was spinning. Was I going to die in a hotel room? Was this Mickey? Then I noticed he was holding a gun in his lap. All the sweat and perspiration I had just washed off in a very relaxing shower, possibly the last one I would ever have, was now back in full force running down my back.

Whatever tiny little bit of adrenaline I had left in my body sparked to life. I was mad.

"Who are you?" I demanded, straightening my posture and readjusting my nightgown. "How did you get in here?"

The man continued to smile and waved his gun at the bed. "Sit down and I'll tell you a story."

I sat down. There was nothing within reach that I could throw at him. A king-size bed pillow wouldn't cause any damage to a man with a gun.

"By the way, nice to actually meet you after twenty years."

Yes, this was dear old dad. Looking closely at him, I did not see any family resemblance whatsoever.

"We don't look anything alike," I stated flatly.

Mickey kind of chuckled. "That's because I'm not your dad."

My eyebrows shot to the moon. "Who are you then?" I demanded. "Aren't you Mickey Rogers?"

Grinning, "Oh, yeah, I'm Mickey Rogers but I'm not your biological dad."

He paused, watching me closely, "Or maybe I am." He shrugged. "Who knows and I don't care."

A gut punch of gigantic proportions hit me. Was my whole life a lie? Had my mother not told the truth about me? Emotions that I didn't know I had welled up within me and I did the most shocking thing I think I have ever done.

I jumped up from the bed and flew the few steps to where he was sitting in the chair. I hit him as hard as I could in the nose. I felt something in my right hand break. I quickly glanced at my hand to make sure all of my digits and knuckles were intact. They were, it was Mickey's nose I broke. Blood squirted out of it.

To say we were both surprised was an understatement. He had let loose the gun in his lap as both hands went to his nose as his head snapped back. Who knew I had such power? I certainly didn't. I had never ever hit someone before. It was weird for me to be this physical with anyone ever. I had the presence of mind to grab the gun and backed up while pointing it at him.

He said a couple of choice words that weren't in the hotel's Gideon Bible. He started to push up from the chair when I snapped, "Don't. Even. Think. About. It."

He laughed and continued to push up from the chair. "You're not going to shoot me."

I felt the gun fire. I swear I don't think I did it. I don't remember squeezing the trigger, although my nerves may have taken over my hands and caused the gun to propel a bullet into Mickey's leg. He screamed. I just looked at the gun, horrified. I am a peace-loving individual or, at least, that's what I've always thought. This was the first time I had ever held a gun in my hands and now I've maimed someone, possibly for life. I was hyperventilating and my hands were shaking uncontrollably. I was afraid to put the gun down because I wasn't sure if Mickey could get to it. My brain was telling me if he could get to it, then he'd probably kill me. He had already indicated that much earlier. I wasn't ready to die.

The hotel phone rang. I carefully eased over to the phone on the nightstand and picked it up. "Hello?"

The voice on the other end said, "Ma'am, are you okay? We've already called the police. Just say 'cat' if you're okay or 'dog' if you need help."

That was a no-brainer. "No, I didn't bring my dog with me."

"Got it. Thank you."

I was trying to take a deep breath, but my lungs were refusing to take in more than a couple of very shallow gulps. Mickey was moaning, bent over holding his leg around the knee area.

"You witch!" Okay, that wasn't exactly the word he used but it was close enough. It wasn't a word I ever wanted to be called. I went out of my way to be nice to everyone.

"Hey, be careful about using that word," I admonished, still pointing the gun at him, "it's not one I like."

He said it again. Much as I wanted to go over and slap him, I had better sense and knew if I got within arm's reach of him, he could probably overpower me and get the gun. I wasn't going to allow that to happen.

Backing up and easing toward the door, I reached behind me to open it just as I heard the slight click of the hotel card being inserted into the reader.

A police officer pushed the door open, holding a gun in his right hand and pointing it into the room. I moved over to the side and dropped my hand holding the gun down.

Another officer entered the room, looked at Mickey, and then looked at me. "Ma'am, what's happening here?"

Mickey was trying to tell his side of the story which did not resemble the truth in any way, shape, or form. Both officers were ignoring him. I guess I looked more harmless than he did. I also surmised that a female holding a gun on a man with both a bloody nose and a bleeding leg might indicate to the officers that said female was attempting to defend herself.

I quickly told him what had happened and then said, "Detective Sam Needles knows me and what's happening."

He just nodded and stepped out into the hallway. I assumed it was to call Sam.

A few minutes later, EMTs came into the room and guided Mickey over to the gurney in the hallway while he was doing the one-legged hop walk.

I was still trying to process everything that was going on. The battery in my brain needed to be recharged.

"How did Mickey get into my room? The door was locked." I asked the first officer. He looked over at the other cop and nodded. He left.

The first officer smiled, I had already given him Mickey's gun, "We'll find out. Do you think you're going to be okay? You've had a lot happen."

Really? I was in such a state of overwhelm I wouldn't have been able to define the word normal if my life depended on it. I suspected it was what most people had in their lives...normal. Boring. Quiet. Something I had in my life for years when I lived in Jacksonville. Ever since I moved back to Palm Park, there was more craziness that seemed to surround me on a regular basis. I missed the quiet, the peace, the boring part of life. I was bordering on longing for it to return.

The other officer appeared. "I've just arrested the check-in guy downstairs. Mickey gave him a hundred dollars for another card to your room. Told the guy he was your dad and wanted to surprise you on your birthday."

I shook my head. "Isn't that illegal? That becomes a major safety issue for single women."

They both nodded.

"By the way, Detective Needles should be here shortly. He said one of us needs to stay with you until he arrives."

That made me feel better. My breathing had finally returned to normal, my heart no longer felt like it was natives from a foreign country jumping up and down and hearing the beat of a different drummer, and my thoughts were starting to make sense...well, at least to me. At this point, I didn't care about what anyone else thought.

I was thinking about what Mickey had said earlier. Dear old dad was trying to rattle my self-confidence by declaring he wasn't my real dad. Even though he had caught me off guard by saying that I had seen my birth certificate, and his name was on there as my dad. Was it possible he really wasn't my biological dad? Yes, of course. Did I believe I was his daughter although I didn't see any family resemblance? Yes, I did. Do I think my mother would have told me if someone else was my father? Yes, I did. Good lord, the woman told me way more than I ever wanted to know about anything and everything growing up. I didn't think she had harbored any secrets about my paternity identity.

Sam walked through the door. "Is there any place in this town where you're going to be safe?"

He said it jokingly. I burst into tears.

Chapter 12

Apparently, my whole psyche was in worse shape than I thought. Wiping the sudden onslaught of tears with the heels of my hands, I muttered, "I'm sorry" several times.

Sam nodded at the officer. "It's okay, I've got it from here."

Turning back to me after the officer left, Sam suggested, "I can see that you need food. Let's go to Huddle House."

With a cheesy grin, he said, "Um, Harper, I think you need to put some clothes on. They're probably not going to let you in there wearing just a nightgown."

I sniffled and nodded. I was also mortified. I hadn't really paid any attention to the fact that I was in my nightgown after my shower. My modesty level had been derailed by seeing Mickey in my room.

A few minutes later after being served hot coffee at the Huddle House, yes I had changed into jeans and a tee shirt, I glanced up at Sam. "Do you have any idea what's going on here? I'm getting tired of dead bodies showing up near me."

Trying to make a joke, I semi-laughed, "Is there something in the water that's causing this?"

Sam's brown eyes twinkled, his dimple deepened, he chuckled, "I'm wondering the same thing, Harper."

"What's up with Mickey? What happened to the box and Fat Freddy?" I involuntarily shuddered at thinking of Fat Freddy.

Sam leaned back in the booth, draping an arm on the back. "I can't tell you everything yet, Harper, but I can tell you that you have helped law enforcement tremendously."

He nodded at the waitress for more coffee. "The box left Duval County and made its way into our county. Once it did that, we could arrest whoever had the box. There are some legal technicalities involved but we did everything by the book. I'm sure you noticed the police cars zooming past you last night."

I nodded while taking a sip of the steaming hot coffee.

"Those were our guys en route."

Interrupting him, I asked, "But what about the flashing lights? Wouldn't that warn them?"

Sam chuckled again. "If they, or anyone, hadn't done anything wrong, they would have slowed down or pulled off to the side of the road to let us pass.

"In this case, we were hoping they would take off speeding, which is exactly what they did. Here's what is interesting. There were two cars hightailing it down the road."

"Wow! That means…"

"Yes, they were both carrying several boxes that field-tested for cocaine. Those boxes are worth hundreds of thousands of dollars on the street."

I just sat there stunned. Poking at my corned beef hash and eggs, I asked, "Do you think it's safe for me to go back home now? I mean, you've got Mickey and, I guess, all of the other guys. I should be safe, right?"

Was I nervous? Yes, of course. What if the sniper hadn't been caught? Was my life still on the line, so to speak? I really wanted to go walk on the beach for solitude. I wanted my soul to be nourished by the waves gently rolling in and splashing the salty water on my feet. I wanted to walk in the water and have all my troubles washed away.

But fear seemed to have fallen on me like an old nasty coat I wanted to be rid of but couldn't make myself throw away because it held too many memories. If I threw away the old coat, would that mean all my memories ceased to exist? Was that a risk I wanted to take? I didn't know. I did want to be free of the fear.

"Harper," Sam's voice was soft, "you can go home, and you'll be safe. The cleaning lady is supposed to come around ten this morning. You can go back to the hotel and sleep or read or watch tv if you want."

Nodding, curling up in hotel soft bedding sounded incredibly enticing, "Sure. I'm ready to go whenever you are."

Back in the hotel room, I didn't bother exchanging my clothes for my nightgown. I simply crawled in bed and pulled the covers over my head. Right before I dozed off, it occurred to me that Sigmund Freud would have a field day with my actions; and, more than likely, turning me into a victim of everything that had happened. I didn't care. Why do these weird thoughts invade my brain at the oddest times? I fell asleep.

Waking up a very relaxing six hours later, I actually felt refreshed and decided to go home.

Sam's cleaning lady was finishing up when I arrived. My apartment looked better than when I first moved in. I tried asking her questions about Sam...like how long she had known him and how long she had worked for him. I received a smile from her. Thinking maybe she spoke only Spanish, I asked, "Hablas ingles?"

She laughed. "Yes, of course, I speak English. It's just that the answers to your questions are confidential. I don't know how Sam would like me to answer them. So..." She spread open her arms slightly with her palms up.

Smiling, I agreed. "Gotcha. Honestly, it's none of my business either. I was just trying to be friendly."

Waving at the clean living room, "This is fantastic! You did a great job of cleaning up all the glass. How much do I owe you?"

I was reaching in my purse for my wallet. Yes, I still carry cash although it wouldn't have surprised me if she had said Venmo or Paypal would be acceptable methods of payment.

"Nothing." She was still smiling. Okay, did this mean Sam was going to expect a 'friends with benefits' thing from me? He was cute but I wasn't sure if I was ready for that yet.

"Um, did he pay you and I reimburse him or how does this work?" I was confused.

She picked up all her cleaning supplies and headed for the door. "Ask Sam."

The plate glass window had been replaced, the apartment was clean, and I saw a note on the counter. Picking it up, "Meet me at the steakhouse at five tonight. Sam."

Chapter 13

I arrived first and got us a table. Deciding to spruce up a bit, I was wearing dark blue slacks, a white blouse, and a red necklace, just big enough to be seen but not ostentatiously huge where it took over my whole outfit.

"You look nice." Sam slid into the red faux leather booth seat. "Special occasion?"

I grinned back. "Maybe. I'm hoping you can tell me more details on Mickey and the drug bust."

The waitress came by, and Sam ordered for the two of us. Normally, I'm not wild about men ordering my food, however, since I've now shared several meals with him, he knew what I liked. I always ordered the same thing.

Taking a sip of iced tea, he nodded. "Yes, now I can tell you everything. The Times Union is going to have a big article on us tomorrow. The news stations are going to have some coverage tonight on their ten and eleven o'clock newscast. This may even make the national news."

I raised my eyebrows. "Really?"

"Mickey played in a band for years and after digging into his background a little bit more, we discovered there was a somewhat surprising connection between the bars or clubs that he played in and how it was always a military town."

"And, let me guess, the clubs were relatively near a base." I grinned, "He was either running drugs or connecting with people who were."

Sam touched the end of his nose. "Bingo! He was actually the connector. He would find a guy, usually an officer who had just returned from an overseas deployment, and then tell this officer that his buddy was killed in action. He had received a box from him right after he was killed. His buddy had told him if anything happened to him, this box needed to go to a specific person on base. How could he find this individual and, more importantly, how could he get the box to him?"

He took a sip of his iced tea. "Here's the kicker, most of the officers would take the box and have it delivered to the guy on base."

"They didn't know they were aiding and abetting someone in a felony crime, right?" I was almost bouncing up and down in the booth. "That's wild!"

Sam agreed. "Yes, even though the military warns about such scams, it's still very easy to pull off. Since Mickey was a musician, he often found an officer who knew how to play a little guitar or who could sing and would offer to let the guy play or sing a song or two on stage in exchange for delivering the box."

"It fulfilled a dream of the officer to play in a band on stage, right?" I grinned. "I'm betting the officer had a couple of drinks under his belt and his guard was down."

"Probably. Mickey also gave them some song-and-dance about getting injured and getting out on a medical discharge. So, he was a brother in arms to these guys."

"Was he ever in the military?" I was chowing down on my steak. I didn't realize how hungry I was.

"Not that we can find. The FBI ran Mickey through their database and, surprisingly, nothing ever showed up on him except those drunk and disorderly charges I told you about earlier. No speeding tickets, no military background, nothing."

Swallowing, "I wondered if he was on their payroll somewhere along on the line."

"Nope."

"Did any of his band members know what he was doing? It seems a little odd that he could have been doing this for years and not gotten caught."

He finished chewing before answering. "Apparently, Mickey's only been doing this for about three or four years."

He held up his hand to keep me from interrupting. "Mickey lost a lot of money, according to him, on the Super Bowl. He was offered the opportunity to work his debt off by delivering boxes to the various clubs in different military towns.

"Mickey's singing like a bird and has admitted that his drug of choice is alcohol and smoking a little weed here or there. He wasn't into coke, which made him a safe bet as far as delivering it."

Pushing back my now empty plate, "So, basically, he was just the mule delivering packages? How did this all end up with Mason being murdered and me being shot at? I still haven't figured that part out yet."

"Crème brûlée?"

This was a man after my own heart! My favorite dessert ever. I nodded my approval. My little fat cells were jumping up and down in sheer happiness. He signaled for two of them to the waitress.

"Kind of a sad thing about Mason..."

I snorted, "Other than the fact he died you mean."

Sam smiled, "Well, there's that. Mason played in the band with Mickey..."

"So, he really was my half-brother?" I was still curious about that.

"Yes. Anyway, Mason played drums in the band off and on for Mickey. The box was given to him by accident. The label said M. Rogers and Mason thought it was for him. He opened the box, discovered the coke, and had a major fight with Mickey. He threatened to go to the police. Mickey, of course, couldn't allow him to do that. Mason got mad and left."

"He went to the beach to think things through," I guessed. "After Mickey was his dad and he was probably struggling with whether to turn him in or not."

Sam nodded, "That's what we think. Mickey panicked, thinking Mason was going to turn him in. He called..."

"Fat Freddy!" we said in unison and gave each other high fives just as the waitress placed our desserts in front of us.

"I've seen people get excited before about crème brûlée but never to the point of high fives," she laughed.

"It's a long story," Sam winked at her.

I gently tapped my spoon on the hardened sugar top and scooped up a mouthful of the delicious custard. I sure hoped this dessert was on the menu in heaven.

"Is Fat Freddy the mastermind behind all of this?" I asked.

"I don't think so," Sam paused for a moment and then continued, "Fat Freddy was controlling Mickey and when Mickey had any problems, he called Fat Freddy to handle it."

Starting to laugh, I sputtered out, "Dear old dad is a chicken!"

Sam nodded, "Pretty much. We know he called Fat Freddy about Mason. We strongly suspect he's the one who had the sniper kill Mason. We can't one hundred percent prove that though."

Holding up my spoon, "Wait! Who owned the condo where the sniper shot from? Is there any connection there?"

Shaking his head again, "Older couple from Miami own it and they were on a cruise."

"But those places have security and..."

"And people hire moving companies all the time to move their furniture in and out. He very easily could have had access to their floor that way.

"Regardless, whoever he was, he didn't leave any incriminating evidence. We're not sure who he is."

With that last statement, all the delicious food I had eaten dropped down to my feet. Fear threatened to crawl up my legs and back into my body.

"What do you mean, 'you don't know who he is'?" I almost screeched.

Sam put his hands out signaling me to keep the noise level down. This wasn't his life we're talking about! Okay, he's a police officer and his life is on the line every day but he chose to do that. I, on the other hand, did not choose to be a target for anyone.

"Is he black ops?" I was still a wee bit too loud.

Sam frowned at me. "Do you mind keeping it down a little? The whole world doesn't need to know this yet."

I glared at him. "It's not your life we're talking about!"

"Harper," he was struggling to stay patient, "do you want to hear the rest or do you want to call it a night?"

I scrunched up my face. Details, I wanted to know more details. "Go ahead."

He almost gave me an eye roll. "Once Mason realized what was in the box, he packaged it back up and had it delivered to you. Before you even ask, Mickey had your address. No, I don't know how he had it, but he did. I guess Mason thought you knew what was going on and that's why he had your name on the paper in his hand when he was killed."

"In other words," I almost whispered, "I'm safe."

Smiling, Sam nodded. "Yes, because you did just what you were supposed to do. You delivered it and left."

"Because I put the tracking device in the truck that's how you knew when Fat Freddy left Duval County and entered ours."

"Bingo."

"So, Sam, if they hadn't panicked, they would have gotten away with coke?"

He touched the end of his nose. He hadn't finished eating his dessert yet and I wondered if I might get that last spoonful. Sam must like me because he pushed the ramekin over to me. "There you go. But, yes, they probably would have been able to continue their little game."

He wiped his mouth. "Mickey sang like a canary when we arrested him. Fat Freddy and his buddy refuse to answer any questions, including their names, and they've already lawyered up."

I just nodded. "One last question, Sam. You said you thought you recognized the sniper's voice on the phone. Did you ever remember who it was?"

He smiled, "I guess I was wrong."

I wasn't sure I believed him but I didn't think he'd tell me.

Taking another sip of his tea, "So, you see, you helped us to make a big drug bust." Sam leaned back in the booth. "You should be proud of yourself."

Strangely, I wasn't. I couldn't really verbalize it. I still had a niggling feeling something was off. Maybe I should talk to Ronnie about everything.

Chapter 14

"You have got to be kidding me!" squealed Ronnie. "Harper, girl, nobody but NOBODY would ever believe this story!"

He held up the newspaper with the bold headline of "Murder at Jax Beach!"

"A lot of the good stuff didn't even make the paper! I love it!"

I laughed. It had only been a couple of days since the news broke about Mickey, the drugs, the arrests, and I had been interviewed on several national tv shows. My book sales were better than they had ever been.

Sitting in the pet store, sipping coffee with my dear, sweet friend, it suddenly occurred to me that moving back to Palm Park hadn't been such a bad idea after all. My hometown was starting to grow on me in a good way. Maybe that's all it took, moving away for a number of years and then coming back. Maybe Thomas Wolf was wrong...you can go home again...but with a different perspective. Letting go of old baggage wasn't such a bad thing.

Ronnie handed me the most darling little Maltese puppy. "She needs you to love on her."

I nuzzled the soft, curly hair on her tiny little head.

"Ronnie, you know what's really odd?"

"What, honey?"

"Fat Freddy and his buddy disappeared with the FBI."

Ronnie chuckled, "Well, you know what they say...politics makes strange bedfellows."

Nodding, I said, "I love my country, it's the government I fear. I doubt we'll ever know the truth about what really happened. Who knows? All of this may be helping to fund some secret boogity-boogity government covert program."

"Who cares? You're safe, honey, and you can bring me coffee whenever you want!" Ronnie held up a puppy for me to pat.

"Okay, girl, no more murders. At least not in Palm Park or Jacksonville."

"Well, there's always St. Augustine."

We laughed.

Murder at Palm Park - Chapter 1

Sarah was slumped over the table, her coffee with an obscene amount of liquid sugar in it was dripping off the edge, so was red fluid. The new barista, well, let's just say he wasn't going to be making any coffee drinks ever again.

I threw up as I was punching nine-one-one. My hand was shaking so badly that I now only had about half a cup of coffee left. I was now wearing the rest of it on my hand, arm, and the front of my shirt.

While waiting for the police to show up, it was only minutes but felt like hours, my thoughts dive-bombed my psyche.

I am a highly paid escort. I am young, cute, and deadly. I am an assassin.

No, no. That's not right. I am an opera singer. Yes, that's it. I open my mouth and beautiful, lyrical notes grace the air in the theatre.

I am a professional liar, and I am paid very well for it. What am I? I could be an actor, an attorney, in sales or advertising, a detective, or a writer.

"Seriously! Get out of your head. I can see story ideas bouncing around in your brain." Sarah had grumped at me. We've been friends since before breakfast. Actually, we've known each other since the fourth grade. We are not best friends...just good friends who know way too much about each other in certain areas of our lives. Still, when Sarah's not craving something to eat every two or three hours, she can be a lot of fun.

"What's wrong with you?" I grinned. It was just so much fun to see how much I could annoy Sarah, especially when I knew she was skating on the edge of crazy without her morning caffeine and sugar fix.

She grabbed her cup of coffee from the new barista at Coffee & Cupcakes, took a sip, put it back on the counter, and pushed it back to him. "It doesn't have enough sugar in it. I specifically asked for six shots. You didn't do that."

The guy inhaled deeply through his nose, letting the air out slowly through his nostrils, "Do you want me to put more in this cup or do you want a new one?"

Sarah snapped, "What do you think?"

"Hey, Sarah, chill." I held up three fingers to the guy. "Just put that many in the cup."

She started to say something, and I decided to shut her down. "Stop it! Tip the man."

Glaring at me, she snatched the mug that now had more sugar in it than our ancestors had had in a year, "No!"

Deciding our friendship probably needed a break, a long break, I tipped the young man. Taking my coffee and ignoring Sarah seated at one of the little tables, I started for the door.

"Hey!"

I ignored her and kept walking.

Looking back on it, I was amazed at how unobservant I was...or, just call it being too self-absorbed with Sarah's bad manners that I wasn't paying attention to the tall individual coming through the door. I was already out on the sidewalk trying to decide if I was going home to start writing a new story or if I was going to go pet the new puppies at Ronnie's pet store when I heard two double shots.

It took a moment for it to register that those were gunshots that I heard. Behind me. In the coffee shop.

Turning around, I rushed through the door. I don't know that I was thinking anything when I entered the store. My brain stops having coherent thoughts when I'm scared.

That's when I saw Sarah and called the cops.

Detective Sam Needles, really that is his name, walked over to where I was now sitting inside the store. "Please tell me you're not rehearsing a scene for a new book or something."

I shook my head. There was a small, unfortunate incident that had happened several months earlier when several mothers at the local park had observed me, Ronnie, Sarah, and Ruthie acting out a scene for a new book, thought we were trying to kill each other, and called the cops. We were but it was because I was trying to figure out the action details and how to describe it in a chapter. I'm a visual person and I needed to see a person's movement before I could write it.

Sam had been dispatched because the local patrol officers were off getting coffee and donuts or something.

Let's just say he wasn't amused when I told him those nosy mothers should have been paying more attention to their precious little progenies rather than adults on the other side of a public park who were minding their own business.

I told him what had happened.

"Was it a man or a woman coming through the door as you were going out?"

I shrugged. "I think it was probably a man because he was so much taller than I am."

Sam tried to keep from snorting. "You do realize you're only about five-three on a good day."

Huffing and trying to stand taller, there's only so much vertical height I can do even with taking deep breaths and blowing it out. "I'll have you know I'm five-four. Don't make me any shorter than I already am."

"So, the person was tall. What were they wearing? Did they have anything in their hand? Hair color or where they wearing a hat? Can you describe anything about this individual?"

Shaking my head, I said, "Um, I was kinda not paying attention. I was irritated with Sarah's poor manners with the new guy, the new barista."

Sam nodded his head. "Did Sarah have any enemies? Anyone she was having a problem with? Owed money to?"

I suddenly realized how little of Sarah's personal life I actually knew. When we got together, all we did was talk about everyday things, nothing important, and nothing really personal.

"Sarah was dating or, rather, had gone out on a coffee date with a guy she met online. But I don't know anything about him."

I hadn't been wild about her picking men out of a lineup on a dating website and told her so. I didn't know the guy's name or anything about him. She told me I was an old fuddy-dud. Seriously? Who even uses words like that anymore? We had exchanged unpleasant words and today was the first day we had seen each other in a week.

With her being so snarky at the barista, I hadn't even cared enough to stay and ask her what was wrong. Maybe my subconscious had picked up bad vibes or maybe it was just me deciding that I'd had enough of her negativity. Whatever it was, I didn't want it in my life.

Maybe I should feel badly about my thoughts and feelings but, to be honest, I really didn't. I was sad she was dead, had been murdered, but I wasn't freaking out about it. My throwing up was more about seeing blood than anything else. I have a notoriously weak stomach when it comes to seeing body fluids, even seeing a kid spit on the ground can cause me to want to vomit. Go figure.

No expression on Sam's face. "Thought you had been friends for years. How could you not know who she was dating?"

Did I dare say we didn't have that type of relationship because that wouldn't make sense...or maybe it did. Just because we were women and friends for years didn't mean we shared all the details of our lives. Or, at least, I don't.

To share all details, intimate details, of my life involved a level of trust that I just simply do not have for most humans. Dogs, yes; humans, no.

Also, I must admit, I truly wasn't that interested in who Sarah was dating right now. Since my own dating life was minimal...who am I kidding? It's non-existent, which means, I wasn't remotely interested in who she was dating. It was different when we were both dating someone because then we had things to talk about but with me not having anyone in the romance department at the moment, I didn't care.

I wasn't sure how to respond to Sam's question, so I shrugged.

To read the rest of MURDER AT PALM PARK, get it at your favorite retailer.

Purchase my books at your favorite retailer

Book 1
A Dose of Nice and Murder

Book 2
A Honky Tonk Night and Murder

Book 3
The Faberge Easter Egg and Murder

Book 4
Little Candy Hearts and Murder

Book 5
Lights, Action, Camera and Murder

Book 6
A Turkey Parade and Murder

Book 7
Cookies and Murder

Book 8
Flamingos and Murder

Book 9
Bowling and Murder

Purchase my books at your favorite retailer

| 101 Summer Jobs for Teachers | Kids Fun Activity Book |  Counting Laughs |

About the Author

I grew up in Palatka, Florida, traveled the Southeast extensively for a number of years, and now make my home in Jacksonville, Florida where I am in the friends witness protection program due to past associations in Palatka. Some folks just don't have a sense of humor.

To join my VIP Newsletter and to receive a FREE book, go to www.SharonEBuck.com/newsletter.

I absolutely love readers because without you I'd be eating peanut butter and crackers. I greatly appreciate you and your support.

People are always asking if I'm available for speaking engagements. The short answer is "Yes, of course." In fact, I can even do a Zoom event for your book club.

Would you be kind enough to recommend this book and share the laughter with your friends? I appreciate it!

Thank you for being a loyal fan!

Acknowledgements

Thank you to my wonderful support team and friends for your encouragement, words of reassurance, inspiration, and belief in me on those days when the blank computer screen would stare back at me like a one-eyed monster daring me not to write anything. I survived and conquered.

In no special order, thanks to the following individuals:

Kim Steadman – There should be a law about how much we're allowed to laugh on the phone. Thankfully, there's not. Thank you for your friendship and the time we spend talking about writing, books, the book business, and just chatting. Visit KimSteadman.com

Michelle Margiotta – Your music has lifted me up when I was frustrated with my writing process, when I had doubts, and it has nurtured the very depths of my soul. Your music is so filled with colors and swirls dancing throughout your compositions that one cannot help but to be totally enthralled and inspired by your incredible gift. Visit MichelleMargiotta.com

Cindy Marvin – my friend and attorney who tries (hard) to keep me out of trouble before I even get into it.

McDonald's Baymeadows @ I-95, Jacksonville, FL - Keisha and her morning crew for serving me vanilla iced coffee every morning. They jumpstart my day with their smiling faces. It's how I start my day.

Southside Chick-Fil-A in Jacksonville, FL – Patty, the awesome marketing manager, and her team who have hooked me on frosted coffee. I am now an addict LOL Every fast-food restaurant in America should take lessons on customer service from them. It's always a delight to go into a happy place of business. I am always treated like a friend, not a customer.

George and Mama at Athenian Owl Restaurant on Baymeadows in Jacksonville, FL –My favorite Greek restaurant and they make me feel at home every time I eat there.

And, lastly, thank you to all my loyal readers and fans. I love and appreciate you!

To God be the glory.

Murder at the Pirate Museum

A Harper Rogers Cozy Mystery

Sharon E. Buck

Southern Chick Lit

Copyright © 2024 by Sharon E. Buck

All rights reserved.

No portion of this book may be reproduced in any form without written permission from the publisher or author, except as permitted by U.S. copyright law.

This book is a work of fiction. Names, characters, businesses, organizations, places, events, and incidents either are the product of the author's imagination or are used fictitiously. Any resemblance to actual persons, living or dead, events, or locales is entirely coincidental.

For more information, or to book an event, contact :
sharon@sharonebuck.com

To join my VIP Newsletter and to receive a **FREE** book, go to www.SharonEBuck.com/newsletter

Cover design by Steven Novak,NovakIllustration.com

Looking for a dash of fun, a hint of snark, a sprinkle of sass, and a whole lot of silliness with a Florida twist?

SCAN ME!
To receive a FREE Book

Join my free, no obligation, twice a month newsletter, and I promise not to send your email address to the "your car warranty has expired" people.

SharonEBuck.com

Contents

1. Chapter 1 #
2. Chapter 2 #
3. Chapter 3 #
4. Chapter 4 #
5. Chapter 5 #
6. Chapter 6 #
7. Chapter 7 #
8. Chapter 8 #
9. Chapter 9 #
10. Chapter 10 #
11. Chapter 11 #
12. Chapter 12 #
13. Chapter 13 #
14. Chapter 14 #

FREE BOOK #

Harper Rogers Series #

Parker Bell Series #

More Books	#
About the author	#
Acknowledgements	#

Chapter 1

I screamed. I felt someone push me and saw something being tossed at me. Since I have the athletic skills of a drunk ninja turtle, I didn't catch it. Clattering to the wooden plank floor was a bloody knife. Next to it was a man lying in a puddle of blood.

I had seen the man when I first entered the Pirate Museum. Thinking he was some St. Augustine timeshare salesman dressed as a pirate, I had ignored him.

Upon looking closer at him, my opinion hadn't changed except to notice that he was dressed more as homeless chic with a blousy dirty shirt and baggy pants. He had long red hair and a pitifully scraggly beard for an adult male.

When I screamed, the other tourists turned toward me. I had already knelt down beside the man to see if I could do anything for him. I also made the incredibly stupid mistake of picking up the knife to move it out of the way when I stood up.

That's what the tourists saw - me with a bloody knife in my hand. Two rather large, dairy-fed women from the Midwest somewhere saw me with the bloody weapon of mass destruction and decided I had killed the man on the floor.

If they had only known the thoughts that were swirling around in my brain looking like Mr. Toad's Wild Ride at Disney World, they wouldn't have bothered trying to save the rest of the tourists in the museum.

They rushed toward me trying to keep me from escaping. I'd like to point out I was standing straight up and had made zero, nada, no attempt to escape, and they started slamming me in my back with their oversized purses apparently filled with boat anchors.

I covered my head with my arms and stumbled forward only to trip over the dead guy, fall, and smack my head on the corner of the display case.

Discovering later at the hospital that I had a concussion and needed three stitches, I'm going to blame everything that happened before the hospital as temporary insanity. Yeah, I'm just going to say I don't remember squat.

***

What I think happened, since I probably had short-term amnesia from the concussion, was, apparently, I continued to scream for help. Evidently, that's not the thing to do in a pirate museum where the cannons periodically erupt with a loud boom and white smoke curls out. It's a tourist thing for someone to scream and the store's staff paid absolutely no attention to the shrieking I was doing.

Not having the sense God gave a goose, I ran out into the store area with the bloody knife in my hand. Yes, there were a lot of tourists wandering around. They pretty much dissipated when they saw me.

The middle-aged cashier blanched, and I saw her push a button under the countertop.

I was blathering and pointing at the inside of the museum. Taking a guess I wasn't making much sense, I turned to go back in and see about the man on the floor when I was attacked again by those two women wielding their boat anchor heavy touristy canvas bags. They continued to whale on me until the cops showed up.

Still prattling on and probably making no sense to anyone, I tried to stand up and explain what had happened when I felt the cold steel handcuffs snap around my wrist. This wasn't good. I had never been arrested before, I was scared, and it occurred to me that I was being arrested for murder. I started to cry. I couldn't even think. My head hurt...and my shoulders...every place those heifer-sized women had hit me with their overloaded bags.

I was yanked unceremoniously up from the floor by a dark blue-uniformed police officer. At least, the women had stopped beating me up with their I Love St.Augustine tourist tote bags.

The cashier had gone back in the hole of the ship's décor and had let loose a blood-curdling scream. "George, George, George! What did she do to you?"

More officers flooded the area. My mind was attempting to mimic a whirling dervish with thoughts that were never going to be formed into complete sentences.

Being pushed roughly into the back of a police cruiser, the officer was not listening to me as blood was running down my face from where I had hit my head on the table corner. My only thought was I didn't want to wear prison orange, that's just not my color.

He did take me to the hospital where I received three stitches and was diagnosed with a concussion.

Finally managing to get my wits to fly in a somewhat uniform manner, I asked, "When do I get my phone call?"

No response. Maybe I didn't speak loud enough. "Hey! When do I get my phone call?"

No one was paying any attention to me. I probably looked like every other crazy person the cops brought to the hospital.

My head hurt. As addled as my brain was, I realized I needed to call for help, and the only phone number I could remember was my best friend Ronnie's. This is what happens when you rely on your cell phone for everything. I'm convinced that part of your memory cells die every time you don't have to recall a phone number.

Now convinced I had no more brain cells left, I was going to end up in prison orange and becoming someone's jailhouse wife.

I threw up. Medical staff assured me it was because that's one of the symptoms of a concussion. I didn't tell them it was from the stress of thinking I was going to be some female prisoner's new special friend...and that I would have to wear orange jumpsuits. I was scared out of my wits...at least the ones that were still intact from not memorizing phone numbers.

At some point, the police did let me call Ronnie.

"Hi, honey, what's happening?" He was chipper.

I started to cry. "Ronnie, I've been arrested over in St. Augustine. Find me an attorney quick."

"Do not, repeat do not, do anything other than give them your name. That's it, nothing else. I'll find you someone who'll get you out. Only your name."

Looking ever the fashionista that I am not, I was back in the police car and hauled off to jail. They put me in a room and not a jail cell.

An officer with a bulbous nose, short salt-and-pepper hair, and having theI've-eaten-way-too-many-doughnuts belly came waddling in the room and plopped down in a chair across the table from me.

"What's your name?"

"HarperRogers."

He sighed, "What's your full name?"

"Harper Elizabeth Rogers."

"Tell me your version of what happened."

"No."This was not a word I used frequently, and it sounded a little unnatural, but I wasn't going to give these yahoos any ammunition to use against me.

"If you don't have anything to hide, why not just tell me what happened?" He sounded bored.

I just looked at him. I'm a writer and I stare for long periods of time at the computer screen, I could keep this up for hours. I was trying to organize my thoughts into a somewhat semblance of order while ignoring him. My head hurt.

If I focused on the new murder mystery book in my brain I was writing, I really could sit and look at this guy for hours, days even. The computer only talks back when I mash a couple of keys. I didn't feel the need to talk. I could feel my body starting to relax a little.

Although I wanted to lie down and go to sleep, I decided to contemplate my day so far.

***

I remembered I was asking myself tons of questions. Did Sir Francis Drake bury his pirate treasure in St. Augustine? Why were there so many pirates in this area? What was their average age? Did they die rich or as a pauper? Did they share the treasure that supposedly every pirate ship had? Who were the female pirates?

All of these and a thousand other questions popped up in my mind as I wandered through the Pirate Museum in St. Augustine. As the oldest city in the United States, it had seen more than its fair share of pirates...Blackbeard, Andrew Ranson, Captain Kid, Sir Francis Drake, and many, many more always looking to plunder whatever valuables they could find.

I remember I had been fascinated with the museum's décor. It held a large collection of artifacts from the seventeen and eighteen hundreds. The museum was designed to look like you were inside a Spanish galleon, dark wood floors with rigging ropes, historical guns, and pottery were carefully secured behind safety where some less-than-honest tourist couldn't put their little grubby fingers on them and heist them back to whatever state they came from.

With over six million people visiting this quaint and oldest city in the United States, smart businesspeople designed their attractions for the tourists to look at things but not be able to touch them.

I was doing research for my new book, and I went to the only museum in the United States that had the largest and most authentic collection of pirate artifacts under roof. Fortunately, it was only about a thirty-five-minute drive from Palm Park.

I had always liked St. Augustine and learning about pirates and their so-called evil ways. It also gave me a great excuse to visit the bakery shop Crème de la Cocoa and get the best macarons ever.

While I was trying to decide if I was hungry or not and needed a macaron fix, I noticed there were signs everywhere alerting tourists that they were being recorded.

My favorite placard warning tourists not to steal anything was:

"Roses are red, violets are blue,
A pirate's heart beats for treasure so true.
With a patch on one eye, and a parrot or two,
I'll chop off a finger or two
If anything disappears with you."

I was chuckling to myself and still debating when I was going to leave for the sugary goodness of a macaron this side of heaven when a long, red-haired, gaunt man with a few wispy red fringes of what was supposed to be a beard sidled up to me. I jumped. I hadn't noticed him. So much for my observational skills.

After living in Jacksonville for a number of years and basically being somewhat paranoid in general, I was convinced that was a good thing for a mystery writer because it added credibility to my books, I glanced at his clothes, they appeared to be homeless chic, and snapped, "Dude, you need to back off."

My mind swirled with different scenarios of what I would do if he tried to attack me. Maybe if I pretended to faint that would work or maybe if I bit him on the nose, he would leave me alone. I saw that in a movie once, or....

"Ah, me lass, you be having a fine time wouldn't you now?"

Oh, mercy, was this a re-enactment or one of the crazies who had escaped cold weather up north and had decided to relocate to sunny, hotter than a fried-egg-on-the-sidewalk, Florida?

I truly don't like engaging in small talk even with friends much less with a total, whacko-looking stranger. I tried ignoring him but, he was persistent. Maybe he was trying to sell me a timeshare while dressed as a pirate. Except, he really didn't look like a pirate. There was absolutely no attempt to dress like a pirate. He had on a way too large blousy shirt that could have been an extra-large from a well-known large discount store with the blue, white, and yellow signage.

His pants looked like they came from Goodwill, and they were baggy. He was also barefoot. He also smelled, I tried not to inhale too deeply but the distinct aroma of garlic and alcohol permeated my olfactory senses. I didn't think he'd had a shower in several days simply because my eyes were starting to water.

How did this crazy person get in here? Maybe an employee let him in and was splitting timeshare commissions or maybe...

See, this is what happens when I've had too much coffee in the morning. It's bad enough that I always have way too many story ideas running loose in my head at any given time but it's even worse when you combine the two together along with my basic up-and-down yo-yo personality.

"Awe, come on, lassie, ye wouldn't be..."

Okay, I'd had enough of this fake dialogue and my fuse, never long to begin with, let loose. "What part of leave me alone do you not understand? I'm a writer, a mystery writer, and I'm trying to do some research on pirates. You're bothering me. Be gone!" I attempted to shoo him away by waving my hands in a dismissive way.

"Ah, me lass, I can be telling you tales that will make your hair and toenails curl."

I shuddered. The very idea of my toenails curling sent my mind reeling back to that iconic scene from"The Wizard of Oz," where the Wicked Witch's toes curled up and vanished beneath the house.

"Where's the director?" I demanded. "I'm reporting you for annoying the customers."

A smile stretched across his face showing fake blackened teeth. I had the horrible thought he might be the director. I was wrong. It was worse.

"Ah, me lass, I'm actually the owner of this wonderful museum celebrating St. Augustinepirates. What would you like to know about pirates?"

I was aghast and before I could stop the words, they escaped from my mouth. "You're kidding, right? You stink. I mean, you literally stink! When was the last time you showered?"

Most normal people would have been appalled but apparently this guy had the social skills of a goat. He laughed.

I could feel my fuse igniting even more. Snarling, "Get out of my way! I'm leaving!"

"Hey, excuse me." Someone was standing behind him and he turned. I whirled around, heading toward the door, hoping the distraction would cause him to leave me alone. I heard a soft oof. Someone jostled me and I semi-turned to see why.

"Here, catch!"

I was so startled at seeing something being tossed at me that I never looked to see where it came from.

Catching anything was not an athletic skill I possessed. That's when I heard the soft oof, looked down, and saw the red-haired guy on the floor.

"Help! Help!" I screamed. There were several other tourists in the museum, who looked over at me, saw the knife, and then they were stampeding for the door shouting and carrying on.

Chapter 2

The police officer must have said something again while I was going over all of the details in my mind. My head hurt and I gingerly touched the bandage over my eye.

"Huh? What did you say?" I asked, glancing around the gray austere room before settling back and looking at the officer.

"I said why aren't you talking?"

"Am I bleeding?" I wasn't sure if the stitches leaked or not.

He didn't say anything.

Blowing air out my nose, "Told you, I don't have to. I'm waiting on my attorney."

Dive bombing back into my brain, whatever information I needed on pirates I could find online. I had only gone to the museum so I could get a feel of what their lives might have been like with the old clothes, guns, and maps.

After looking at those clothes, the texture and the weight of them in the steamy, unairconditioned, humidity of the Sunshine State, I was pretty sure pirates would not have had the most pleasant of personalities. St. Augustine was originally located in the middle of nowhere on the edge of swamps filled with mosquitos, rattlesnakes, and alligators. It would have been a smorgasbord for mosquitoes wanting to feast on a naked arm.

I was trying to figure out the basic plot line of my new book when a woman popped through the door, never looking at the bored officer. "You can go now. I need to talk to my client."

Hurray, Ronnie had come through for me! That's what BFFs are for. She looked vaguely familiar, but I couldn't place her.

Her warm smile put me immediately at ease. "Hi, Harper. Ronnie told me you needed my help."

Nodding borderline frantically, I tried to smile. It probably came out as a grimace.

"You may or may not remember me from high school. I'm A.B. Read."

Frowning slightly, my brain was spinning feverishly trying to put a name and a face together. I wasn't having a whole lot of luck with this. I'm blaming it on the stress factor of sitting in jail and being blamed for a crime I didn't commit.

"I went by Anne in those days." Her smile was bigger. She had placed her briefcase on the table and pulled out a legal pad. "Give me the short version of what happened."

Not caring what her name was umpteen years ago, I was only concerned about me, myself, and I getting out of here.

I told her everything, she nodded, standing up, "Give me a moment."

Oh, great! Now I've been left alone in this room with nothing to focus my thoughts on except...nothingness. I laid my head on my arms on the table. I went to sleep. Stress will do that to me. Also, a concussion will do that as well.

It was probably another hour before Mr. Personality opened the door and motioned for me to follow him.

A.B. was standing at the police countertop, smiled, and said, "Come on."

I must have looked confused.

"It's time to go home." She turned and I followed her to the parking lot.

"Um, A.B., do you think you could give me a ride home?"

She laughed, a little twinkling-type of laugh. "You don't think I'm going to leave you out here in the parking lot, do you?"

Neither one of us talked in the car. I almost ran to my apartment. I couldn't wait to get in the shower and wash the nastiness of the past twenty-four hours off. I gave serious thought to throwing away the clothes I had been wearing, but I'm parsimonious and didn't want to get rid of perfectly good clothes.

What does parsimonious mean? I'm cheaper than dirt, also known as what is the real value of something that I'm willing to part money for from my tightly clenched little fist.

Hearing a knock at the door. I peeked through the keyhole. I was surprised to see Detective Sam Needles standing there. Sam and I had dined together on several occasions. I wouldn't call it dating exactly, it was more along the lines of friends with no benefits.

Did I mention he was cute? Dark hair, dimples, and a killer smile.

"Hey, Sam," I smiled as I opened the door, "what's up?"

He wasn't smiling. "Were you at the Pirate Museum in St. Augustine earlier today?"

So much for a warm and fuzzy hello.

"Yes." I was puzzled.

Sam cleared his throat. "Harper, did you have an argument with George Cloise?"

"Who?"

"The pirate museum owner." Sam wasn't smiling. A faint tingling of less-than-positive vibes was making its way through my body. I wondered if I should be calling my attorney.

"That's his name?" I was stalling for time. "I didn't have an argument with him. He was being annoying. Do I need to call my attorney?"

He frowned, "What is the bandage on your head for?"

"I fell and hit my head on a display table. There are three beautiful stitches under the bandage. Why are you asking me these questions? Anything that happened yesterday was in St. Augustine, not Palm Park."

"I know. I heard it through the grapevine and…"

Laughing, I said, "Marvin Gaye. I know that song."

Shaking his head and closing his eyes, his mouth turned into a grin. "That was a bad choice of words. Hopefully, this doesn't mean I need to dance now."

"No." We were both laughing and headed to sit on the couch. "So, what are you really doing here?"

He shifted his weight on the couch and crossed one leg over the other. He appeared to be a little nervous.

"Just thought I'd come over and see how you were."

My brows furrowed and my eyes narrowed. I was suspicious. Had Sam been sent over to see what information he could obtain from me about that debacle in St. Augustine?

Clearing his throat, he said, "I heard you were the last one in the museum?"

"Oh, not true! Not true!" I borderline shrieked. I almost jumped up from the sofa. "There were two tourists in there who started beating me up with their purses. There's no way I was the last person in there!"

I was breathing deeply, and I was mad.

"Your fingerprints were found on the knife, and..." Sam paused, "you were seen on tape shoving him."

I stood there, blinking. He was a spy. He had been sent to see what other information he could get.

"Are you arresting me?" I was trying to sound brave when every fiber of my being was screaming "I can't go to jail. I don't look good in orange."

Sam shook his head. "No, of course not. You are a person of interest in this case." He stood up. "Don't think about leaving Palm Park."

I could only nod. I felt immobilized. Sam left. I was still standing in the middle of my living room and knew I needed a salted caramel macaron I had stashed in my freezer. There was a black vortex swirling around in my brain sucking out any coherent thoughts.

Why was George murdered? I crunched down on my brain cells while savoring the macaron to see if I remembered who was standing behind him. Much as I hate to admit it, I was probably too self-absorbed to even notice what other tourists were looking at the pirate artifacts. It's bad enough I can be that obtuse in general but it's even worse when I'm researching something, which is what I was doing.

The delicious sugar concoction I was holding in my hand found its way to my mouth. I could feel the velvety softness almost melting in my mouth. Maybe it was the sugar burst winding its way through my body or maybe my brain cells had kicked back into gear.

I called A.B. Searching through long-ago memories, she and I had gone to high school together, I vaguely remembered she'd scored a perfect SAT score for the whole state of Florida, causing a great deal of stress amongst the educated elite in the school system because they were sure it couldn't be done. She proved them wrong. What was even funnier was she was from Palm Park, a rural, economically depressed little town on the beautiful St. Johns River in northeast Florida. No one expected anything like this from Palm Park.

She had won numerous scholarships and graduated magna cum laude from the prestigious University of Florida Law School. Why she had come back to Palm Park was beyond me, she could have practiced anywhere and probably made a lot more money.

"A.B. Read Law Office." The voice was crisp, sharp, and had that gatekeeper attitude.

I didn't like attorneys in general. They always seemed to be so smug that they were smarter than you. Bad memories of my Jacksonville divorce attorney surfaced; although I had to be fair, she did keep my ex-husband from benefiting from my intellectual property. I probably would have killed everyone in sight had I had to share my book royalties with him.

"Um, this is Harper Rogers. May I speak with Anne? We went to high school together."

"She goes by A.B. now. Let me check to see if she's available." Attorney speak for "Let me see if she wants to talk to you."

I didn't have to wait long. "Hey, Harper, how are you doing?"

I relaxed and started to tell her about Sam showing up and asking questions when she interrupted me. "Come in at nine tomorrow morning and we'll talk. Oh, bring four glazed doughnuts with you. Brenda will love you for it."

Indulging in watching "Funny Girl" with Barbra Streisand for the two thousand and twenty-ninth time, I had a very peaceful evening at home.

Chapter 3

Entering through the heavy doors, I vaguely wondered why so many law offices have hard-to-open doors. Maybe they're just making sure you really want to hire them.

The lobby area was very tastefully appointed, a fancy word for decorated, with expensively framed artwork depicting various scenes from the St. Johns River, St. Augustine's Castillo de San Marcos, and, what's this? A painting of female pirates Anne Bonny and Mary Read? That's interesting.

Anne or A.B. entered the lobby, smiling and holding out her hands. "Harper, so nice to see you again. This time not at the jail."

Grinning slightly, I handed her the four glazed doughnuts. Her smile became even bigger, and her blue eyes sparkled. "Why, thank you so very much, Harper. Brenda, two for you, and bring the other two into the office."

A.B. turned and I followed her. I stopped once I walked through the door. Her office had numerous paintings of Anne Bonny, Mary Read, Grace O'Malley, and a few other female pirates I didn't know hung on the walls. There appeared to be a number of pirate-type artifacts in glass display cases around the room. To say she was enamored with female pirates was an understatement. I was impressed.

In fact, the office was decorated to look like a captain's cabin. This was every bit as nice if not better than the Pirate Museum's décor.

A.B. took a seat at the round ruff hewn wood table next to a massive ornately carved wood desk. I sat down to her left.

Behind the desk was a pirate ship that appeared to be bobbing up and down on the St. Johns River. I don't know how that was done but it certainly gave the appearance that pirates may be close by.

Of course, maybe it was a warning to clients that they had better make sure they paid their invoices on time or maybe it was simply a reminder that women could be every bit as intimidating and in control of their destiny as male pirates.

Smiling, she said, "Welcome to my world. Now, tell me everything."

I proceeded with everything that had happened and ended with Sam ordering me not to leave Palm Park.

"They don't have enough evidence to arrest you or they would have. They're merely trying to put the fear of God into you. If they have the tape of you shoving George, someone tossing something to you, then the tape will show everything."

"Here's the thing, A.B., only one person was watching the cash register at the entrance. There were a lot of tourists in the shop and the museum."

We chatted a few more minutes catching up on our lives since high school, I wrote her a modest retainer check in case anything happened and left feeling a little better.

Stopping by my friend Ronnie's pet store, I knew I could always hug one of the little Maltese puppies he had in the shop. They were such a little bundle of joy and love all wrapped up in baby soft hair. If it weren't for the fact that I'd be an awful puppy mama, I'd have a dozen of them.

Ronnie swears I would forget to feed them and take them out to do their business. Unfortunately, he's right. When I'm in the midst of writing a new book, I'm pretty much oblivious to anything else.

I have to order take-out most of the time simply because I've burned so much food on the stovetop and in the oven that even my cleaning lady doesn't want to clean it. Martha Stewart doesn't have to worry about my domestic skills upsetting her as the queen of all things domestic.

Although my ex-husband never mentioned my lack of housekeeping aptitude in the divorce, it was the standard "irreconcilable differences", I'd like to point out the man simply expected dishes of food to be placed on the coffee table and then they disappeared when he was through eating. He had no clue on how to do anything in the kitchen...or the garage...or the yard...or...you get the idea. He did, on the other hand, know how to find a sweet young thing who thought he was the greatest thing since sliced bread. I was more than willing to let her have him at this point. I don't know what we ever saw in each other, but we parted amicably.

"Oh, honey, honey!" Ronnie rushed toward me with his arms outstretched for a hug. He was almost as much fun as the little furbabies he had in his store. Bussing me on both cheeks, he leaned back and said, "What's going on? I can feel it. Harper Elizabeth Rogers, no keeping secrets from me…because you can't!" We both laughed.

Here's a little background on me before we go any further. My mother had a wicked sense of humor because, yes, my initials do spell HER. That is certainly preferable to dear old dad wanting to name me Harper Olivia Rogers aka HOR. As my mother explained many years later, she wasn't going to have a daughter where the initials spelled out an euphonism for a common street walker.

Ronnie was chattering up a storm, picking up and handing me little white wiggly puppies who couldn't kiss me enough. I was in love and every time I came to the shop, I swooned over them again and again.

Finally, holding one of the precious little ones next to my heart, I told Ronnie what had happened at the pirate museum.

I think Ronnie knew virtually any important person in what I fondly referred to as the Northeast Florida version of the Bermuda Triangle – Jacksonville, Palm Park, and St. Augustine. It seems like I was always going out from Palm Park to either Jacksonville or St. Augustine and then being snapped back to Palm Park like a rubber band that had been stretched too tight.

"Honey, you've got to tell me what happened! George was looney tunes to begin with and had absolutely no fashion sense." He sniffed.

I laughed silently. This was coming from a man who was wearing black and silver striped pants with a black vest and white shirt with a little red western string tie, and black ankle boots.

"I take it you didn't like him," I grinned.

"Oh, he was okay. He just wouldn't dress like a pirate and, honestly, if it weren't for Vykky deBurgo, the museum wouldn't exist."

My ears picked up and my internal radar started spinning around like sugar in a cotton candy machine. There was a story here, I just knew it.

"Tell me more, tell me more," I singsonged at him, smiling.

"Oh, honey, you're such a wonderful person but please don't sing. You can't carry a tune in a bucket." Ronnie rolled his eyes and giggled.

I couldn't argue with him on that. It was true. I could sing four notes on key, but they weren't necessarily all together at the same time.

"Are you going to tell me the low down or are you going to make me pull those silly Christmas lights out of that thing you call a beard?" I laughed.

He pretended to be hurt but I knew better. Ronnie had found some sparkly battery-operated lights online that he could put in his beard. Always the fashionista.

"Vykky deBurgo is a member of one of the founding families of St. Augustine and..."

"Let me guess, she spells her name in a unique way." I rolled my eyes. In my limited experience, I had discovered folks of a certain upper echelon evidently wanted to be thought of as very special and, thus, spelled their names in an uncommon fashion.

Wiggling his bushy black eyebrows, "But, of course, my darlin'. Her real name is Victoria, and she goes by V-y-k-k-y."

Scooping up one of the bouncy Maltese puppies and touching his nose to her nose, "Vykky is the patron saint of the museum. George used to be a diver and went on numerous treasure-hunting dives with a lot of famous people including Mel Fisher.

"George had the artifacts but no money to set up the museum and he was truly convinced the public, and especially the tourists, would be willing to pay money to see his pirate treasures."

"Well, he was right, I suppose." Although the people in the store and the museum I saw didn't equate to him being a rich man with this particular business venture but, then again, I could be wrong, and it could have been just to be a slow day when I was there.

"Think about it, Harper, there are more than six million visitors to St. Augustine every year, and even if only one percent of them go to the museum, George's making somewhere in the one million two hundred thousand range. That's not too shabby and a great return on investment."

"This doesn't make any sense, Ronnie. If he's making that type of money, what does he need Vykky for?"

Smiling, "Remember, she set him up in business. She's probably getting half of whatever he's making. So..."

"So, she's a smart businesswoman," I finished for him.

Ronnie was so dramatic. Looking to his left, then to his right, leaned forward, and whispered, "She's looking for a specific type of treasure."

I laughed. "Ronnie, you know the puppies aren't going to tell anyone, right?"

He looked a little sheepish.

"What kind of treasure is she looking for? I would think she would have found it by now."

He shrugged.

The bell over the door tinkled letting us know that someone had entered the store.

It was Sam. Usually he was smiling when he saw us. This was not one of those times.

"Harper Rogers, you're under arrest for the murder of George Cloise."

I ceased to breathe, there was no oxygen in the air, and I was pretty sure my eyes had rolled back in my head giving the appearance of a dead person. Ronnie told me later no such thing had occurred and that I had laughed when Sam told me that.

Isn't it funny how the same incident can cause two different perceptions from two people witnessing the exact same thing and both of them be right? I'm guessing that these different perceptions of life are what cause eyewitness descriptions to be notoriously unreliable in the law enforcement field.

Trying to be funny, I stuck both arms out and grinned. "Okay, go ahead and slap my wrists now."

Sam obviously doesn't have the same sense of humor I have because the man actually slapped handcuffs on me before I could retract my outstretched arms.

As he proceeded to read me my Miranda rights, as shocked as I was, I did manage to eke out, "Ronnie, call A.B., tell her I've been arrested again, and that I don't look good in orange." This last part I almost wailed.

"She doesn't, you know," said Ronnie, turning to Sam.

Sam blinked his eyes a couple of times. "She doesn't what?"

"Really, Sam, you don't know this?" Ronnie sounded almost exasperated. "Harper doesn't look good in orange."

Shaking his head in disbelief, he probably couldn't fathom how both Ronnie and I agreed that I did not look good in orange because it clashed terribly with my pale complexion. If I were being realistic, he probably thought we were both looney tunes looking for our own reality TV show.

My emotions were swirling like crazy: disbelief, shock, anger, and total confusion. How could this possibly be? I'm the good girl who never gets into trouble. Just because I've had a couple of murders happen near me since I moved back to Palm Park doesn't count. I've lived for years with nothing nefarious happening anywhere close to me. Palm Park must be a weird vortex of some off-the-chart quantum physics and they, for some reason, have attached themselves to my energy vibrations. Yeah, that sounds a little woo-woo. Even I don't think I buy into that explanation.

My only real explanation is maybe I've been good for way too long and strange things just happen in life. Although, admittedly, I don't think most people have these types of occurrences in their lifetime. Maybe it's come about because I'm a mystery writer and I need new things to write about.

Do I dare admit that these thoughts are zooming through my brain at the speed of Superman jumping over a locomotive?

"Harper, how many times do I have to tell you to get a move on?" Sam sounded irritated although he wasn't making a move to drag me kicking and screaming out to the squad car. I'm not prone to screaming and kicking in general. It's not a becoming look for a child, and certainly not for an adult.

"I don't want it to look like you're resisting arrest. That won't look good in the report."

He had me there. If this ever went to court, it definitely wouldn't endear me to the judge.

"Ronnie, call A.B." I was urging him to hurry up. I didn't want to spend the night again in jail which, unfortunately, is what happened before A.B. could get me bailed out. It takes hours to get sprung once you're thrown in jail.

The good news was there were several prostitutes in the holding cell. While some folks refer to them as ladies of the evening, I will testify that these women were not ladies in any sense of the word. They were foul-mouthed, stunk, and were dressed every bit as bad as what you might suspect. These women were not highly paid escorts, they were low-level street walkers where the cops used them to make their monthly quota of arrests.

Once they discovered I was a writer, yes, I told them hoping no one would beat me up, they told me some great stories – many of them funny. They all asked if I would put them in one of my books. Of course! They could become new readers and buy my books. Also, my premise was they wouldn't hurt me if I promised to put them in a book.

A.B. escorted me out of jail again six hours later and took me home. She didn't say much, I didn't say much. All I really wanted to do was take a long hot shower. I wondered if all the negativity of these two jail experiences could be washed off my body, find its way down the drain, and out of my life.

Crawling into bed although it was now daylight, something tickled my brain that Ronnie had said. Vykky was the patron of the museum. Why wasn't she an owner?

Right before my eyelids drooped shut, I decided to call and see if I could do an interview with her. As a writer and successful author, I could tell her I was working on a new book and, with her being one of the founding families of St. Augustine, I needed her unique perspective of the oldest city in the United States.

That was an idea that would come back and bite me in the fanny.

Chapter 4

"No." Vykky was short when I called and asked for an interview. Although I am a wimp in person, I can be very assertive, okay, maybe aggressive, on the phone.

"Ms. deBurgo, since your family was one of the founding members of St. Augustine..."

She interrupted me. "What part of no do you not understand?"

I grinned. I had her now. As long as she stayed on the phone, I had a pretty good chance of getting her to see me.

"You know, we can do a Zoom meeting where we don't actually have to meet in person." I was being coy, "Unless, of course, you're not that familiar with Zoom."

"I certainly do know how to use Zoom," she snapped. "I use it all the time for various meetings."

"Great! Are afternoons or mornings better for you?" I was mentally high fiving myself. I was using the old tried and true sales method of using the assumptive close technique. The person has to make a choice and you're leading them to the close.

"Ms. whatever your name is, I see what you're doing, and it won't work with me." She sounded triumphant.

"Great! I'll see you at the Old Café at ten a.m." I disconnected the call laughing. She wanted to be in charge, I got that. I also guessed that she would show up simply to see who had the audacity to manipulate her into doing so.

I spent the next couple of hours researching her on Google and ended up calling Ronnie for the information that couldn't be found on the internet; specifically, what was her personality really like.

"For that type of information, Miss Harper Rogers, I'm going to need a grande double espresso butter pecan coffee." I could hear the laughter in Ronnie's voice.

"I'll be there in about twenty. Anything else?" I was trying to be accommodating. Food and coffee were the fastest and simplest ways of getting the scoop on anyone from Ronnie.

"There's a new puppy you can play with, honey. See you!" He disconnected with a lilting laugh.

Doing a slide-and-glide through the local coffee drive-thru, I was at the pet store in record time. I didn't even spill any coffee in the car. I'm prone to do that on occasion.

Doing a Zumba hip move with ease to open the pet store door, I wondered why I couldn't do it in class without creating undue pain in my lower back and down my legs. Life wasn't fair and it was unkind to me in the area of exercise and balance. I've been known to smack into doors quite unintentionally.

Scooping the coffee out of my left hand and replacing it with a sleepy Maltese puppy, Ronnie almost started slurping the coffee before I realized what was going on.

"I so needed this today, honey! Thank you, thank you, thank you!"

Curiosity will override anything else going on in my life. I could wait to ask questions about Miss Vykky.

Snuggling the sleepy puppy closer to my chest while juggling my coffee, "What's going on, Ronnie?"

"You'll never guess who called me asking about you?"

Okay, this was never a good thing when someone wanted to know more about me. I didn't want, need, or even desire to have a stalker in my life. I really just wanted to be left alone and write; well, except I did need to be around people from time to time to help keep me sane. Although that last point may be debatable among certain people. Of course, these people were not my tribe, my peeps, or whatever the phrase-of-the-moment happened to be for people I didn't want anywhere near me.

My mental rolodex was spinning like crazy trying to figure out who could possibly want information about me. I am actually a boring person. I like to write, I'm borderline obsessive about it. I'm a workaholic. I have fun. Maybe not your definition of having fun but you're you and I'm me.

All of these thoughts were shooting at the speed of light through whatever dimensions my brain operated in.

"Vykky deBurgo!" Ronnie was gleeful. I'm not quite sure why but he was.

"Yes, and..." I was cautious, not about Ronnie but about what Vykky wanted to know. As much of a gadabout as Ronnie was, he was very discreet when it came to dispersing gossip and details. I trusted Ronnie.

"She wanted to know who you were, what you were working on, and who you were related to in St. Augustine. I told her you were a bestselling author. I knew you were working on a pirate book, that seemed to really pique her interest, and that you weren't related to anyone in St. Augustine."

Okay, that was all good and it also meant she would meet with me tomorrow morning.

"What else did she say or want to know?" It would be interesting to see what else she wanted to know.

"That was it except that she was meeting you tomorrow morning for coffee." Ronnie giggled, "She did say she didn't appreciate how you manipulated her into doing that except that she'd give you brownie points for your technique."

I told him how I'd done it and we both got a laugh out of it.

"What's the scuttlebutt on her? What's her personality like? Details, Ronnie, details." I looked over the lip of the Styrofoam coffee container.

"Normally, I'd say she's not someone you want to have coffee with but, obviously, you are." He laughed. "She's a little paranoid about people knowing what type of businesses she's involved in. She does loan money to small businesspeople but takes a huge position in their company."

"She's a loan shark."

"Honey, I wouldn't call her that. She's more like a naughty, greedy venture capitalist. To be fair, she does know how to pick winners. The sad part is the business owner is usually desperate for the influx of money and will agree to her terms, which is very advantageous for her and not so much for them."

"Rumors, Ronnie, I want the rumors."

He sighed. "Okay, but you didn't hear it from me. Rumor is she's been looking for a map of buried treasure in St. Augustine where Captain Kidd allegedly hid it.

"It's been heavily rumored for years that John Jacob Astor found the treasure and that's how he got his start in business. He ended up being the first multi-millionaire in the United States."

Ronnie paused, taking another drink of his grande double espresso butter pecan coffee. "Vykky's quite convinced that Captain Kidd's treasure still exists and has never been found. Kidd left a series of numbers or coordinates to his wife that may or may not have been directions to the treasure. That's the reason why she invests so heavily in pirate-related hunts. Regardless of what's found out in the ocean, everything seems to bring treasure hunters back to St. Augustine."

I chuckled. "Well, there's so much history here and I would think the treasure or map or whatever it is would have disappeared a long time ago or, at the very least, still be buried. St. Augustine has a ton of archaeological digs going on at any given time and it seems like something new is discovered every couple of months or so."

Ronnie pranced around the puppies playing with them. "Drake was here before the Old Fort was built. What if the map was buried under the fort?"

We chatted for a few more minutes and then I left. Something was flitting in and out of my brain. It was probably just a butterfly let loose and hadn't discovered its way out yet.

The next morning, I was sitting in the coffee shop waiting on Vykky when it occurred to me I really didn't know what she looked like. As is the case with many women, she changed her hair color and style frequently based on the photos I had seen on Google. A tall, thin woman with black hair pulled back in a severe bun swept into the coffee shop with all of the energy of Attila the Hun. To say this woman was intense was like saying jackhammers don't shatter concrete sidewalks.

Her eyes raked the room, missing nothing. I could feel the blood draining from my heart, I glanced down at my feet to make sure blood wasn't pooling around my toes.

I felt like shooting Ronnie for not telling me her energy level was like that of the space shuttle blasting off from Cape Canaveral.

Virtually, every nerve in my body was shriveling up as her piercing eyes landed on me. Laser-focused, she headed right for my table.

I vaguely wondered if, by osmosis, I could capture some of that energy and bottle it for those days when I felt wimpy...like right now.

Standing up, I held out my hand. She ignored it as she sat down across from me. "Black Americano."

Blinking my eyes several times, I wasn't sure if she was telling me to get her a coffee or was trying to insult me since my skin is a porcelain shade of white or if the coffee shop personnel were being commanded to bring her a cup of the dark brew.

"Do what?" Let me be the first to admit, my brain cells don't always fire on all cylinders particularly when I am exceptionally nervous, which I was.

She waved her hand dismissively at me. "Not you, them."

Attitude, she was all about attitude, with a dash of a sense of entitlement. Considering that her family was one of the founding members of St. Augustine and still owned a great deal of land downtown, maybe she just felt everything was owed to her. In a literal sense, she was right because the store and building owners were paying her rent for their businesses on her property.

Her eyes bore into mine. I think dead shark eyes have more personality. It was like looking into a dark black vortex where there was no bottom. She must have had a vacuum in there somewhere because I could feel myself being sucked into her world and into the hole. It was the strangest of feelings. I was here physically but felt like I was on a highway speeding to an unknown destination.

I blinked my eyes and that broke whatever spell I was under. It jolted me back to looking at Vykky. Her eyes were dark brown. She either had great youthful genes in her DNA or she'd had plastic surgery done. I was betting on plastic surgery.

To say that her makeup was professionally done was an understatement. It looked fabulous. I was actually a little envious. I could spend twenty minutes putting on makeup and it still gave the appearance of either someone who didn't care about their looks, I sort of do, or the artistic skills of a pre-pubescent female teenager. I couldn't even brag that my skills were better than a mortician's, sad to say.

Vykky could be anywhere from thirty-five to seventy-five. Based on what Ronnie had told me and what I was able to glean from Google, she was probably in the neighborhood of a very youthful sixty.

"I normally don't do this type of thing." She was haughty.

For some unknown reason, uncontained and unfiltered words burst out of my mouth and into the atmosphere at the speed of light. "What? You don't have coffee with anyone who's not on the social register?"

Her eyes flashed so quickly I almost missed it, but I thought I saw a spark of amusement. Maybe she wanted to be called out. Maybe she was tired of people kowtowing and appreciated a brief moment of spontaneity from someone who wasn't worth a million dollars or more.

One of the staff brought over her coffee in a delicate white China teacup with a saucer and placed it gently on the table. My coffee was in a cardboard-type cup with a plastic lid. The rich do live in a different world.

"What do you want?" She got right to the point, I had to give her credit for that. She took a sip from the cup.

Throwing all caution to the wind, I plunged ahead hoping she wasn't going to stomp out of the shop. "You're the richest woman in St. Augustine. You are an angel patron to many people and a venture capitalist to business owners."

She merely blinked her eyes and sat the cup back down in the saucer. Her fingertips were lightly resting on the table.

"You also believe Captain Kidd's treasure is still somewhere here in St. Augustine and you want it." I paused, hoping air had somehow magically managed to find its way into my lungs and inflate them so I could breathe without fainting. I was nervous.

She tapped her manicured first fingernail on the table. I couldn't tell if she was annoyed or thinking. I did have the sense not to say anything further. He who speaks first loses is an age-old sales technique. It also usually worked for me in interviews. Most people can't stand the silence after ten to twenty seconds. The longest I've ever had anyone go was thirty seconds before breaking down and answering my questions.

"What's your book about?" Her voice was flat with a slightly curious tinge to it.

"I write murder mysteries and..."

"You want to know if I had anything to do with the murder of George Cloise." She took another sip of coffee.

That thought really had not crossed my mind but now that she had planted it, I was going to run with it.

"Maybe," I was hesitating just enough to pique her interest, "but I'm not investigating his murder."

A slight smile creased her face. I guess she hadn't gone for the Botox treatments because her facial muscles did move.

"You probably should since you're being charged with it."

Chapter 5

News travels fast in the northeast Florida Bermuda Triangle - Jacksonville, St. Augustine, and Palm Park.

I just blinked at her. On any other person, her smile would be a smirk; however, a shark devouring its prey is what popped into my mind.

Lifting her cup to her mouth, she said, "If I'm not mistaken, you weren't supposed to leave Palm Park, yet here you are."

Much as I hated to admit it, she was right...and I knew it. I hoped Sam or one of his buddies in blue didn't suddenly pop through the door and drag me back to Palm Park. My logical mind told me the chances of that happening were between slim and none, and Slim had gone to the Bahamas.

Setting her cup down, "I don't think you have any clue as to what George was doing, what he had, or even what he knew."

She tilted her head to the left slightly. "George was a very unique character who had great contacts in the treasure-hunting field. He knew everyone and, yes, he was on some major finds."

I was watching her body language. She was poised, elegant, and relaxed as a hoot owl getting ready to swoop down and grab a frightened mouse for dinner.

I was the mouse. I was already tense. My stomach needed antacids for the Spanish flotilla swimming around in my belly.

Debating whether to tell her about the person who had tossed the knife at me, I really thought she probably already knew and was playing with me, trying to mess with my psyche. She was doing a fine job of it. I decided not to mention it.

Taking a deep breath, I said, "Tell me...tell me your version." I smiled and hoped my lips weren't trembling as a dead giveaway as to how nervous I was. I held my breath knowing that sooner or later she would tell me something.

"George has something of mine," she paused, taking a tiny sip from her cup, "or, at the very least, knows where it is."

Something suddenly clicked in my brain. "Was George getting Spanish artifacts for either your private collection or for you to sell to a high-end collector?"

Her eyes narrowed. As many times as I've watched snake shows on the National Geographic Channel, I don't think I've ever seen a snake's eyes constrict that quickly.

Gathering my courage, I continued, "That's the reason why you've been his patron for so many years. Let me guess, he keeps leading you on, so you'll continue to sponsor him."

Setting her cup down, daintily patting her lips so her lipstick wouldn't smear, she said, "My dear, you certainly have a vivid imagination but, then again, I guess you would since you're a writer."

She stood up, nodded at the barista, and walked out the door.

If I had to guess, I'd say I may have hit a sour note with her. It also occurred to me that I probably needed to get back to Palm Park before she alerted law enforcement that I had left the county and was probably subject to arrest.

Taking the back way home, I did pass several highway patrol troopers but thankfully, they were not interested in me. I was also going just a couple of miles over the speed limit but not enough to raise any suspicions.

My phone rang. "So did you enjoy your trip to St. Augustine this morning?"

Rats! Sam knew, maybe he had a tracker or something on my car but that didn't really make any sense.

"Did you want to go for coffee or is this call for something else?" I tried very hard to sound cheerful.

He sighed. "Harper, seriously, don't leave the county. If..."

"Sam, I'm not under arrest and I'm pretty sure I can go wherever I want."

There was a long pause. "Harper, when a law enforcement officer asks you not to leave the county, did you think that was a guideline for other people?"

I couldn't help it, I giggled. "How did you know I left the county?"

"The person you met with for coffee has a lot of contacts and a lot of pull, Harper. That individual has also let it be known that you are casting dispersions on her character. She's also let it be known that if you continue to do that, she might be inclined to file a lawsuit against you."

Now, I burst into outright laughter. "Are you serious, Sam? We were having a private conversation, no one was close by, and our entire meeting was probably no longer than fifteen minutes. If she is threatening a lawsuit over something this frivolous, then she's got something to hid. The question is what.

"By the way, she said I was under arrest and I'm not, am I?"

"Not at the moment. You don't want to swim with the sharks, Harper. Have a great day."

The call was disconnected. I looked at my phone and shook my head. I think Sam was trying to warn me about Miss Vykky but for what purpose I wasn't exactly sure.

Deciding Ronnie probably had the answer for this, I did a slide and glide through the coffee drive-thru and got two coffees and four doughnuts.

Ronnie's such a ray of sunshine and I appreciate his friendship. He's always so happy to see me when I come through the pet store door especially when I'm bearing gifts.

"Oh, honey, look at what you've brought me! You are so sweet! I love, love, love you, honey!" He was doing air kisses while gently easing one of the coffees from my hand to his.

As he was nibbling on the doughnut between sips of coffee, I told him everything that had happened.

"So, do you think Vykky had George killed?"

"Well, here's the thing, Ronnie. She didn't get upset until I basically implied that he was blackmailing her."

"That would do it, honey," he took another sip. "Particularly, since you insulted her intelligence and..."

"Whoa! Wait up right there, Ronnie! I never said the woman was dumb or stupid."

He waved his hand at me as little sugar flecks fell off his doughnut. "You told her that George was leading her on and that's the reason why she continued to be his patron. That's saying she wasn't smart enough to find out what he had, and she was paying for the privilege of being stupid."

Crap doodle! I hadn't even thought of that. It never occurred to me that what I meant could be misconstrued that way. If I wrote that scene in a book, I would have caught it but being in real life, words have a nasty way of causing me all sorts of problems. Things that simply would never occur to me normally. Maybe there is something wrong with my brain. Whatever filters had been given to most people apparently were rather scarce in my brain.

"Honey, don't worry about it. I love you anyway." Ronnie stood up and gave me a platonic hug. "However, it does sound like you may have stepped on Vykky's toes and that's probably not a good thing."

We chatted for a few more minutes and I went home, had an early dinner, and was just getting ready for my shower when my doorbell rang. I looked through the peephole and saw Sam. Grinning, I opened the door.

"Harper Rogers, did you threaten to murder Vykky deBurgo?"

Chapter 6

"**No**," **I stuttered. My brain** was swirling. What was going on? Was Vykky threatening me to leave her alone with some bogus, trumped-up charge?

I think I started hyperventilating because I do remember Sam sitting me down on the couch and handing me a paper bag. I didn't realize I had one in the house or maybe he just always carried one when he was the bearer of bad news.

"Am I being arrested?" I huffed out trying to catch my breath. I was sure my brain had been deprived of oxygen. Nothing was making any sense.

"No," he paused, "Not at this time. Do you want me to get you a Coke or something to drink?"

"Why...why...," I took a deep breath, "why are you here then?"

Sam squirmed, cracked his knuckles, and looked uncomfortable. "You realize that there are certain things in life one must do to appease the higher ups, right?"

My mind snapped back into gear. Oxygen flooded into my lungs and rejuvenated my blood cells so I could think clearly. I was no longer spinning like a Jewish dreidel at Christmas time. I hissed, "You were told to come over here and threatened or intimidate me to leave Vykky alone? You do realize I only spoke to her on the phone once and met her in person for about fifteen minutes, right?"

He shifted and couldn't seem to get comfortable on my sofa. Sam wouldn't look at me. This meant he was being forced to do something he disagreed with or that he knew had zero merit and that it was a complete waste of time.

"So, this is her method of intimidation? To get local police to warn me to leave her alone?" I snarled, setting the brown paper bag aside. "One would think you have something better to do than this, Sam."

He almost squirmed on the couch and looked away. What kind of detective was Sam if he was this uncomfortable answering my questions? I'm going to go with it was probably because we were friends, and he didn't like this aspect of his job.

He suddenly stood up. "Harper, this is as a friend," Ha! I was right. "You don't want to mess with Miss duBorg."

I pointed to the door. "You can tell your superiors I am not easily intimidated. Oh, yeah, ask them why they're giving warnings for someone who doesn't even live in our county."

On a roll, I continued, "You do realize this is like Mafia tactics, don't you?"

He shook his head, exhaled deeply, opened the door, and said, "I'm just saying, Harper, be careful. She's got a lot of tentacles and you don't want to be caught up in them."

I shut the door a little harder than I meant to...sorry, I lied. I really meant to slam it but I didn't whip my arm back far enough to slam it like a cat five hurricane attack.

I called A.B.'s office and told her what had happened. Her only response was, "That's interesting. Keep working on your book."

Probably good advice but things kept whirling around in my mind. Had I inadvertently stumbled onto something that Vykky didn't want me to find out about? She was definitely warning me away. I'd like to tell her 'foolish woman' but I had better sense. I don't think this had to do with my inadvertent suggestion that she had been played by George.

I needed to do more research on George. I wondered if he had any other patrons for his business or treasure-hunting expeditions.

After several hours of going down the Google rabbit hole on George, his treasure-hunting expeditions, and then turning my attention to the ever-curious Vykky. She's to the point of massive intrigue for me. She's revved up my curiosity level. Before she was only mildly interesting, now I want to know what makes her tick. Once I know that, I can either annoy her greatly or figure out a way to make her neuroses work for me. Of course, I was now borderline paranoid about everything.

My phone started playing. I picked up without looking at the caller I.D. I thought it was Ronnie calling me. I was wrong.

I answered the answer without the butterflies in my stomach flying in unison. I hoped my voice didn't sound as shaky as it felt.

"Hello."

"You really don't want to mess with me." The call disconnected. What did the caller I.D. say? Vykky duBorg. Shut the front door!

Chapter 7

That was certainly something I wasn't expecting. At least, I was able to keep breathing at this point. That's progress.

My nerves were shot. Vykky's call sounded like a threat. I called my attorney who was now not only on speed dial but I had also memorized her number in case my phone was ever taken from me.

"A.B., what does that mean for me?" I'm not going to lie, I was scared. "Um, if I were thinking out loud, should I plan on moving to Costa Rica or the Virgin Islands?"

She ignored my question. "Don't worry about Vykky unless she starts making five or more calls in a day and then we can file harassment charges against her."

Disconnecting my phone, it rang again almost immediately. The good news was it interrupted the downward spiral of negative thoughts that were threatening to overtake my brain and causing it to shut down.

"Honey, what is going on with you?" Ronnie sounded a little distraught. "I'm bringing pizza over."

There's always time for pizza. Ronnie was my BFF and was so incredibly thoughtful. Every girl should have a guy friend like Ronnie.

I had two Cokes waiting when I heard the tapping at my door. Call me gun shy but I did look through the peephole to make sure it was him and not Sam coming to deliver another nasty message from his superiors again.

Opening the door, Ronnie borderline pranced in. "I got the PMS special!" He announced gleefully.

Shaking my head, "Only you call it that. It's pepperoni, mushrooms, and sausage to most normal people."

"Oh, honey, that ship normal sailed a long time ago." We both giggled.

Chowing down on the pizza, I caught him up with everything that had happened and ended with, "Nothing is making any sense."

"What does A.B. say about all of this?"

Shrugging, "Not much. She told me to ignore Vykky unless she starts blowing up my phone. By the way, who did the interior design in her office? I absolutely love it!"

"Some gal out of Atlanta." Taking a big gulp of his Coke, "Don't worry about a thing, A.B. will take good care of you. I think Vykky doesn't like you."

I snorted. "Ya think? I'm wondering if I should retaliate against her."

Ronnie looked up, his eyeballs peeking over the top of his glasses. "Seriously, Harper Elizabeth Rogers, that is not one of your better ideas. You're already being investigated for murder. Adding another one to your list of things to do will not, repeat will not, help you in a court of law. Don't even think about writing it down as a book idea."

Wiping his mouth, "All of this being said, I think Vykky thinks you know something about Captain Kidd's treasure. She's going to put enough pressure on you to make you cough up Anne Bonny and Mary Read!"

"Who never came to St. Augustine!" I grabbed another slice of pizza. "What do you think happened to Kidd's treasure?"

He grinned, "I think it's already been found and different parts of it have already been sold to high-end collectors. That being said, I don't think the majority of it has been dispersed. I think whoever found it wants to keep it in that one location."

"Gives a whole new meaning to pirate booty, doesn't it?" I laughed. "But there's a whole school of thought that says the treasure is over in South Africa somewhere or maybe that was Sir Francis Drake. I get the two of them confused."

Ronnie wiggled his eyebrows at me. "See? That's half the fun of trying to figure out where pirate treasure is supposed to be buried. I honestly don't think it's about the actual worth, the dollar figure, of the treasure. I think it's more about discovering what no one else has been able to find. I think that's the juice that drives treasure hunters."

I needed to give A.B. another check just to make sure she was at my beck and call in case those folks dressed in blue with shiny badges decided I needed to be re-introduced to their facility.

Bopping through A.B.'s office doors, I had the good sense to bring doughnuts for Brenda who barely acknowledged my existence. She simply pointed at the inner sanctum doors for me to enter.

A.B. wasn't at her desk when I entered. Since her office was designed in pirate girl décor, I started to wander around the room. She had vibrant colored paintings of various female seafaring entrepreneurs hanging on the walls with a framed placard detailing their escapades. A couple of them had maps underneath the portraits with the always popular 'X marks the spot' on them. I guess pirates all went to the same school of name it and claim it on their buried treasure maps.

She entered through a hidden door I hadn't noticed before. She was grinning. "You really like my office, don't you?"

Smiling, "I think it's a great testimony to female pirates, certainly to the power of women, and I love how you have the treasure maps next to everyone's painting."

Looking around, I said, "Captain Kidd is the only male pirate you have in your office."

"Oh, that," she waved her hand and semi-laughed, "theoretically, his daughter is my great, great, umpteen greats grandmother."

I was fascinated by that. "Really? That's cool. Um, I thought Vykky might be related to him and that's the reason why she has the hots for buried treasure."

A.B. smiled, "Vykky couldn't find Kidd's treasure if it came up and bit her on her Botoxed face."

Meow! I wondered if there was something between Vykky and A.B. I started to ask but A.B. started discussing my case with me and I forgot. I'm easily distracted, what can I say?

Leaving her office, I was encouraged that nothing was going to happen to me. I wasn't going to go to jail. I wasn't going to have to wear orange. I don't know what strings she pulled or what favors she called in, but I was free to roam the Northeast Florida Bermuda Triangle and I could go to St. Augustine any time I wanted. I was a free woman.

I had no sooner gotten home than my phone rang. I didn't look at caller I.D., I probably should have.

"Yo, what's up?" I really thought it was Ronnie. I couldn't have been any more wrong.

It was Vykky.

Chapter 8

I gulped and then flattened my voice. I certainly wasn't happy to hear from her. She had caused me a great deal of grief and aggravation.

"Yes, Vykky, what do you want?"

Her voice was well-modulated. "I'd like to know how you managed to use a get out of jail free card."

I couldn't help myself. "I passed go and collected two hundred dollars."

Assuming I had annoyed her greatly because it took a moment or two for her to say anything. "Who's your attorney?"

"Nunya."

"Nunya," she repeated slowly, "what does that mean?"

"None of your business." I disconnected the call and blocked her.

Why do I fascinate this odd woman? Now I was more determined than ever to find out what the connection was with George and this socialite businesswoman. There had to be more than just Vykky financially sponsoring him. It occurred to me that he was blackmailing her. If that were true, what did he have on her that was worth his death? More importantly, chances were, she didn't have it in her possession. She obviously either thought I had it or knew what it was.

What was I wearing that day? Did George slip something in my pocket or purse that day unbeknownst to me?

I wasn't sure which purse I was carrying that day because I frequently changed them. I usually only pulled my wallet out of one purse and put it in another one. I typically didn't see what else was in the purse.

Going into my small closet, I pulled the straw tote out and turned it upside down on my bed. I didn't see anything in the contents that looked unusual – a handful of tissues, a ballpoint pen, a band-aid, and three single dollar bills. I was rich!

Putting everything back in the tote, I placed it back on the closet shelf. Grabbing the black purse, I dumped everything on the bed. How in the heck did I get dust bunnies in my purse? That didn't make sense and I usually kept my purses zipped up when I wasn't using them. This time, the bag was unzipped. The little dust bunnies looked like tiny little cotton buds that had escaped from the end of a Q-tip. There were six of them laying on top of my tissues, a band-aid, yes I carry band-aids in all of my purses in case I suffer a painful papercut during my travels, and my sunglasses. I wondered where I had lost them. Other than the weird dust bunnies, nothing seemed to be unusual.

I only had one other purse to peruse and that was the current one I was using. I turned it upside down on the bed cover, a little piece of paper floated out and laid on top of the tissues, band-aid, and my wallet. It looked like a Chinese fortune cookie message except there wasn't a printed message. It was a handwritten note with 29°53[]41[]N, 81°18[]52[]W scrawled on it.

After plugging that into Google, it only came up as St. Augustine. Well, that wasn't particularly helpful. St. Augustine sprawled almost eleven square miles where roughly eight and a half miles was land, and the remaining two and a half miles was water. It did occur to me that Kidd's treasure might be in the Inland Waterway or that when it was being dredged umpteen years ago, the construction crew had already found the treasure, divvied it up, and spent it. I didn't think so, but you never know.

Deciding this might be something A.B. needed to know, I called her office, told Brenda I needed to speak to her, and the soul of brevity put me through.

"What's going on, Harper?" A.B. always sounded happy to talk to me, despite her seeing me several hours earlier.

I told her about the little piece of paper with the latitude and longitude written. She asked me what it specifically said and the only response I received was, "Humm, that's interesting."

"Why?" I was curious.

"If I remember correctly, I think that's really close to some property Vykky owns."

Yes, I thought it beyond interesting that my attorney would know the latitude and longitude of any piece of property anywhere much less that it was close to property Vykky owned.

"A.B., are you related to Vykky by any chance?"

She laughed. "That's an amusing thought, probably more to you than me or Vykky."

Was this a non-denial denial or just the basic I'm-not-answering-any-questions attorney jargon?

"Bring it down the next time you come this way. Put it somewhere out of sight though."

"So, it might be important then?"

"Who knows? Maybe but probably not."

We rang off.

It was time for me to visit Ronnie. I had a ton of questions. If anyone would know, it would probably be Ronnie.

Yes, I was going to bribe him with doughnuts and coffee. I'm surprised neither one of us was obese from the amount of caffeine and sugar we consumed on a weekly basis.

"Ronnie," I singsonged entering the Furever Love Palace, "guess what I have."

Zooming from the back of the pet store to the front, I was surprised the man had never tried out for the one-hundred-meter dash in the Olympics.

He snatched the Brazilian coffee out of my hands and took a big gulp before I had the opportunity to warn him it was different from butter pecan and was exceptionally hot. He almost gagged and I could almost see his eyeballs spinning around with the extra caffeine.

"Honey, honey," he sputtered, "are you trying to kill me?"

I was bent over with laughter. "If you would have waited for a couple of seconds, I would have told you it was something different."

"This is rocket fuel," he choked out. "What are you trying to find out today by bringing this to me?"

"Is A.B. related to Vykky in some way?"

Shaking his head, "I don't know. I don't think so but, then again, Vykky doesn't admit to being related to anyone other than her mother and father and the founders of St. Augustine. I'm not even sure if she has any brothers or sisters. If she does, I'm sure they don't live in St. Augustine."

Taking a small sip of his high-octane caffeine fuel, "I simply don't ever remember hearing about her having any siblings. Maybe her mom and dad decided she was perfect enough, they couldn't do any better, and they stopped making babies."

I had picked up one of the little fluffy balls of Maltese love and told him about the note in my purse. "Don't you think it's odd that A.B. would know the latitude and longitude of St. Augustine?"

"Nope." He opened the doughnut bag and pulled the glazed yeast deliciousness out. "Remember, A.B. blew out the SAT test for the state of Florida when she was a senior and you were a sophomore. That perfect score had never happened before and has never occurred since. It caused all those academic types to wonder what they did wrong and how a high school senior could score perfectly on their test.

"The woman remembers all sorts of things. I think she told me once she has an eidetic memory. She sees it once and it is set for life in her brain."

A.B. was brilliant and I was happy to have her as my attorney.

"Ronnie, why is she practicing law here instead of some big law firm in a large city?"

He laughed, "Because she can work when she wants to. You do know that she came up with and patented Scrubby Bubbles, right?"

I shook my head.

"Yeah, about eight years ago she appeared on Shark Tank and one of the sharks wanted to buy the entire company for something like a million dollars. A.B. retained a three percent share, smuck insurance as she called it, and sold the company to the shark. Then four years ago, the shark sold it for seventy-five million dollars and her three percent share ended up being something like two point two five million dollars. A.B. doesn't have to work unless she just wants to."

Oh.

We chatted for a few more minutes and I headed home where I discovered Sam waiting by my door with a pizza in his hand.

How much pizza can a girl eat in a day?

Chapter 9

I almost fainted. I felt like I was in the wind tunnel of a tornado. I was Dorothy in the Wizard of Oz, and I hadn't been smacked in the head with a flying window from a Kansas tornado. Taking a deep breath, I noticed Sam had placed his hand in the middle of my back. I was assuming it was because if I did faint, it would make it easier for him to guide me down to the floor.

"What are you doing here, Sam?" I managed to take a deep breath. "Are you coming to give me another warning from your head honchos?"

Unlocking the door, we walked in. He put the pizza on the countertop and took a couple of glasses down from the cupboard. Placing them under the ice cube dispenser, he filled the glasses up. Unscrewing the top from the large Coke bottle I had sitting on the counter, I waited until it quit hissing and poured it over the ice. The crinkling sound of the cubes gave me a few more minutes so I could gather my thoughts.

Smiling so that his dimples showed, "It's a peace offering, Harper. I'm on my own time and not police time."

I snorted, "I thought cops were always on duty."

"I'm a detective, remember?" His smile was still there. "And, no, I'm not always looking for criminals. It wasn't fair for me to do that the other day and I apologize."

My little radar was going ninety-to-nothing wondering what the real purpose of his visit was. I'd like to think it's because he likes me and we're friends. The suspicious part of me didn't believe he was only here because we were friends in the slightest.

"What? You look like you don't..." His smile widened.

"I'm not buying what you're selling." I was trying to sound firm when I was getting little vibrations throughout my body. There are days I'd like for us to be more than friends, but this wasn't that day. Maybe. Nope, nope, nope, I had to remind myself to stay firm in my resolve not to drop my guard against a bona fide detective.

"Um, Sam, does Vykky duBorg have a sister or any other relatives that you know of?" I started nibbling on a slice of pepperoni pizza.

"You know, I'm not sure." He took a swig of his Coke. "I had heard at one time, and this was a bazillion years ago, and..."

I couldn't help it, I started to laugh. "Bazillion?"

Sam looked puzzled and did a semi-shrug. "I don't understand."

"Really? You used the word bazillion." I continued to laugh and tried not to choke on my slice, "Who knew that you would ever use that word?"

He started to laugh. "It's as good a redneck word as any."

The little bit of tension in the air dissipated. Because I can be annoyingly focused...or so I've been told...I asked him again, "Does her Royal Highness Vykky have any siblings or cousins or anything?"

"Oh, yeah, back to that, huh?" He took another sip of his Coke. "I had heard years ago that her mother had a sister, but she didn't live in Florida."

He shrugged, "That's all I got and I'm not even sure that's true. All of this was," he grinned again, "a bazillion years ago."

We laughed again and chatted about nothing. I didn't tell him about Vykky calling me. For the time being, I wanted to keep my cards close to my vest. I didn't think he was a wolf in sheep's clothing this go-round but, still, I was a wee bit cautious.

I decided to step out on a limb. "Sam, what do you think this whole thing is about with Vykky?"

He lifted his shoulders and dropped them. "Other than the fact you've really riled her up, I don't have a clue."

Grinning, "Maybe, in your research, you've stumbled onto something about her or something that she wants, and you just don't know it."

"The only thing I've been researching are pirates. I wasn't even interested in their treasure. I'm predominantly interested in their clothing, what their eating utensils were, and their weapons." I sighed, "I can't imagine how cranky they must have been in those heavy clothes in Florida's heat and humidity."

"You're not interested in their treasure?" Sam was incredulous.

I shook my head. "You can look up clothes and everything online but until you see how heavy the clothes were, it really doesn't register."

"No treasure?" Sam was still shocked.

"No. Honestly, Sam, that's it. I was just doing research. I'm not one for digging around in the dirt or going underwater to find treasure. Let someone else do it. Remember, I work really hard on this porcelain white skin. I don't like to be out in the sun all that much."

"Living room light bulb tan then, huh?" We both laughed.

My phone pinged. "Hold on a second, my attorney is calling me."

At least he was a gentleman, "I'll step out into the hallway to give you some privacy."

"Hi, A.B., what's up?"

"Is anyone with you?" Her voice sounded very happy.

"Well, Sam came over, brought pizza, and now he's stepped out into the hallway."

She laughed, "Are you two dating?"

I sighed and rolled my eyes. "It's more like friends with no benefits."

Chuckling, "I understand. Okay, I've been able to see the video from the Pirate Museum and you're completely in the clear."

I sat down on the sofa and felt like the weight of the world had been lifted from my shoulders. No longer was I Atlas, the mythological god banished to carrying the world on his shoulders.

"Wha...what does it show?" I was anxious and curious at the same time.

"There was a guy behind George with a ball cap on. He was very careful to make sure his face was never shown from the time he entered the Pirate Museum lobby to actually going in the museum and then his hasty exit."

Yes, she really does talk like that.

"And..."

A.B. continued, "It appears that he stabbed George in the back and as George was turning, he stabbed him again. It is very clear in the video that your back was to George when all of this was occurring. You didn't turn around until the assailant tossed the knife at you and then you promptly dropped it." She paused for a moment, "Because you never actually caught it to begin with."

She started to laugh. "Harper, if I remember correctly from high school, you have absolutely no athletic coordination skills whatsoever, do you?"

As embarrassing as it was, I have to admit it's still as true today as it was during my high school years. I nodded my head and then realizing A.B. couldn't see me doing that answered with a pitiful sounding, "No, I don't."

"That totally lets you off the hook for the murder of George Cloises."

"What happened to the guy that murdered him?" I couldn't recall a single thing about the man.

"He ran out the Employees Only door."

Taking a deep breath, I let it out slowly. "Let me guess, there's no cameras in there and there's probably not any outside either, right?"

"Bingo."

"So, A.B., does that mean he got away with murder?" Wild thoughts were dashing around in my head equivalent to the spin cycle on a washing machine. I was a little apprehensive. "Do I have to worry about him coming to get me?"

"Probably not, Harper. I think you were a person of opportunity for him."

"A.B., last thing, what do you think this is all about?"

"Not enough information to make a guess at this point, Harper. Have a great day."

Relief was an understatement. I almost bounced over to the door to let Sam back in.

He saw me grinning like the proverbial Cheshire cat. "I take it everything's good."

"Yes!" I looked him directly in the eye. "Did you know the video shows me with my back to George?"

His eyes widened, okay, so he didn't know. "No, I didn't know that. How did your attorney get the tape and we didn't?"

Interesting choice of words. I was smug, "Probably because it happened in St. Johns County where you don't have any jurisdiction and not here in River County."

He nodded, looking thoughtful. Okay, I opened a can of worms on that but, realistically, he didn't have any jurisdiction for the St. Augustine area, and I doubted they'd share the information with him or even his supervisors. Law enforcement likes to keep things to their own agency so they can receive all the glory in the news media when they solve a crime.

Looking at me, "Mind if I make a quick phone call?"

I didn't think it made any difference what I told him, he was going to do it anyway.

"As long as I can listen in." I smiled sweetly. It's my apartment and I didn't want to go stand in the hallway.

"Sure." He punched in some numbers, glanced at me, and said, "Hey, it's Sam. What do you have on the video of Harper Rogers and George Cloises at the Pirate Museum?" A couple of ums and hums then, "Okay, thanks."

With raised eyebrows, I looked at him.

"How did your attorney get the Pirate Museum videotape? St. Augustine PD hasn't seen it yet."

Chapter 10

"**You really should back off** if you know what's good for you."

Vykky looked at her phone with the blocked number. Her eyes narrowed. How had someone gotten her personal phone number? She always used her other phone for everything related to business. Very few people had this number.

"What..."

The caller had already disconnected. Vykky's jaw tightened. Murmuring to herself, "Harper, dear, you're going to pay for that."

Chapter 11

"You know, Sam, there are some things in life I don't need to know about. You know, like electricity. I don't care how it's made, just that when I turn on the switch my light comes on."

"Harper..."

I grinned. "Seriously, I have no clue and, no, I'm not going to ask A.B. I can't be charged with anything and if Vykky decides to continue to make my life miserable, I'll just turn everything over to A.B. and let her handle everything."

He wiggled his eyebrows. "I don't think you want to play hardball with her. She's got more money than you and can make your life really miserable."

"True," I agreed, "however, I'm a very small fish to her and I would hazard a guess that she would get tired of me pretty quickly."

He left shortly thereafter, although, he did kiss me on the cheek. That was a surprise, and, yes, it did make me feel all tingly. Maybe there was something there after all. A girl could hope.

Calling Ronnie, I spilled everything to him. It's a good thing he couldn't see me through the phone because I was actually blushing like a schoolgirl from her first kiss.

"Girl, I've told you before, you both have sparks for each other. Just that neither one of you will admit to it." He sighed and almost giggled, "I think I know the two of you better than you know yourself."

At least I was smart enough to realize that he knew me better than I understood myself. Even though I have rampant thoughts merrily tap dancing their way through my brain, I just don't think I'm that personally aware. I'm a writer and I live too much in my brain anyway.

Deciding to sleep in the next day, I was rudely awakened by my phone ringing.

Struggling to become awake and find my phone at the same time was meant for someone who was physically more coordinated than I am. I knocked it on the floor. I finally found it under the bed but it had already stopped ringing. Looking through the recent calls, it was A.B.

She could wait until I had coffee. I'm not a very nice person before coffee. If Sam and I ever hooked up, I should probably tell him that.

After I'd had my second coffee, coming awake, and having my brain cells flying somewhat in formation, I returned A.B.'s call. The efficient Brenda did her standard 'let me see if she's available' thing.

It took a moment or two before A.B. came on the line. I could tell she was busy because she got right to the point.

"Harper, the St. Augustine P.D. has I.D.'d the man who murdered George Cloises."

"Wonderful!" I exclaimed. "Has he been arrested?"

"No. They found him in the dumpster behind the Pirate Museum. He's dead. Looks like he was shot in the forehead with a pirate's gun."

My head was swimming. "What do you mean he was shot with a pirate gun? Don't they make a lot of noise?"

"It was an English flintlock fifty caliber and, yes, they make a fair amount of noise. He was found this morning when one of the employees came to work."

"Whoa, A.B.! What do you think happened?"

"Shear speculation. Whoever hired him to kill George killed him and dumped his body."

"A.B., who was this guy?" I was curious. Did I know him? Was there some weird connection between us? I knew I was in the clear but this was all so very strange.

"Some guy by the name of Todd Stein. Had an arrest record as long as my arm, been in and out of jail since he was a kid, and had only been out of prison for a couple of weeks. Do you know him?"

She caught me off guard. I was going through names in my head. "Um, no, I don't think so. Do you know him, A.B.?"

She sort of laughed. "No, if I did, he wouldn't have spent as much time in jail as he did."

"A.B., don't you think it's weird that he was shot with a pirate gun? Why would someone do that?"

She started to say something when I interrupted her. "Wait, wait! There aren't any cameras by that door, are there? This means someone knew that and it also means someone had access to one of the pirate guns."

She was brisk. "Yes to your first question. Possibly to your second comment. Someone could have had a flintlock pistol in their own home versus taking something out of the museum. No, they don't have a suspect at this time. Talk to you later."

Questions were swirling as I sat at my laptop and started typing. If the guy was in the dumpster, that meant either a hefty person, probably a male, lifted the body up and pushed it into the dumpster after he was shot or someone had this Todd person sit on the edge of the trash container and when he was shot he fell backward into the container. I didn't know anyone who would willingly sit on top of a trash container strongly suspecting their immediate demise.

I googled Todd Stein, found his jail log information, and looked at the ever-popular jailhouse photo – black barber apron around his neck and only his face showing. He looked to be a slim man, maybe in the one forty – one fifty pound range.

Who could lift a man in that weight category? I wondered if I could do it. Pondering on that for a few minutes, it suddenly occurred to me that I probably could if, and only if, he were standing on a box. If he were standing flat-footed, chances were I wouldn't be able to lift a lifeless body into the dumpster.

This begged the next question, were there two people involved?

I was still of the opinion Vykky had something to do with this. I just didn't know how yet. She might not have been there or even shot Todd but, the more I thought about it, the more convinced I was she was behind two murders.

The next question became who was closest to her and had been with her or in her employ for a number of years.

I called Ronnie.

"Hey, honey, I need a coffee. Miss Priss and Mr. Randy Dandy are trying to have conjugal relations and it's really too soon for them to be doing that. I'm stressed, honey!"

Knowing that I probably shouldn't laugh but I did anyway, I agreed to bring him a coffee.

Because I have a whacky sense of humor, I stuck my hand holding the coffee through the store's door.

"Oooo, girl! Thank you!" I heard him squeal. It was safe for me to enter.

"Ronnie, it has..." I never got to finish my sentence because he started sputtering.

"Do you hate me so much that you can't be bothered to tell me what coffee you are bringing me?" He tried to sound upset but was kind of chuckling at the same time. "Does this have espresso in it?"

I was almost doubled over with laughter. "Yes. Ronnie, I was going to tell you but you snatched it out of my hand so quickly I didn't have a chance to tell you."

"You lie!" We both laughed. "Okay, Miss Trying-to-Butter-Me-Up-and-Ask-Questions, what do you need to know now? And I'm guessing it has to do with Vykky."

"Yes, who does she have, a man, who's been with her the longest?"

Ronnie paused and stroked his beard. "Probably Raoul. He's her handyman. He's not much bigger than me but he's incredibly strong."

"Do you think he could lift a hundred and fifty pounds of dead weight from the ground and throw it over his shoulders?"

He nodded. "He could probably do two hundred pounds pretty easily. He used to do all of Vykky's landscaping and gardening. He lifted a lot of mulch, grass pallets, that type of thing."

I thought I was getting close to what had happened to Todd Stein.

"How loyal is he to Vykky?" I held my breath. Ronnie knew everything. I never asked him how or where he got his information. Some things I don't need to know.

"Well, I know she brought his family over from Venezuela a long time ago and bought a house for his mom and sisters. Then a couple of years ago, she bought him the house he was renting. It's about a mile from his mom's house. We were at a club one time with a bunch of other people and he said he would do anything for Vykky because she had saved his family from all of the political upheaval in Venezuela. Apparently, Vykky pulled a few strings and they were able to immigrate here. I think she might have gotten them here by asking they be given political asylum."

Vykky was resourceful, had the money and means to do something like that, and what better way to ensure someone's loyalty forever than by taking care of the one thing they value the most – family.

I told Ronnie what I suspected had happened to Todd Stein.

"Probably so," he agreed, "but, here's the thing, Harper, there's still no motive as to why George was murdered. You're focusing on the wrong thing."

"But, but, another man was killed," I sputtered. I hated to admit that I had been distracted by this new murder and not focusing on the why of George's murder.

Somewhat humbled but refusing to admit it, I asked, "So, what's your theory on why George was killed?"

Ronnie laughed, sounding like a little boy who had just caught a jumping frog. "Harper, you're the one with all the ideas. You go first and then I'll tell you."

Rats! Ronnie had outplayed me once again.

"Honestly, Ronnie, I'm not one hundred percent sure. I think he found or knew of some more Spanish treasure. I'm guessing it was substantial and he was going to sell it to another museum or collectors so he had enough money to buy his way out of Vykky's grasp and she wasn't having it. She probably wanted the treasure and to keep him under her thumb. When he refused to tell her, she had him killed."

Ronnie shook his head. "Nope, not all of that makes any sense. She wasn't about to kill the goose that laid the golden egg."

Rolling my eyes, I demanded "What's your theory then? Remember, stabbing is up close and personal. This wasn't a warning shot she was firing at him."

"I think he did find the map to some treasure, whether or not it was to Captain Kidd's alleged bounty, who knows. But I do think he probably showed her some artifacts or doubloons."

Dubious, I waved my hand at him to continue. Picking up Mr. Randy Dandy, one of the overly exuberant Maltese puppies trying to mate with Miss Priss, he grimaced, "Harper, what am I going to do with these two? They're not old enough to be doing the naughty-naughty."

I laughed and picked up Miss Priss. She snuggled up against my shoulder and cheek. "And..."

"And I'm going to have to keep them separated." He sighed, "What's a daddy to do?"

Rolling my eyes, "Ronnie, focus. What do you think happened?"

Putting Mr. Randy Dandy in his own little playpen and watching the overly excited puppy run around with his tongue hanging out, he sighed and shook his head. He turned back to me, "George found some type of treasure, didn't offer it to Vykky but asked how much would it take to get out of their business deal. Vykky probably smelled a skunk right from the beginning because she knew George didn't have any money to buy her out.

"That could only mean one thing to her, George had found some pirate treasure, probably a lot of it, or he had found a map or both. Regardless, she was going to be cut out of what she probably thought was a substantial amount of money."

"Okay, that makes sense," I nodded.

Ronnie continued, "I would hazard a guess that Vykky thought she was being double-crossed, wanted the treasure or map, and if she had that, she didn't need George anymore."

Putting Miss Priss in another doggie playpen, I asked, "But why would she kill him if he had all of this information?"

Ronnie smiled, "Because there were only two places George would have kept a map – either on his person or in the cannon barrel. Chances were he'd put it in the barrel."

Snapping my fingers, I exclaimed, "Of course, then whoever murdered him could come back at any time and get the map. Wait! How do you know where George would put a map?"

"Some things, honey, you just don't need to know." Ronnie winked at me. I really didn't need to know the answer. Some things are just better left unknown.

"Except when Todd Stein came back to find the map, it wasn't there," I surmised.

"Probably," he agreed. "Vykky might have thought she was being double-crossed again and had him murdered also."

"And she still doesn't have the map!" We said in unison, high fiving each other.

After giggling for a few minutes, I said, "She's got to be one frustrated woman."

"Probably in more ways than one," grinned Ronnie wiggling his eyebrows. I playfully slapped him.

"Well, I need to get back to work on my murder mystery."

"What's this one about, Harper?" Ronnie was being polite, I knew he was more into movies and the club scene rather than the printed word.

"Originally, it was going to be about the pirates sailing around Florida, looting everything, and murder on the high seas." I shrugged, grinned, and rolled my eyes. "You know, kind of a historical murder mystery. Nothing like what's going on now. I might have to change what I'm writing."

"Naw, keep doing what you're doing."

"Seriously, Ronnie, all I was really doing at the Pirate Museum was looking at the pirate clothing, guns, and anything related to the way they lived their life. My research really had nothing to do with treasure or anything like that. How I ended up being involved in a murder is beyond me."

"Dead bodies do seem to show up around you on a somewhat frequent basis," he said, not looking at me.

I huffed, "I'd like to point out that I never had anything like this happen to me when I lived in Jacksonville. I move back to Palm Park and weird stuff happens. I believe it's something in the water."

I'd had several really unfortunate incidents over the past however many months where people just up and died near me. I didn't commit any of them, I swear it! Did I end up solving the whodunnit factor? Well, yes, and that's how Detective Sam Needles came into my life but that's another story. My brain had probably morphed into Stephen Hawking's black hole theory where things just disappear forever...or, they change into another life form, I don't know. All I do know is I have thoughts circulating in my head that I'm pretty sure other human beings have never had cross their minds.

This whole thing with Vykky was one of the universe's black holes for me. I felt like I was being sucked into another galaxy and there were no answers for anything. It's bad enough I can do this on my own since I'm a writer but to have external forces creating this havoc in my brain really just wasn't acceptable to me. The question became what was I going to do about it?

I left the Furever Love pet store and headed home. The front door opened way too easily. All I did was put my key in the lock and it opened.

If I'd had the sense of a goose, I wouldn't have walked into my own apartment and called the police instead but since, obviously, whatever few precious brain cells I had went the way of a cat playing with a twisted feather boa, I entered my abode and discovered someone had thoughtfully rearranged my carefully feng shui placed furniture.

What's the short version? Some jerk had trashed my apartment. Everything was turned upside down and my sofa looked like it had been shredded by an untrained puppy on some hallucinogenic drug.

I punched Sam's number on my phone. "Hey, do you think you could send someone over here? My place's been completely trashed." My voice was a little shaky. My apartment had been rearranged several times over the past however months and each time it was because of me being involved in solving a murder. I'd like to point out that none of them had attended the Martha Stewart School of Interior Decorating.

The inside of my brain was turning into a ping-pong match of errant thoughts. I think the Chinese were winning at this point.

"Don't touch anything, Harper," ordered Sam. "I'll be right over. I'm assuming you don't have anyone else in the apartment with you."

Um, I hadn't thought to look but I didn't think so. "No."

I did look around my formerly tidy place but I didn't see anyone hiding behind upturned furniture.

Sam showed up ten minutes later. Palm Park is a small town and you can go from one end of town to the other in about fifteen minutes.

He looked stoic. "Harper, have you ever thought about moving back to Jacksonville?"

Well, yes, the thought had occurred to me on more than one occasion but I wasn't going to admit that to him. Why, I don't know, but I just didn't feel like sharing that priceless bit of information.

He continued, "I'm surprised your rental insurance company hasn't dropped you from your policy."

Sam was starting to annoy me. He was supposed to be here to help or, at least, that's what I had anticipated him doing.

He walked over to the kitchen countertop. "Do I dare ask what this note is about?"

I was so intent on seeing what other damage had been done to my apartment that I hadn't even noticed the note. That's probably the reason why he's a detective and I'm not.

"What does it say?" I asked. Yes, I was nervous. I hoped I wasn't on the Let's-Scare-and-Kill-Harper list.

He glanced over at me and I could tell he was trying hard not to laugh. "Where is it?"

"Where's what, Sam?" I was confused. Well, not so much confused as to wondering what it was he was talking about. Okay, that's what confused means. Words are spinning in my head out of control.

"That's what it says, Harper, 'Where is it?' What do you think that means?"

Oh, I had a pretty good idea. And, it was scary. Did Vykky now think I had the pirate treasure map? How would I have gotten it? The more important thing was: did it really exist?

Something existed, that was for sure, but I didn't know what it was – treasure, Spanish doubloons the pirates had hidden, a map, or something else entirely. Maybe whatever it could be was more valuable than pirate plunder. I couldn't imagine what that might be except maybe valuable real estate.

Contrary to what you might be thinking that's not a far leap...at least not for Florida. Real estate is a very valuable commodity particularly in St. Augustine since there are always ancient artifacts being found.

They're also, theoretically, protected by the state but we all know that's not necessarily true.

I personally knew construction people over the years who had found silver and gold coins while they were working on various job sites. Road crew guys found all sorts of things when they were digging in the dirt.

One guy I used to date, before my ex-husband, had found a small chest of silver coins and had sold them to a collector for an obscene amount of money. He basically retired in his thirties until he went fishing on the beautiful St. Johns River, fell in love with the serenity of fishing, and decided to become a fishing tournament professional.

"Harper, did you totally zone out?"

"Huh." That sounded really intelligent but, yes, I had zoned out. I blinked my eyes a couple of times to refocus. "Um, Sam, I have no idea what that note means."

He stared at me for a few minutes and blew his breath out. "Why do I think you're not telling me the truth?"

Grinning inwardly, I have a perverse sense of humor what can I say, and shrugging outwardly. "I don't know what it means."

"Harper, does this have anything to do with Vykky and the Pirate Museum? Cough it up."

"Like a hairball?" I laughed. Apparently, Sam wasn't wearing his sense of humor today.

"Harper," he snapped, "what makes you think Vykky has anything to do with this?"

There was no real concrete evidence that she had anything to do with it except I was sure she was behind it. Then the lightbulb went off in my head.

"Sam," he just looked at me annoyed, "do you remember the last time my apartment was rearranged and you told me to get a surveillance system or at the very least a camera?"

He nodded, still semi-frowning.

"I bought one. It's over there in my African violet pot." I walked over to it and pulled out a teeny tiny little camera. Unless you knew where to look in the plant, no one would ever see it.

A slight smile creased his face but not enough that his dimple showed. "Do I dare ask if we can take a look at it and see who entered your apartment?"

I had two printers next to each other on the little area behind my desk. One was a legitimate printer, the other was my secret hidey-hole spot. I had taken all of the innards out of it and had several things stashed in there including another cell phone. My premise was if something happened to my primary phone I had a backup with everything already set up in another phone.

On this phone, I could look up the app showing, hopefully, who the intruder was. I punched, I scrolled, and I swiped before the information I wanted showed up.

"Okay, this is interesting," Sam said watching the app's display. "I know who this is."

"Is he a local guy?" I didn't recognize him.

"No." Sam paused, "He's from St. Augustine but he used to come to Palm Park frequently."

"DUI?" I asked. I was starting to guess who it was. The puzzle was starting to come together. I didn't like the picture that was emerging.

Sam ignored me, punched a couple of numbers in his phone, and said, "Raoul Sanchez, b-and-e, Palm Park, he's on camera. He works for Vykky duBorg. Also, suspected for the murder of George Cloises and Todd Stein. Yeah, yeah, okay."

My eyes were the size of saucers. This really was all tied to Vykky. Still, I didn't have a motive or real proof of her involvement. Everything was still very circumstantial.

"Harper, you need to let your attorney know everything."

"Why?" I was truly puzzled. A.B. wasn't going to do anything about this and she wasn't having to bail me out of jail.

Sam didn't answer me. Instead, he took some photos and picked up the note. "Mind if I take this with me?"

"Let me take a picture first." I did.

Sam turned to me as he opened the door, "Call A.B. and tell her what's going on. Tell her I told you to call."

I nodded. Even as squirrelly as my brain cells could be in swirling through the black vortex of life, this really didn't make any sense to me.

Getting the gatekeeper Brenda to let me talk to A.B. proved to be a wee bit of a challenge; however, once I said Sam told me to call her, it was surprising how fast I was able to get through to A.B.

I understand the reason for gatekeepers but it doesn't mean I have to like them. I thought we had food-bonded over the heavily sugared and calorie-laden doughy delights. Obviously, I was wrong. She couldn't be bribed. No more doughnuts for Brenda.

Relaying everything to A.B., I finally said, "I don't understand why I needed to tell you everything because I don't think any of it really applies to me since I've been cleared on everything thanks to you.

A.B. semi-chuckled. "Life is always interesting, Harper. I'm not sure either unless it's to say Vykky's got something else up her sleeve. Let me know if you hear anything from her."

Chapter 12

My phone went off at two a.m. I wasn't a happy camper. I'm very much a day person. My energy kicks off at five a.m. and doesn't really drain until about eight o'clock at night. Someone calling me at two a.m. had better have a really good reason for calling me at o'dark thirty.

My voice sounded a little raspy as I answered, "Yeah, hello."

"How much?" It was a female's voice but because I was fuzzy from my sleep being interrupted, I wasn't sure who it was calling me. It didn't sound like A.B. or Brenda.

"How much what?" I was trying to sit up in bed and hoping the spun cobwebs in my brain were dissipating. Finally, I was sitting upright with my legs dangling off the edge of the bed. No answer so I repeated my question, "How much what?"

"What do you want? I know you've got it."

Because I had not gotten my eight hours of beauty sleep before being awakened so rudely, I was a wee bit cranky. "Look, whoever you are, you're going to have to be a lot more succinct because I have no clue what you're talking about. If you want me to ghostwrite your book or anything related to writing, talk to my agent. That info is on my website. Good night."

"Stop!" This time the voice was louder and very authoritarian. No doubt about who it was.

"Who do you think you are, Vykky duBorg, calling me at this time of the morning?" I snarled. "I have zero knowledge as to whatever it is and you can call me at a decent hour in the morning. That does not mean seven a.m. either!" I disconnected the call and powered off my phone. I said several not nice things about her ancestry and went back to sleep.

Needing to get back to my book, I was working diligently and realized about noon that I had not had any phone calls or text messages. That was pretty rare because Ronnie and I usually messaged each other a couple times a day. Glancing over at my phone, it suddenly occurred to me that my screen was black; that's when I remembered I had powered down my phone last night. Turning it back on, I saw three calls from an unknown number but no messages and fifty million texts from Ronnie. The last one said, "gurl where u b i worried bringing pizza at 1230 2 make sure u ok."

I heard borderline frantic knocking at my door. I scurried across the living room and opened the door.

Ronnie threw his arms around me while holding a hot pizza box in one hand. "Oh, honey, honey! I'm so glad you're okay! I was worried sick about you!"

He was such a good guy and I knew how fortunate I was to have a great friend like him. I smiled, "Let me tell you about last night."

Placing the pizza box on the countertop and flipping open the lid, he said, "Did you have a special night with a hottie detective?"

I couldn't help it, I started to laugh. "Oh, I wish! But, no." And then I proceeded to tell him about Vykky calling me, all of the calls this morning, and finished with, "She must be desperate, otherwise, she wouldn't be calling me like this."

Scarfing down another slice of pepperoni pizza, he said, "Sure sounds like it, doesn't it? Harper, should you call A.B. and tell her what's going on? Isn't this harassment?"

I shook my head. "Probably not because she's not leaving any messages and it's circumstantial as to who it is making the calls."

Picking up a slice, I glanced over at him. "No PMS special – pepperoni, mushrooms, and sausage?"

"Honey, I was just so nervous about you that I don't think I could have eaten anything other than pepperoni." He was reaching for a third piece. I shudder to think how many slices he could have eaten if he weren't nervous. I've seen the man consume an entire large pizza by himself...and not gain an ounce.

My phone rang with Unknown Caller on the I.D. Pointing at the screen, "Gotta be Vykky."

Wiping my hands on a paper towel, I didn't want to get pizza grease on my phone, I answered on the third ring. "Hello."

"Where is it?" The voice was flat, slightly irritated, and demanding.

"Vykky, I have absolutely no clue what you're talking about." I had put her on speaker and motioned to Ronnie to be quiet. "Would you care to enlighten me as to what you think I have or know about?"

I could hear her tapping her nails. She must have me on speaker phone as well. She might have been debating what to share.

"I want the map and I want the silver bars."

Ronnie and I looked at each other, our eyes wide. So there was a treasure map and pirate plunder.

"Vykky, what on God's green earth makes you think I have any of that? More importantly, how would I have gotten that from George?" I was trying to sound a little peeved but it came out more like I was seriously annoyed, borderline angry.

She ignored my questions. "How much do you want? Name a price."

Ronnie poked me, his eyes still the size of dinner plates, and he was rubbing his fingers together indicating big money.

"You're a businessperson, Vykky, so what's the real reason why you want the map and the treasure? Is it for the notoriety? Are you going to sell bits and pieces of it for outrageous prices? Is it for your own private collection or..." a thought just occurred to me and I snapped my fingers, "are you the middleman and selling it to someone else?"

While I personally didn't know anyone with millions and millions of dollars who could buy the Spanish artifacts, I did strongly suspect Vykky did.

There was a long pause then, "What I want it for is none of your business. How much?"

I had to give the woman credit where credit was due, she was focused on what she wanted.

"Why did you send Raoul to trash my apartment?" Enquiring minds wanted to know.

"Who?"

Now I was angry. I don't get angry very often simply because I'm lazy and don't want to waste my energy on negative things. "Stop pretending you don't know who he is, Vykky. In fact, since you are apparently exhibiting signs of dementia, let me refresh your memory."

I took a deep breath, "Raoul is your landscaping all-around handyman who you bought a house for his mother after you helped get them out of Venezuela. He's been with you for years.

"More importantly, I have him on camera breaking and entering my apartment and trashing my place."

"What someone in my employ does on their off time is none of my business." She was haughty to the core. Sad to say, she was going to throw a loyal employee under the bus and let law enforcement do what they wanted with him. Providing for his mom to continue to live in the lifestyle she had become accustomed was probably a very small price to pay for Raoul's silence. I wasn't a fan of that school of thought; however, I wasn't as successful a businessperson as Vykky and she probably simply considered this as a cost of doing business. I still wasn't a fan of doing this to someone regardless of how pretty the package was with a big red bow tied around it.

She wasn't going to admit to anything.

"So, how much?"

I sighed, "Vykky, I truly do not know anything about a map or treasure. I was really just doing research at the Pirate Museum. I don't know what George knew or found. I'm truly not interested in the pirate treasure, although if you wanted to throw some bucks my way, that would be great."

The phone disconnected.

Chapter 13

Vykky was irritated and tapping her red lacquered nails on her desk. Her personal phone rang.

"So did you decide on a price?" she asked.

"This isn't Harper, Vykky."

"Why are you bothering me now? The game's not over yet."

"Vykky, Vykky, Vykky..."

"I hate it when you do that." She was livid.

"You weren't supposed to murder anyone, much less two people. George really would have told you I have the map and the treasure which, by the way, is on property I own."

"How long have you had the map?" It suddenly occurred to Vykky that she had been played.

"Oh, for quite a while now but, Vykky, the map's not what is the most important thing." The caller paused, "The most important thing is the treasure chest that was filled with gold, silver, gems, and jewelry. Vykky, it was all the way to the top. It was packed."

"How much?" Vykky's voice was frosty.

"It's not for sale and, even if it were, you don't have that type of money. The land's not for sale either."

Another pause, "You cheated, Vykky. You weren't supposed to kill anyone."

She huffed, "I'll have you know I didn't kill anyone."

"You're talking semantics, Vykky. You didn't kill someone directly, but you ordered it. Same thing."

"How did you get the map and find the treasure?"

"My secret." There was a soft giggle.

"Wait! How long have you had the map?"

"Well, cuz, for quite a long while." There was a pause, then a smirk. "Let me think for a moment. Oh, yes, I've had it for a couple of years. When you attended Flagler College and you had that little incident with the board of directors, your mother apparently decided you couldn't be trusted, and she gave the map to my mother."

Vykky gasped. "My, my mother had the map?"

"Um, humm, she gave it to my mother and..."

"My mother hated your mother!" Vykky almost screamed into the phone.

"True but they had made an agreement, a legal agreement, that whichever one of their daughters could figure out where Kidd's treasure was buried, they could have it."

Vykky was breathing heavily into the phone, not saying anything.

"Vykky, you knew the rules of the game. Find the map, find the treasure, no killing. You didn't do either of the first two things and you did have two men killed. You lose. I have the map and I have the treasure."

Hissing, Vykky said, "I've looked for that map for years. You won't get away with this! Kidd's treasure is mine."

"You underestimated me, cuz." The voice was taunting now. "It was so easy to have George tease you with a map that didn't exist and to give you a couple of doubloons."

"You played me, Anne Bonny Mary Read!" screamed Vykky.

"It's all about the game, Vykky. You know that. Please, call me A.B. everyone else does."

Vykky was seething. "I'll kill you personally! I'm not hiring anyone to do my dirty work this time."

"Vykky," A.B.'s voice was soft, "didn't your mother ever tell you to not mess with a woman with two female pirate names? Goodbye."

Turning to Detective Sam Needles, A.B. said, "I think you've got enough to arrest her now."

He nodded. Looking around A.B.'s law office with all of the pirate portraits, maps, and artifacts, he said, "Love how you've decorated the place, A.B. Any of it real?"

A.B. grinned, "What do you think?"

Chapter 14

I had taken coffee over to Ronnie at the pet store. I needed a Maltese puppy fix with their cute little faces and personalities, not to mention their soft fur and little kisses.

"Can you believe it, honey? I had no clue A.B. and Vykky were related." Ronnie was holding up a newspaper where the headlines proclaimed Vykky's arrest in big letters. That was not a flattering picture of her on the front page.

I agreed. "I didn't either. This only goes to show you what greed can do to a person. A.B. comes out looking like a champ."

Ronnie grinned, "So does your hottie, Detective Sam."

Blushing, I said, "Well, we kinda do have a dinner date tonight."

High-fiving me, he only said, "Life is always good in Palm Park."

Looking for a dash of fun, a hint of snark, a sprinkle of sass, and a whole lot of silliness with a Florida twist?

SCAN ME!

To receive a FREE Book

Join my free, no obligation, twice a month newsletter, and I promise not to send your email address to the "your car warranty has expired" people

SharonEBuck.com

Purchase my books at your favorite retailer

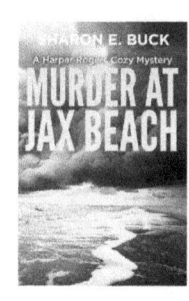

For the Parker Bell & Lady Gatorettes series, turn the page.

Purchase my books at your favorite retailer

Book 1
A Dose of Nice and Murder

Book 2
A Honky Tonk Night and Murder

Book 3
The Faberge Easter Egg and Murder

Book 4
Little Candy Hearts and Murder

Book 5
Lights, Action, Camera and Murder

Book 6
A Turkey Parade and Murder

Book 7
Cookies and Murder

Book 8
Flamingos and Murder

Book 9
Bowling and Murder

Purchase my books at your favorite retailer

101 Summer Jobs for Teachers

Kids Fun Activity Book

Counting Laughs

About the author

Hi, Friend,

Yes, we're now friends because you were kind enough to buy this book and I want you to know how much I appreciate that!

You know how most authors write dull, boring, "this is about me" author bios? Yeah, well, that's not me. I do a lot of fun, silly, off-the-wall crazy stuff, and funny seems to follow me everywhere. I'm happy to share funny with you and, hopefully, make you grin or laugh...thus, interrupting the craziness of your every-day life. Blatant plug, hop on over to my website and sign up for my twice-a-month newsletter (you'll also receive a free book) SharonEBuck.com

Solving crimes between sips of coffee and cookie crumbs!

Sharon

Acknowledgements

Thank you to my wonderful support team and friends for your encouragement, words of reassurance, inspiration, and belief in me on those days when the blank computer screen would stare back at me like a one-eyed monster daring me not to write anything. I survived and conquered.

In no special order, thanks to the following individuals:

Cindy Stavely at The Pirate Museum in St. Augustine for her kindness in letting me view and take notes of The Pirate Museum. This is a fun adventure for your family, friends, or even just by yourself. Visit ThePirateMuseum.com

Kim Steadman – There should be a law about how much we're allowed to laugh on the phone. You get me. Thank you for your friendship, and the time we spend talking about writing, ideas, books, ideas, the book business, ideas, laughing, ideas, and just chatting. Did I mention ideas? "Focus, Sharon, focus" and "Keep the main thing, the main thing." Visit KimSteadman.com

Bellamina Court – Who would have ever thunk that we would hit it off as author sisters Inkers Con 2024? We may have been twins at birth who were inadvertently separated at birth by different mothers hundreds of miles away. We are like two peas in a pod in so many ways. Thanks for all the laughs, giggles, and just sheer silliness we come up with in addition to all of our writing escapades. You get it. Thanks for the unique spelling of Vykky for this book and the great tagline for About the Author. Visit Bellamina-Court.com

Terezia Barna – Thank you for your encouragement, kindness, laughter, and phenomenal email program. Visit TereziaBarna.com

Cindy Marvin – My friend and attorney who tries (hard) to keep me out of trouble before I even get into it. She may or may not be a character in this book. Interestingly enough, her dad went by A.B. And, no, I did not know that when I wrote the book.

Michelle Margiotta – Your music has lifted me up when I was frustrated with my writing process, when I had doubts, and it has nurtured the very depths of my soul. Your music is so filled with colors and swirls dancing throughout your compositions that one cannot help but be totally enthralled and inspired by your incredible gift. Visit MichelleMargiotta.com

George and Mama at Athenian Owl Restaurant – Yes, there really is a George and Mama! And, yes, George really is a Greek Adonis. My favorite Greek restaurant in Jacksonville and they make me feel at home every time I eat there. Visit Athenian Owl

And, lastly, thank you to all my loyal readers and fans. I love and appreciate you!

To God be the glory.

Milton Keynes UK
Ingram Content Group UK Ltd.
UKHW030104081124
450874UK00001B/49